Until June

Aurora Rose Reynolds

June Mayson and Evan Barrister's whirlwind courtship resulted in a secret marriage right before he left for boot camp. Evan knows deep in his gut that June is too good for him, but after getting a taste of the beautiful life they could have together, he's unwilling to let her go. June promises to wait for him, knowing neither time or distance will ever change her feelings for Evan—that is until she's served with divorce papers while he's overseas and she's forced to let him go.

With her marriage and divorce being a well-kept secret, the last person June expects to run into when she moves back to her hometown is Evan. Angry over the past, she does everything within her power to ignore the pull she feels whenever he is near. But how can she ignore the pain she sees every time their eyes meet? How can she fight the need to soothe him even if she knows she's liable to get hurt once again?

Is it possible for June and Evan to find their way back to each other again? Or will they be stopped by an outside force before they ever have a shot?

Table of Contents

Dedication

To my boys the carriers of my heart.

Until June

Prologue

LOOKING AT MY reflection in the mirror across from me, I cringe. My hair is a disaster, there are bags under my eyes, and the nightgown I have on isn't even one of the cute ones I normally wear. It's the one my sister December got me as a joke, but I wear it occasionally, because it's comfortable, even if it was made for a woman three times my age. Resting my elbows on the desk in front of me, I run my fingers through my hair, pulling the strands back away from my face.

"I hate men," I whisper into the empty interrogation room, where I was told to wait over an hour ago after the police kicked in my door and dragged me from my bed. Lifting my gaze, I look at myself in the mirror again and vow that whenever I get out of the mess my ex-boyfriend has gotten me into, I'm going to learn how to be a lesbian, even if I'm not sure that's actually possible.

"June Mayson." I glance over my shoulder at the now open door behind me, and my eyes meet those of a man who reminds me of my dad. He looks to be in his mid-forties and is one of those men time has been kind to. He's built with dark hair that's cut short and parted on the side. His eyes are a blue that stands out against his dark lashes and tan skin. "I'm Officer Mitchell and this is Officer Plymouth." He nods behind him and is followed in by a man who must be playing the roll of "Bad Cop," judging by the frown on his face and the look he gives me when our eyes meet. Time hasn't been as kind to him. He looks like he has enjoyed one too many beers. His middle is round, and his skin doesn't look healthy, in fact it looks yellowish.

Nodding, I cross my arms over my chest and run my hands down the bare skin of my biceps that's chilled from the cool air coming from the vent above me.

"Would you like something to drink?" Officer Mitchell asks as he walks fully into the room.

Shaking my head, I mutter, "No, thank you."

"Hot chocolate?" he offers, and I feel tears burn the back of my eyes. Since I was little, whenever I was having a bad day, my dad would offer me hot chocolate. His hot chocolate has magical powers that always make everything seem okay, but I doubt police station hot chocolate would have the same effect.

"No, thanks. I'd just like to know why I'm here," I tell him as he takes a seat in the metal chair across from me and places a thick folder on the table between us.

"We may be here awhile, Miss Mayson, so I'd like you to be comfortable," he says gently. I look at Officer Plymouth, who is leaning against the wall, then back to him.

"I don't mean to be rude, Mr. Mitchell, but I'd really like to get to the point. I have class in a few hours and I really need to make it on time."

"I'm afraid you're probably going to miss your class today, Miss Mayson."

Closing my eyes, I open them slowly and ask, "Can I get a sweater?"

Surprisingly, Officer Plymouth slips off his suit jacket and walks it over to me, placing it around my shoulders.

"Thank you," I whisper up at him, and his eyes soften around the edges. Pulling my eyes from him, my gaze goes back toward Officer Mitchell.

"How long have you known Lane Diago?" Officer Mitchell asks, and I sit up a little taller.

"I don't know anyone by that name," I tell him, and he opens the file folder, fanning out a few pictures of my ex-boyfriend Aaron and me directly in front of me. Each of them were taken while we were a couple, showing we had been followed more than a few times. Him coming to my apartment...him kissing me outside my car...at the store, walking hand-in-hand down the aisles...at the movies...out to dinner...both of us doing normal couple things.

"You mean Aaron?"

"That what he told you his name was?" he asks, and I nod looking up at him.

"I've known him for about a year," I whisper, dropping my eyes to the pictures again, realizing I actually didn't know him, since his name isn't even Aaron.

"How long have you two been dating?" he inquires, and my eyes drop to the pictures once more.

"We dated for about four months. I broke up with him a month ago," I tell him truthfully as a feeling of sadness hits me unexpectedly. I wasn't in love with Aaron—or Lane. Not even close. But I cared about him and believed he cared about me as well. That was, until he sent me a text to meet him at his house. When I got there, one of his roommates let me in, and I found him up in his room with Susie Detrei's mouth around his cock, proving I was wrong about him.

"You were close," Officer Mitchell states, and I nod because we were, or I thought we were. "Can you tell me who this man is?" he asks, pulling out a picture of Aaron's—*Lane's* cousin, or at least the guy he *told me* was his cousin when he introduced me to him.

"Aaron...I mean Lane's cousin Cody. He lives in Mississippi."

"Did you ever overhear them talking?"

"Overhear them talking?" I ask, looking at a picture of Cody and Lane sitting in what looks like a bar. Lane is holding a bottle of his favorite beer in his hand, and Cody has a short, wide glass with dark liquid and ice on the bar top in front of him, his hand wrapped around it while he laughs at something.

"Overhear them talking about anything out of the ordinary?" he clarifies, and I shake my head.

"No."

"Are you sure about that?"

"Maybe if you told me exactly why I'm here, I could give you the information you're looking for."

"Lane Diago's uncle is one of the biggest distributors of illegal narcotics in Alabama, Kentucky, Tennessee, Mississippi, Georgia, and South Carolina."

"What?" I whisper as my eyes focus on one of the pictures of Lane and me standing outside my apartment. I was wearing a short, colorful summer dress and gold strappy sandals, and Lane had on a pair of black cargo shorts and a plain white tee. His head was bent toward mine, my hand was resting against his chest, and his was wrapped tight around my hip. It was our third date and our first kiss. I had waited forever to even go on a date with him, because I wasn't ready for a relationship. I finally gave in to him, because he was so persistent. He asked me out every time we saw each other, and he was always dramatic in the way he did it, which I thought at the time was kind of cute.

"Did you ever see—"

"I never saw anything," I cut him off. "Lane didn't even smoke pot, and almost everyone I know smokes pot," I whisper, pulling my eyes from the picture to look at him.

"You two were together a lot. You dropped him or picked him up from buyers." He shifts through the stack of photos and pulls out one of me parked outside a house where I had been waiting for Lane. "My men saw you on more than one occasion."

"To friends' houses," I tell him, suddenly finding it hard to breathe. "If he asked me to drop him off at a friend's, pick him up, or to run him somewhere when we were going out, I would. But I never witnessed him doing anything illegal."

"Do you understand you can go to prison if we find out you spent any of the money he earned from selling drugs on things for yourself?" Officer Plymouth asks, crossing his arms over his chest.

Laughing, I cover my face with my hands and lay my head on the table while I try to pull myself together. I probably shouldn't be laughing right now but it's either laugh or cry.

"What do you find funny about this?" Officer Plymouth asks, and I lift my head to look at him.

"I paid for us to do things more than once. He even asked me for gas money a couple of times. I never, not once, took money from him, not even for a coffee," I tell him, and his eyes go to Officer Mitchell, who mutters, "Fuck."

"He cheated on me a month ago, and I haven't talked to him since then," I tell him, and he shakes his head.

"We have time stamps for phone calls between the two of you over the last month."

"Did you ever look at how long those calls lasted?" I ask, knowing that if he did, he would know we didn't actually talk. "He called. He called over and over. Finally, I had to pick up to tell him to stop calling me. I didn't want anything to do with him a month ago, and I sure as hell don't want anything to do with him now."

"Another fucking road block," Officer Plymouth grumbles, and my head swings to him.

"I'm sorry. I swear that if I knew anything, I would help you out, but I don't. Lane never told me anything, and I sure as hell didn't see anything. If I had, I would have talked to my uncle about it."

"You're sure you didn't see anything, hear anything?"

"I'm sure," I tell him, wishing I did know something, not because I'm a rat, but because I know what drugs can do to people. I know not everyone dies from using drugs, not everyone's life goes to shit from using them, but my roommate during my freshman year of college overdosed and died, and that was after she turned into a completely different person. Someone I didn't like much. Someone I couldn't trust. So, there's no way I would ever protect anyone who is responsible for supplying those drugs, no matter how much I cared about them.

"Would you be willing to get back in touch with Lane?" Officer Plymouth asks, bringing my attention to him. My heart flips in my chest at the thought, but I don't get a chance to answer, because someone bangs on the glass mirror in front of me, causing my reflection to go funny.

Chapter 1

June

"YOU HAVE GOT to be kidding me." I turn around, slamming my front door behind me, and walk right back into my house. I stride past the stack of boxes near my front door, down the hall, across the living room—where the furniture is all piled in the middle of the room, because I haven't had time to think about how I want it placed—and into the kitchen. Picking up my cell phone from the counter, I dial my cousin and listen as it rings while nausea and anger fill my stomach.

"Why is Evan parked outside of my house?" I ask on a growl as soon as Jax answers, and I don't even give him a chance to reply before I continue on a hiss, "I want him gone, *now.*"

"June, you know that's not going to happen. Your dad's worried about you. I'm worried about you. Uncle Nico's worried about you. Everyone's worried about you right now."

"He's in jail. Nothing is going to happen to me," I tell him, trying to sound calm, even though I feel as far from calm as someone can possibly be.

"Until he's sentenced, you're gonna have someone watching over you to make sure nothing happens to you," he states, and I want to scream at him. I want to tell him to send someone—*anyone*—else, but I can't, because he has no idea Evan is my ex. Worse, he's my ex-husband. No one knows that, and I don't want anyone to know.

"I appreciate you looking out for me. I really do. But this is totally

7

unnecessary, Jax, and you know it."

"Evan's solid. You won't even know he's there—unless you feel like being nice and want to invite him in, so he doesn't have to sit out in the heat."

"I'm never inviting him in," I whisper to myself, but Jax hears me anyway and chuckles, probably thinking I'm being dramatic.

"He's not that bad. I'm sure he'd even help you set up your furniture if you'd ask him to."

He laughs again, and my eyes squeeze closed as I whisper, "I gotta go," and hang up, without even saying goodbye. Just the idea of Evan anywhere near me sets my teeth on edge. "He can roast for all I care," I tell myself, even though I know it's a lie. Love sucks. Love sucks, because sometimes even when you don't want to love someone, you still do. No matter how many times I've tried to convince myself that what I shared with Evan is over, I still hurt. I hurt because I still love him, and I do not want to love him.

Not at all.

Pressing my fingers into my eye sockets, I let out a groan of frustration. I need to get to the store and pick up some groceries. That's what I planned on doing when I went to leave and saw him standing outside next to his truck, looking more beautiful than ever, which doesn't make sense. When we were together, I knew he was the most beautiful man I had ever seen, and it sucked big that he hasn't changed in our time apart, that he hasn't grown a third eye or turned into a slimy green alien with big bulging warts covering his body. He's still the same beautiful Evan Barrister I fell in love with the moment our eyes locked.

His dark hair and warm brown eyes, that glittered when he smiled, were what caught my attention. But the first time he held me in his arms, the first time I sank myself between his broad shoulders, I knew he was it for me. I knew he was everything to me. It wasn't about the way he looked, even though I knew he was the kind of man most women fantasized about. The kind of man you would see on the street and stop to stare at, because you knew you had never seen a man like him in real life and needed to remember every detail, since you would likely never see his kind of beauty up close again. It wasn't about that at all. It was the fact that when I was with him, I knew it was where I belonged. Right down to my bones, I knew that, I was meant to be his and he was meant to be mine.

Pulling my fingers away from my eyes, I open them wide, not wanting to remember the feelings I felt for him, even knowing there's not one damn thing I can do about it. He's ingrained in me, a part of me I know is gone forever, but wake up everyday thinking will come back.

"You are not going there, June Mayson," I scold myself as hot tears burn the backs of my eyes. Blinking rapidly, I pull in a breath through my nose, toss my cell to the counter, and head for the front door. There is no way in hell I will let him take over my life again…no way I will stop living.

Not again.

I did that when he went away. I did it when he had his mom deliver divorce papers to me, too. I died inside when I knew there was no longer an us, and I just fricking *finally* got myself back. So no way will I allow him to stop me from moving forward with my life.

Not a chance.

Swinging open the front door, I plow down the steps to the sidewalk, keeping my eyes to my feet as I go. Just because I may be over him, doesn't mean he doesn't affect me, and he can do that, but I don't want him to ever see he does.

I don't want him to have even one single piece of me.

Pressing the button on the remote in my hand, I hear my doors unlock at the same time I put my hand to the handle, swinging open the door to my platinum grey with chrome everything Beetle R-Line 2.OT SE and slide in. I love my car. It's a chick car, but it's the first real thing I ever bought for myself with money I earned. My dad shook his head when he saw it, but my mom, she was a whole different story. She hopped in, and we went cruising around town with the windows down and the music up to the perfect decibel—*loud*.

Sadly, the cops felt differently about the volume of gangster rap coming from my car and informed my mother and me of that when they pulled us over. They went as far as to explain exactly what a "trap queen" was, only doing it smiling as they wrote me a noise violation ticket. I didn't care about the ticket one bit. I was with my mom, and we were having a good time being silly. As soon as the cops were back in their car and out of hearing distance, my mom turned the volume right back up, smiled, and then yelled, "Drive, June Bug!" over the music pumping from my car's speakers. I did, and we drove around for another half hour before my dad sent a text to my mom, telling her to get her ass home. Then we giggled all the way back like two kids. It was a blast.

Coming out of the memory, I smile, put my car in reverse, glance over my shoulder, and back out of the drive and onto the street—all the while avoiding looking in Evan's direction. I don't even have to peek in my rearview mirror to know he's following. His truck's so loud, the sound of it rumbles through my car like a constant reminder.

When we were together, he had a car. It was a small two-door Honda. It was old, but it was reliable. His dad, who hadn't done much for him, helped him rebuild the engine the summer he graduated high school, and he cherished that car, because it was one of the few good memories he had with his father.

Now, his Honda is long gone to parts unknown, and he drives a truck. Only his truck doesn't look like any run-of-the-mill truck. It is huge and black, down to the rims. I have no doubt he could turn out the headlights at night and go invisible. But I'm not going to think about that, even if I really want to know what exactly he is doing working for Jax.

Swinging into the grocery store parking lot, I find a single space in a row with cars ten deep on each side and pull in, making it so that if Evan wants to park, he has to do it somewhere not close to my car. Putting the Beetle in park, I grab the small envelope of coupons I keep in my glove box, open my door, and get out. Spotting Evan pulling in to a space across the lot, I quicken my steps into the store and grab a cart. Knowing I need everything, I start in the produce section so I can work my way down each aisle of the store. When I finally reach the cash register, my cart is overflowing. I not only picked up the basics, I picked every single food item that caught my eye. This means I have a cartful of mostly junk food, because I'm shopping on an empty stomach. Lucky for me, I have a boatload of coupons and know my junk food binge isn't going to send me spiraling into debt.

"June?"

Hearing my name, I turn and feel my shoulders stiffen slightly when I come face-to-face with a guy I dated in high school, a guy who—even at seventeen—played me for a fool. He was the first, Evan was the second, and the third was Lane. He would be the last, though. I was now going to bat for the other team, or at least pretend to.

"Matt, how are you?" I ask, even though I couldn't care less. I'm not a bitch, or at least, not normally, but he did a number on my teenage heart. I may not be a bitch, but I can definitely hold a mean grudge.

"Good, just moved home. I'm working for my dad." He smiles.

"Sweet." I semi-smile back then turn my body partially away from him when the cashier asks for my coupons.

"Are you home?" he asks, and I direct my attention from the cashier to him and start to reply, when I feel heat hit my side. I know *he's* there. I can tell from his smell and the heat coming off his body, but when his arm slips around my shoulders in the familiar way he used to hold me, my body stiffens and my eyes fly up. All I see, though, is the set of his jaw.

"Evan." He sticks his hand out toward Matt, and my breathing becomes choppy as Matt's eyes scan between my ex-husband and me.

"Um…Matt," he says, returning the handshake before looking at me. "I…I'll see you around," he mutters then disappears out of sight so fast I don't even see him go.

"Honey," the cashier calls, and I turn to face her, dislodging Evan's arm from around me while taking a step to the side to put farther distance between us. "You okay? You look like you just saw a ghost," the woman says softly, and I take in her worried look then inhale a deep breath.

"Yeah…um, what's my total?" I whisper, and her eyes soften then look past me, and I feel the warmth of Evan leave my side.

"You sure you're okay?" she asks quietly.

"Sure." I smile, and she nods like she doesn't believe me, but that's okay, because right now, I don't believe myself.

"One hundred and seven, sixty-two. You saved over fifty dollars." She grins, and I attempt to smile again as I hand her the money, but my face feels like it may crack when I do it.

"Thank you," I mumble, taking my change from her, then I thank the young girl who just bagged my groceries, wrap my hands around the handle of the cart, and push it out of the store, ignoring the fact I can feel Evan trailing close behind me.

"June."

"Don't." I shake my head, not even looking in his direction. I can't deal with him, not now. Loading all the bags in the trunk, I jump into my car, buckle up, reverse, and head for home, avoiding looking in my rearview or thinking about what just happened, though I can feel it clawing at my insides even as I park in my driveway.

"Did you just move in?" a woman's voice yells as soon as I swing the door to my car open. Looking around for where the voice came from, I get out and slam the door shut. "Over here, honey!" the voice calls again, and I find a petite woman with black hair standing on the porch of the house next to mine with her hands on the railing and her body hanging half over.

"Hi!" I call back, and she smiles.

"So, are you moving in?" she asks, and my guess is she missed the moving truck in the driveway this morning.

"I am, or I did this morning," I reply, moving toward my trunk so I can get my groceries out.

"Hold on. I'm coming to introduce myself," she yells once more, and I start to giggle, surprised she didn't just shout her name to me and have me holler mine back. Leaving my groceries in the trunk, I meet her halfway on the lawn between our houses, wondering how the hell she is capable of walking through grass in her heels. I would be on my face if I were her, but she looks like she does this every day.

"I'm JJ." She smiles once she's close, and I notice that her hair isn't just black; it's black with large chunks of purple running through it that make the grey of her eyes pop. "Just two of the letter *J*, not the actual name Jay spelled out twice." She grins, and I grin back, sticking out my hand.

"June, like the month June."

"So you moved in this morning?" she asks, looking at the house behind me.

"I did."

"I was at work," she mutters then jabs her thumb toward her house. "My old man was asleep 'til I got home, so he missed you movin' in too."

"Well, it's nice to meet you now." I smile again, and her eyes scan over me then go kind of squinty.

"You ain't got no problem with bikers do you?"

"Um...no..." I shake my head and my smile widens.

"Good. Not that it happens often, but my old man's boys do sometimes show up, and when they do, things can get loud. If you have a problem, you can come over and tell me. If you don't have a problem, you can just come over and have a beer." She grins, and I laugh, thinking I like JJ already.

"I'll probably take you up on that offer."

"Good, now I gotta ask, who's the hot guy in the truck?"

I don't turn around. I know without looking who she's talking about as her chin lifts behind me. "Umm…" I wonder how the hell to explain Evan to her.

"Never mind. I can see you don't want to talk about it right now. I'll stop by and bring tequila tomorrow. You can tell me then," she states, inviting herself over.

"His story will probably take two bottles of tequila," I mumble, and she smiles again, this time bigger.

"I can already tell you're my kind of people." She looks me over then peeks over my shoulder again. "You two fit, and from the way he's looking over here, I'm guessing he knows that, but like you said, that's a story for tequila, so I'll let you go and we'll talk about him tomorrow."

"Tomorrow," I agree, reaching out to squeeze her hand. "It was nice meeting you, JJ."

"You too, girly. Tomorrow." She smiles then turns and flounces through half my yard and hers, heading up to her front porch. Just as she gets there, the door opens and a big, bearded man—who is not at all unattractive—steps out onto the front porch, takes her hand, and lifts his chin to me. Giving him an awkward wave, I watch JJ smile up at him and say something that has him grinning while shaking his head before dragging her through the door and closing it.

I know it right then and there—I'm going to love my new neighborhood…or I will love it once I don't have Evan standing guard outside of my house.

Chapter 2

Evan

"YOU'RE MY EV," she whispers, looking down at my ring on her finger while her thighs press tight to my hips.

"Always, beautiful."

Her gaze meets mine and she pulls back, causing her dark hair to glide softly across my chest as she sits up. My eyes drop to my hands and I watch as they move up the silky skin of her thighs, the soft curve of her waist, and then over her breasts, the weight filling my hands.

"Ev." She slides me inside of her, and my hips surge upward, sending me deeper. My eyes move to hold hers as she lifts then falls slowly, so fucking slowly that I know she is going to kill me. But I wouldn't mind dying like this, deep inside of her, surrounded by beauty.

"Fuck," I breathe, and she smiles. She's the most beautiful thing I have ever seen in my life. Nothing better than her. Perfection. "Kiss me." I slide one hand around her back and pull her forward, taking her mouth and tasting her on my tongue. Nothing sweeter than her, fucking nothing.

"Oh, God," she whimpers down my throat as she convulses around me.

Blinking my eyes open, my pulse races and I wrap my hand around my cock, squeezing tight as I mutter, "Fuck," to the ceiling while trying to catch my breath. When I first got home from Afghanistan, my dreams were the nightmares I lived there, the nightmares of losing men I considered brothers. Now my nightmares are the loss of her—June.

Rolling out of bed, I move to the small, attached bathroom, turn on the faucet, lean forward, cup the water in my palms, and splash my face, letting the cool liquid wash away the last of my dream. Resting my palms on the edge of the sink, I drop my head forward and squeeze my eyes closed, wondering how long the memories of June and me will haunt my nights. Lifting my head, looking at myself in the mirror, I stare at the man before me—knowing I'm everything my father said I am.

"*Fuck!*" I roar, pulling back my arm and swinging, watching the glass shatter as my fist makes contact and my image disintegrates.

Chest heaving, I drop my head again, pulling in ragged breaths.

Heading down the hall, I see Harlen coming out of his room and lift my chin.

"You heading to work?" he asks, stepping in sync with me as we move down the outside corridor of the compound toward the kitchen/cafeteria.

"Yeah," I mutter, lifting my chin to Z when I spot him sitting at a table as we enter through the door. The large room, which used to be the lunchroom when the factory was working, now holds a few round tables near the entrance for the kitchen. An eighty-inch flat-screen TV is hung with a warn leather couch in front of it, and two pool tables are set up in the back corner. Most days, the room is packed with the men who either work or live here, most of them are transitioning from military to civilian life.

"You still looking for another bike?" Harlen questions from my side, bringing me out of my thoughts as I pour myself a cup of coffee.

"Yeah, I just haven't had a chance to look. Not sure I want new," I mutter, watching him nod and cross his arms over his chest.

"I might have something for you. A bike came in yesterday, and the guy mentioned selling. I'll feel him out when he comes in today."

"Let me know," I mumble then look at the clock and see I need to pick up Sage at the office in ten. "Later." I lift my chin to Z and head out to my truck. Climbing in the beast, I put my coffee in the cup holder, back out of the parking space, and head toward town where the office is located.

"What the fuck is the deal with you and June?" Sage asks, hopping into my truck, setting his cup of coffee in the cup holder between us, and buckling up. I wasn't going to answer his question. One, it isn't anyone's fucking business. Two, he and Jax have no fucking clue that me and June had a history, and they weren't going to learn that shit from me. June didn't tell anyone about us when we got together, not even her sisters, who she told everything to. I didn't understand her reason for keeping us a secret. I didn't fucking like it, but it was what it was.

When we got married, she still didn't share about us. I was okay with that. She said she had a plan and was going to tell her parents while I was away. That way, they had time to settle into the idea that their daughter was a married woman, and then when I got home, she would introduce me to them. My headspace at the time was completely jacked, and like I said, I didn't think much about it. The only thing I knew was I had a good woman, a woman who loved me, a woman I loved, so I was letting her lead where her family was concerned.

Obviously, shit went down when I was away, and I ended our relationship, permanently. So there was no longer a reason for her to tell anyone she had been married, which she didn't, and I wasn't going to enlighten them to the fact we had history.

"She fucking called Jax this morning, telling him to keep you away from her," he continues, and I feel my muscles tighten.

Yesterday was a fuck-up on my part. I should have kept out of the way, but I couldn't stand the idea of that little fucker asking her out and her saying yes, so I stepped in.

"Are you even fucking listening to me?" Sage demands, and I turn my head and raise a brow. "I know you were married," he whispers, and my muscles that were tight wind even tighter. "Know it wasn't long, but do know she was your wife. I don't know what the fuck happened, but I have to tell you. I like you, man, but you fuck with my cousin's head, do something to hurt her again, and you'll answer to me."

"Do not," I breathe, "fucking threaten me."

"It's not a threat, brother. It's a promise. I know she was fucked up for a while. Everyone knew she was fucked up, but she wouldn't talk about it, about what happened. Now I know her fucked up came because you guys ended."

"She moved on," I say, reminding myself of something that fucking kills me every time I think about it.

Snorting, he shakes his head. "If you really think that shit, then you're fucking stupid."

"Whatever," I mutter instead of punching him in the face then put my truck in reverse and head out toward town to meet up with a potential client.

"I SEE HE'S back," I hear JJ say just as June opens the front door to her house. Seeing her, my hands form fists. Her dark hair is down around her bare shoulders. The black, cotton strapless dress she has on makes her skin look even more golden, and her face is completely free of makeup. I know if I were close, I would see the light scatter of freckles across the bridge of her nose and the golden flecks in her eyes.

"I'm working hard at pretending he's not," June tells JJ, who holds up a bottle of tequila, the same bottle she walked out of her house with. She shoves it toward her, laughing as she says, "This will help you forget."

Taking a step back with the bottle close to her chest, she lets JJ inside, and I hear her quietly reply, "Not sure about that," her eyes move through her yard to me. My heart stops the same way it did the first time we met, only this time, instead of her lips parting and her eyes shining in wonder, her eyes narrow, her lips tighten, and she closes the door, giving me everything and absolutely fucking nothing.

"Fuck," I rumble, tilting my head back. The first time I saw June, I had been walking out of the auto supply store where I worked when she had been walking in. I was off for the day, but when she tilted her head back toward me with her lips parted, whispering, "Thank you," as I held open the door for her, I knew I needed to talk to her, so I followed her back inside.

She didn't talk much. She told me what she was looking for, and I showed her where she could find it. Her cheeks were an adorable shade of pink by the time she checked out, and then got even darker when I asked her for her number as I walked her to her car. I knew the second I met her there was something different about her, something I couldn't put my finger on, but I knew she was going to become important to me.

She wasn't important—she was fucking vital, the best thing that ever happened to me. But then I had to let her go so my fucked up didn't ruin her.

Getting in my truck, I start it up and stare at her house, knowing there is no way anyone will fuck with her, not while I'm out here or JJ is inside. No one would be stupid enough to court the kind of repercussions they would receive from Brew if they fucked with his old lady. And I would kill someone without blinking if they got too close to June.

She was fucked up. Sage's words have played in my head over and over today. When I was with June, we talked about our future a lot and made a million fucking plans. She knew I owed at least four years to the marines. I signed up for the service before we met. I didn't have the money for school and the marines gave me the opportunity to get an education and make some money while doing it.

June was on my orders, and after boot camp, we were scheduled to go to Germany. She wanted to see the world, and I was happy to have the ability to give her that. She knew we would be there for two years but also understood two years wasn't long and that when the time was up, we could move back stateside or find somewhere else to explore. She was excited to be with me, to start a life, and to see the world.

I just didn't bank on me being one of the top shooters in my class. I had never held a gun in my life and knew jack-shit about shooting. But the moment they placed that piece of metal in my hands, it became an extension of me. I was good—so fucking good that they sent me to Afghanistan on the first tour out after boot camp. Seeing what I saw, living through what I lived through, I knew I couldn't touch June again. She deserved more, she deserved everything, and I would never be worthy of her.

Hearing a bike pull up behind me, I look in my rearview mirror then smile when I see Harlen swing himself off his Harley.

"Heard you were over here," he mutters, hefting himself up into the passenger seat of my truck and slamming the door.

"Sweet of you to come keep me company." I grin, and his eyes narrow.

"We're gonna look at the bike I told you about this morning. Owner's part of Brew's crew." He lifts his chin toward Brew's house. "He's meeting us here."

"Thanks for looking out."

"You don't have the right equipment, and you're too big to ride bitch when your piece of shit bike breaks down." He grins, and I feel my lips twitch then look in the rearview mirror when the roar of the pipes hits the block. I watch as a Harley Fat Boy cruises down the street past my truck, and pulls into Brew's driveway.

Getting out of the truck, we walk across the yard, stopping next to the bike as the owner gets off.

"Shock," Harlen greets the guy with a handshake then dips his chin to me. "This is Evan."

"What's up, man?" Shock rumbles as we shake hands, and he steps away from the bike and crosses his arms over his T-shirt-covered chest. "This is her. I hate parting with her, but I'm upgrading," he says as I walk around the bike. The matte black paintjob sliced between with liquid black is seamless. The chrome all looks new and well maintained. "It's a '94, but it has a 127ci Ultima engine and six-speed transmission, with less than five hundred miles on it. The engine also has a polished Mikuni carburetor and a Dyna 2000 ignition system. She's the shit wet dreams are made of."

"You'd say that, since that bike got you more gnash than you know what to do with," Brew says, walking toward us down the driveway. Shock doesn't reply verbally, but his smile broadens and he smacks Brew's shoulder when he's close and then looks at me.

"You wanna take her on a ride?"

Looking over at June's, I start to shake my head.

"No one's gonna fuck with her while I'm standing on my front lawn," Brew promises low enough for just me to hear. I look at him and dip my head then look at Shock.

"Toss me the keys." Catching them when they fly through the air, I swing my leg over the bike, start her up, and back out of the drive. I don't go far, but pull out onto the main road and open her up, hitting forty-five. I grin—the fucking sound alone is enough to draw attention, but the bike is a work of art. The power and body is exactly what I was looking for. Pulling back onto the block, I glance at June's front door and see her and JJ standing in the doorway. Lifting my chin at them, JJ smiles, but June…June doesn't. No, her eyes go dark, and not in a bad way. They go dark in a way that makes me want to see them change like that up close. Pulling into Brew's driveway, I shut off the bike and look at Shock as I swing my leg over.

"How much are you asking?"

"Nine. A quick sale, cash only." He grins.

Pulling in a breath, I look at the bike then back to him. "You got a deal." He chuckles then pats my back.

"I'll get your info from Harlen. We can set up a meet tomorrow, or I'll swing by the shop in the morning."

"Sounds good," I agree and chance a look at June's front door. This time, it's closed and I rub my chest over my heart, wondering when the fucking pain there will go away.

Chapter 3

June

MOVING AROUND MY room after adjusting the sheets, I toss the duvet from the floor onto the bed. I sleep rough; I always have. I know there are people who can fall asleep in one position then stay that way the whole night, but that's not me. I move constantly, so much so that I've fallen off the bed in the middle of the night more times than I can count.

Grabbing the ends of the duvet, I struggle to lift it like they do in laundry detergent commercials then give up, letting it fall into place messily. When I bought it a year ago, I didn't go cheap. It's probably three-inches thick, full of feathers. Between my duvet and the feather-top mattress pad on my bed, I fall asleep in heaven every night. Tossing the pillows on next, I then fling the throw blanket, which serves no other purpose than to be cute, onto the corner then stand back, admiring my handy work.

I love the bedroom set my mom picked out. I told her what I wanted when I knew I was going to buy my house, and she took over from there. The distressed wood of the bedframe, dresser, and side tables make the room feel warm, while the dusty purple duvet cover that looks like velvet, and grey toss pillows and sheets, make it elegant. Creating a mental list to pick up curtains and to find lamps, I head for the bathroom to finish getting ready, since my dad will be here to take me to lunch soon. Turning on the bathroom light, I sigh when I see my reflection. I don't like wearing a lot of makeup, but the dark circles under my eyes leave me no choice. Digging through my makeup drawer, I find my tube of concealer and go to work.

Seeing Evan again is taking a toll on me. I can't sleep, and my mind is in a constant state of turmoil. I wake up in the middle of the night from dreams of us. The memories of him, of us, are too much. Some memories have the ability to heal, the ability to light up the dark, because the beauty of the memory is so bright, you're still able to bask in it.

But the memories of us are killing me slowly. They remind me that for one moment, I had everything, while reminding me it's gone. It's the realization that we're done that's torturing me. The realization that I can see him but can't touch him, that he exists but he's not mine, is agonizing. Hell, yesterday, when me and JJ watched him ride down the block on his motorcycle, I swear I wanted to push the door open, run into his arms, and beg him to take me. He looked...he looked—well, I guess there are no words for the way he looked. All I know is between the tequila and seeing him ride, when I went to bed last night, I took my BOB with me and spent an ungodly amount of time getting off.

Pulling my face away from the mirror, I check my work. The bags are not as noticeable anymore, and hopefully, with some bronzer and blush, my dad will be none the wiser. Stepping into my closet that's attached to the bathroom, I push boxes aside until I find the one I marked *Dresses*, rip the tape off, and dig through until I find what I'm looking for. Taking off my shirt, I drop it to the floor, not bothering with a bra because I have no boobs, and slip the dress on over my head. The slim straps and thin cotton material is perfect for the humid Tennessee heat. Grabbing a pair of simple leather sandals, I push my feet into them then head for the door when I hear a car pull up outside.

"Hey, Dad." I smile, opening the door for him before he even has a chance to knock, then step back and let him into the house.

"June Bug." He leans down, kissing my cheek. When he pulls back, he engulfs half my face with his big hand. "You look tired," he states quietly as his eyes study me.

"I'm okay. Moving always sucks." I let out a breath and look away to finish my lie. "I want everything unpacked already, so I've been staying up late and waking up early to get it done."

"June, what's going on?"

"Nothing." I smile, and his voice drops to the 'dad tone' that says, *Don't lie to me.*

"June."

"I'm fine, Dad. I promise, just tired." I wave my hand around and start to head for the living room to grab my purse, but his hand grabs mine, stopping me in my tracks, and I turn to face him once more.

"I know you're lying." He shakes his head and continues quietly, "Not sure when my girls all started keeping shit from me, but I gotta say, I don't like it." His hand comes back to my face and his eyes search mine. "I love you, more than anything in this world, and nothing will ever change that." He kisses my forehead then leans back, catching my eyes again. "If you need someone to talk to, I'm here, and if not, your mom doesn't love you as much as I do, but I'm sure she'd hear you out too." Rolling my eyes at the comment about Mom, I wrap my arms around his waist and squeeze.

"I know. Love you, Dad."

"Always, baby girl." His lips touch the top of my head, where he asks, "You ready to go eat?"

"Yes, can we take my car?"

"Fuck no," he replies immediately without even thinking about it, and I can't help it, I laugh leaning back. "It would make me feel better." I pout, and he shakes his head.

"Not happening. Get your bag. I'm driving." He lets me go and I do as he says, before meeting him back at the front door so he can drive us to lunch.

"Thank you." I smile at our waiter as he slides a double cheeseburger and onion rings in front of me and the same thing in front of my dad.

"Let me know if you need anything else," he returns then walks off. I have no idea why this is my favorite place to eat; the customer service is lacking big time. I don't think I've ever seen anyone who works here smile. Then I take a bite of my cheeseburger and remember why I don't care that the people who work here are rude.

"When do you start your new job?" Dad asks, squirting ketchup on his plate.

"Next Monday." I swallow my bite of cheeseburger then dip one of my onion rings in ranch dressing. "It's not ideal teaching summer school, but the principal told me that with me working now, he can pretty much guarantee me a spot when summer ends."

"I'm proud of you."

"Thanks, Dad," I mumble, watching him lift his hand and wave over my shoulder. Glancing behind me, my lungs freeze when I see my cousin Sage followed by Evan heading toward us.

"Yo," Sage greets, grinning.

"Hey, bud." My dad scoots over in the booth, and Sage leans over to kiss my cheek, mumbling, "Hi" before taking a seat next to him.

"Mr. Mayson." Evan shakes my dad's hand then looks down at me, and I scoot over without thinking, making room for him. He takes a seat next to me…right next to me.

This cannot be happening.

"You know my daughter, Evan?" Dad asks, and as Evan turns to me, there is something in his eyes I can't read, but it doesn't look good. My heartbeat kicks up as his eyes go back to my dad.

"We've met."

"Forgot you've been helping keep an eye on her," Dad mutters, taking a bite of his burger then swallowing. "What are you two doing today?"

At Dad's question, I tuck myself tighter against the wall, because Evan is taking up the whole seat, and I can't focus while his body is brushing against mine.

"Normal stuff," Sage says as his eyes move between Evan and me. His shoulder bumps Dad's and his eyes light with mischief.

"Don't they make a cute couple?" He grins, and I narrow my eyes on him at the same time I feel Evan's body still.

"Don't be a pain," Dad mutters, but his eyes move between the two of us, and I wonder what he's thinking about, because his eyes change ever so slightly.

"I'm gonna go order. We should eat on the road so we're not late," Evan says to Sage, and I let out a breath I didn't know I was holding before saying goodbye to both of them as they leave me and my dad sitting in the booth.

"Evan's a good guy. Your cousins like him," Dad adds, but I don't acknowledge his statement. Instead, I dip another onion ring into my ranch then shove it into my mouth, chewing slowly. I need to do something about Evan. Obviously, things are not going to be as easy as avoiding him forever. He works for my cousin, lives in the same town as I do, and is somehow friends with my sister July's husband's biker friends. His life and mine have intertwined.

"What are you thinking about so hard?" Dad asks, bringing me out of my thoughts, and I scramble for something to say.

"Do you think we can stop at Minx before we head back to my house?" I ask when I swallow, and his eyes narrow. "I'm guessing that's a no," I grumble under my breath while fighting my smile.

"Ask your mom."

"'Cause she loves me more?" His lips twitch, but he doesn't reply. My dad hates shopping, so his response is not a surprise. "I'll ask mom," I agree then pick up my burger and take a bite.

LOOKING THROUGH THE window next to the door, I watch Jax and Evan talk next to the front of Evan's truck. I don't know what they're talking about, but whatever it is has both of them laughing. Moving away, I go down the hall to my room and grab one of my sweaters from the closet, admiring my new curtains and lamps on the way through my room.

Instead of my dad bringing me home after lunch, we went back to my parents' house, so my mom and I could take her Suburban to Minx, where I found two very cool amber glass lamps with shades the color of cork, along with silvery grey curtains. When my mom and I arrived at my house, Jax was here for "June duty." I don't think it's necessary for anyone to watch me. Lane is awaiting trial, and I wasn't a witness to anything he had done. My family, on the other hand, obviously doesn't agree with me on the matter. Since Jax was at the house anyway, Mom and I put him to work, hanging the curtain rods and curtains. Not long after he was done, my mom took off, and Jax stayed and had a beer then went out to talk to Evan once he showed up.

Moving back toward the window, I see Jax pat Evan's shoulder then head for his car. Debating with myself, the same way I have done all day, I give up and walk to the front door and swing it open as Jax turns at the stop sign at the end of my block. Watching him drive out of sight, I turn my gaze to Evan and find his eyes already on me.

"Umm..." I murmur, wondering, *What the hell am I thinking?*

"You okay?" he asks, taking a few steps toward the house, but stopping halfway across the lawn.

Fuckity, fuck, fuck.

"I...I'm fine. I was..." Jesus, my stomach is in knots and I feel like I'm going to be sick. *This was a bad idea.* "Can we talk?" I ask after a moment, and I watch his eyes shutter as he nods once and heads toward me. Stepping back so he can enter the house, I lead him down the hall to the living room. "Would you like a beer?"

"I'm good," he replies, stopping in the middle of the room, and I look around as he does. My entertainment center is one my parents had. It's black with doors on the bottom and sides and has a shelf above, with a space for the TV in the middle. The sectional up against the opposite wall is big enough to fit my entire family. The standing lamp on the far side of the wall is perfect for reading, since the shade is directly over the side of the couch with the footrest. I haven't put up any of my pictures, so everything is bare.

"Do you want to sit?" I ask, taking a seat on the edge of the couch clasping my hands in front of me.

He looks at me for a long time—so long that I start to feel uncomfortable—then wanders across the room and takes a seat on the end of the sectional, facing me. His presence is so big that even from where he's sitting across the room, it feels like he takes up the whole space. Worse, I can't read his expression, so I have no idea what he's thinking.

"What did you want to talk about?" he asks, studying me.

"I feel…" I pause to take a breath and get my thoughts in order, because I have no idea what exactly it is I want to say to him. "You…" I cut myself off again, covering my face with my hands. "This was stupid. I don't know what I'm doing." I uncover my face and look at him. "Sorry, you can go," I whisper while standing then head for the hall toward the door.

"I'm sorry." At his words, my body locks and tears creep up my throat. "I wasn't…I'm not good enough for you." Pressing my lips together, I fight the pain in my chest then turn to look at him when I have it locked away.

"I know," I whisper, ignoring his flinch as I walk to the door and open it. Looking at my feet, I hear him come down the hall and see his boots when he stops in front of me. I don't look up. I can't—the pain in my chest is too intense. Feeling his lips at the top of my head, a tear falls to the ground at my feet.

His fingers at my chin force my eyes to meet his. We stand there for what seems like forever looking at each other before he speaks. "I wish things were different, I wish I was good enough for you." His softly spoken words do nothing to mend my broken heart, do nothing to help ease the pain in my chest, if anything they cut me deeper.

"I wish that too." I whisper, dropping my eyes to the ground. His hands drop away and he leaves, taking everything I have left inside of me with him when he goes. Shutting the door and locking it, I slide to the floor, wrap my arms around my legs, bury my face against my knees, and cry.

HEARING SOMEONE KNOCK on the door, I try to open my eyes, but they feel like they're full of gravel. It took me forever to find sleep once again last night… and judging by how my body feels, that wasn't long ago. Hearing the knocking turn into pounding, I scream at the top of my lungs, "I'm coming! Hold your horses!" then stumble from my bed and head for the front door.

"Took you long enough," July says, pushing into the house, followed by Wes, as soon as I open the door.

"What's going on?" I frown, watching them walk toward the living room.

"You may want to put some pants on." July grins, and I look down at my heart-covered cotton underwear and throw my hands up in the air then stomp back to my room to pull on a pair of sweats. Already in my bathroom, I decide to brush my teeth and my hair. When I make it back to the kitchen, July and Wes are making themselves comfortable in my kitchen, starting coffee.

"Do you want to tell me what's going on?"

"We just wanted to come check on you," July says, and I feel my eyes go squinty when I look at the clock on the wall.

"It's eight in the morning," I point out, glaring between the two of them.

"Evan got trashed last night," Wes states, and my heart drops into my stomach as July hisses, "Wes."

"What?" He frowns, and she rolls her eyes.

"You saw him, babe. He was a fucking wreck."

Fuckity, fuck, fuck.

"You're telling me this, why?" I prompt evenly, even though my stomach is turning with nausea.

"He's hurting," Wes says quietly, and I wrap my arms around my middle as I swallow through the lump in my throat. I also remind myself that his feelings are no longer my problem.

"I don't want to sound like a bitch, but why is that my problem?"

"Why?" he repeats softly, and I grit my teeth as I watch disappointment flash in his eyes.

"Yes, why?" I whisper and drop my arms.

"I think you know the answer to that," Wes says, and I pull my eyes from him to look at my sister.

"You told him?" I guess, and she pulls her bottom lip between her teeth and nods.

Closing my eyes, I run a shaky hand through my hair while I try to get my thoughts in order then open them when Wes speaks again.

"You love him?" he asks, cutting me off before I can say anything, and I take a step back, feeling the color drain from my face. "Yeah, you love him," he whispers and his eyes go soft. "I don't know what happened between the two of you, but I know Evan. I know he's a good man who was dealt a fucked-up hand in life. His dad's a piece of shit, and when his mom isn't drinking, she's okay, but she's normally drinking." He lets those words hang then drops his voice even more. "He went to war and watched men he cared about die. My guess is, he's thinking a sweet, beautiful woman like you deserves more than a guy like him," he says, and that lump in my throat aches as the words Evan said last night replay in my head.

I'm not good enough for you.

I'm not good enough for you.

I'm not good enough for you.

I'm not good enough for you.

RUNNING FOR THE bathroom in the hall, I flip up the lid on the toilet and drop to my knees as I lose everything inside my stomach. Somewhere in the back of my head, I register my sister's comforting presence with her arms wrapped around me, whispering into my ear, but my heart, which I thought had been broken, shatters into a billion tiny pieces.

I'm not good enough for you.

"All I wanted was him," I whisper.

"I know, honey."

I'm not good enough for you.

"Only him."

"I know, sis.

"What am I supposed to do?" I whisper, taking a wet rag that's dangled in front of my face and pressing it to my mouth.

"Honestly?" Wes asks from behind me, and I nod, not lifting my head to look at him. "Don't let him push you away."

"It's too late," I breathe, feeling my heart pound and bile crawl back up my throat.

"Is it?" he questions softly, and I squeeze my eyes closed, knowing it is. It's way too late. There is no way I would ever put myself out there again, not like that, not with him. He didn't hurt me, he obliterated me.

"Maybe you could be his friend," July suggests, and I look at her.

"I don't think that's possible."

"You're both hurting, honey. I…" She pauses, pulling in a breath, and looking up at Wes who reaches down, running his fingers along her cheek. I love that my sister has what she has with Wes, but as much as I love it for her, I hate the jealousy I feel when I see them together. "I want you to be happy," she continues as her eyes drop to meet mine. "I don't think you'll be able to move on to your own happy until you figure out how to move past the hurt you feel."

Even knowing she's right, I don't know if I will ever be able to do that.

Chapter 4

June

"YOU CAN DO this," I whisper to my reflection in the rearview mirror. Moving my eyes to my lap, I mutter, "Why the hell did you let your sister Jedi mind trick you?"

Dropping my head to the steering wheel, I rest it there, resisting the urge to pound my head against it. July and Wes somehow talked me into meeting up with them at the compound. They said they were having a party and that I needed to get out of the house. I did need to get out of the house, but a party where Evan would be didn't seem like something I needed to do. In fact, I'm pretty sure I need to do the opposite, but still, I'm here, parked outside with the engine off, trying to build up enough courage to actually get out of my car.

Running my hands down the front of my bright orange sundress, I deeply breathe, open the door, and put one beige, sandal-covered foot on the ground then the other, proud of myself for at least making it out of the car. Shutting the door behind me, I look across the parking lot and pull in another deep breath before heading for the door next to the large gate, which will allow me into the open court where the party is. As soon as I'm there and pull the door open, I'm bombarded with the sound of rock music playing in the background, people talking and laughing, and the smell of booze, cigarettes, and pot.

"This is a bad idea," I whisper, scanning through the crowd of jean-and-leather-wearing men and barely dressed women for my sister or

Wes.

"Pardon?" a deep voice asks from my side, and I jump and turn my head to search the dark. A man steps out of the shadows, causing me to back up. He's not much taller than me, with blond hair that hits his broad shoulders. He's pretty, in a masculine way, with a square jaw, full lips, and big blue eyes surrounded by thick lashes.

"Sorry, I was talking to myself," I tell him, and he grins an eerie grin that doesn't quite fit the way he looks.

"Do you do that a lot?" he asks, taking a step closer to me, and I instinctively take another step back, wanting to keep space between us.

"Um…" I look around again, praying I see someone familiar.

"What's your name?" His eyes roam over me as he takes another step closer then reaches out and grabs a piece of my hair, wrapping it around his finger. Alarm bells are going off in my head, telling me to get away, but I feel like my feet have frozen to the concrete below them.

"I…" I pull my head back, taking my hair with it.

"I?" he prompts, tilting his head and taking a step closer.

"Jordan, back the fuck up."

My head swings around, and my heart, that was beginning to race, topples over itself when my eyes collide with Evan's. Closing the distance between us, he takes my hand as soon as he's near.

"Aw, I was just gonna have a little fun with her," Jordan says, and Evan tugs my hand, forcing me to collide into his side.

"Come near her and I'll have some fun with you, the kind of fun that will leave you in the hospital," Evan spits out, sounding serious and scary.

Jordan holds up his hands, scans me once more, sending a wink in my direction, and then turns around and walks back into the shadows, which is not only weird, but is also a little creepy.

"Are you okay?" Evan asks, and my gaze moves from where Jordan disappeared to his eyes.

"Yeah, he just startled me," I tell him quietly, feeling his hand wrapped around mine, his fingers over the pulse point of my wrist. His touch sends tingles up my arm, causing my breath to come out funny as his eyes roam my face. His touch is so familiar yet so foreign. Even if it's only a small part of me he's touching, I feel it everywhere. Dropping my hand, he runs his fingers through his hair, and I immediately miss the way it felt being connected to him. I know it doesn't make sense, but if it were possible for someone else to have your heart inside of their body, I know he would be carrying mine around.

"I didn't know you were going to be here," he says after a moment, and I bite the inside of my cheek to keep from asking if it would matter had he known.

"Wes and July asked me to come. I can go if you don't want me here," I whisper, and he closes his eyes for a brief moment. When he opens them, he pins me in place with his stare. I see it then, through the yellow light shining around us coming from the fires in barrels and the low lighting off the building above us—

Pain.

A pain so deep that it tears at my soul, ripping it to shreds inside my chest. A pain so harsh, I can feel it like it's my own.

"Evan," I exhale, taking a step closer to him, placing my hand on his bicep.

"Don't."

"I…" I shake my head, blinking back tears.

"Don't," he repeats, taking a step back, and my hand falls from his arm to my side. "Your sister's inside. Go find her. There are a lot of people here tonight, so stick to her or Wes," he says sternly then turns and starts to stalk off.

I don't know what comes over me, but the words are out before I can even think about keeping them in, or filtering them. "I lied." I'm not sure if my voice is loud enough to be heard, because my heartbeat is thumping wildly in my ears. He stops walking away, and I see his shoulders rise and fall. "It might not matter now…" I pause then pull in a breath through my nose. "I don't…maybe it never mattered." I shrug, even though he can't see it. "You were all I ever wanted," I say then continue on a whisper, "I believed in you. I believed in us. There was never a time you weren't good enough for me." When I finish, I feel my face heat in embarrassment and aggravation. Before I can make an even bigger fool out of myself, I hurry away in search of my sister and alcohol.

"SHOT! SHOT! SHOT!" I chant loudly, along with everyone else at the table, as my sister shoots back a shot of tequila. Her eyes meet mine as she slams the glass down on the tabletop, and I giggle at the pinched expression on her face.

"Your turn," she yells, pointing at me, and I pick up my shot glass and shoot it back, feeling the burn in my chest as the heat of the alcohol hits my system. It's not my first shot; actually, I'm pretty sure it's my twelfth. I'm feeling good.

Happy…

Relaxed…

After my talk with Evan—or my weird outburst, I should say—I found July and Wes in what they consider the common room. My sister, being my sister, took one look at my face and yelled, "Harlen!" and the second Harlen, who I'm pretty sure is a real-life giant, appeared, we started trying to outdrink him. I have no idea why. The task is pointless; the guy looks like he could drink a bottle of tequila alone and still not feel the effects.

"You know you girls are never going to be able to outdrink Harlen, right?" Mic, one of Wes' friends, asks from my side, and I turn my head and grin at him.

"I know." His eyes drop to my mouth and he smiles. Biting my lip,

I look away from him. He's definitely good-looking, like super hot, but I vowed to stick to my story of lesbianism. I'm not even sure if that's a real thing, but I need a man like I need a hole in my head.

"Caaan someone call me a cab or Lüber or whatever?" I slur, looking around the table. I need to get out of here. The alcohol I've drunk is floating through my system, making me feel loose.

"You're not leaving, are you?" my sister says with a pout from across the table, taking another shot.

"I need to get home before I do something stupid," I tell her honestly, hearing a few chuckles from the men surrounding us.

"I'll give you a ride," Mic says softly next to me, and my eyes slide to him.

"*You* would be the somethin' stupid," I tell him, and he smiles bigger, placing his hand on the back of my chair and leaning slightly in to me. At his move, I lean back and blurt, "I'm still in love with my ex-husbeen."

Blinking, he leans back then rumbles, "Fuck."

"Ezzactly." I nod then let out a breath, looking around the table. Everyone has been drinking, and my dad taught us from the time we were young to never, not *ever*, get in a car with anyone who has even had one beer.

"You hab your phone?" I ask my sister sitting across the table from me when her eyes meet mine.

"It's in Wes's room. Where's yours?"

I bite my lip again. I never have my cell. The stupid thing is annoying, so I constantly leave it behind. I should probably start carrying it. "At home," I tell her, and she nods like it makes total sense then looks at Wes.

"Can we give her a ride?" she whispers, or she tries to, but she's so drunk it comes out loudly and everyone at the table looks at her.

"She can stay here," he replies, running his thumb over her bottom lip.

"Can we stay here too?" she asks, leaning in to him and biting his thumb. His answer is a growl. Dragging my eyes from them, I look around. I don't want to stay here, but I'm so drunk, things are starting to look a little—or a lot—blurry.

"Come on. I'll get you settled," Mic says quietly, helping me out of the chair I planted myself in a few hours—or minutes—ago. I'm not sure how long it's been.

"Thaaanks," I slur, leaning in to him. I don't even know where he leads me. I hear him talking to someone, but my mind is so fuzzy I can't even tell what he's saying. The second I'm directed to a bed, though, I lie down face-first and pass out.

I SEMI-AWAKEN AS I feel warmth and smell something I swear my soul recognizes as its own. I don't want to open my eyes. I don't want this feeling coursing though me to end. Breathing steadily, I let my body absorb the feeling of the hand wrapped around my waist, the steady breath at the back of my neck, and the weight settled against me. I know I'm going to wake up and this is going to be a dream, so I want to consume all of it, memorize every single second. This is like every other time I've woken up thinking Evan is with me—that his arms are holding me, that he still loves me—only now I know what we had isn't what I made it out to be.

A hand rises, cupping my breast, and the hard length of a man presses against my ass. Squeezing my eyes closed, I pray I'm still dreaming, pray I didn't do something fucking stupid last night and didn't make my fucked-up life even more fucked up.

Cracking my eyes open, I see a plain white wall in front of me. My eyes drop to my chest, and sure enough, there's a large hand wrapped around my breast.

I have no idea what I did last night. The whole night is a complete blur, but I don't remember getting into bed with anyone. Scooting carefully across the expanse of the bed so I don't disturb my bed partner, I finally get free and roll off the side, putting one knee and one hand on the floor at a time until I'm on all fours. Lifting my head over the edge of the bed, I see…Evan? His eyes are closed, his face soft in sleep.

"How the hell did you get here?" I ask under my breath, dropping my forehead to the floor.

"I put you here last night," Evan answers from above, but I pretend I don't hear him as I attempt to scoot under the bed to hide, but the frame is too low to the floor.

His hand touches my back and my head flies up.

"Morning," he whispers, running his fingers along my hairline.

Blinking, I look around. Even knowing he's talking to me, I still try to see if there is someone else he's talking to so softly. I've missed his gentle voice more than I will ever admit. I missed all of him, but I really missed how soft he always was with me, how he treated me like I was something delicate, something he needed to take care of, something he cherished above anything else.

"Why…what am I doing here?"

His eyes run over my hair and face for a moment and he looks toward the door. "I came back last night and you were trashed," he says with his eyes on the door while running his hand through his hair.

"I asked for a cab," I tell him, and his gaze drops back down to me.

"I wanted to keep an eye on you. You were pretty out of it, and I didn't want you to be alone if you got sick."

"Oh," I whisper, sitting back on my knees and wrapping my arms around my waist. This is awkward—or more than awkward, whatever that is.

"It's not even six. Come back up here. You can get up in a bit," he says quietly, and my eyes move around the room. It's small, with a double bed, and a single dresser under a small window. There is nothing personalizing the space, but it's clean and I see a bathroom off to the side.

"I should go. Do you mind if I use your bathroom before I do?"

His answer is a jerk of his chin, so I get up off the floor and head for the bathroom. Closing the door, I look at myself in the mirror above the sink. My image is distorted through the shattered glass. Raising my fingers to the broken mirror, I see blood imbedded between the broken pieces. Pain slices though me, along with understanding. I'm not sure what happened to Evan when he left, but the man I saw last night—the guy who spoke to Jordan like he would lay him out and not stop to check his pulse—isn't the guy I fell in love with. This Evan is different. He's scary and angry, and I can tell he's fighting demons, but even with all that, I find myself wanting to soothe him.

Biting my lip, I turn on the water and splash my face to get rid of the tears that started to fill my eyes. I want to fix him, or hug him.

Yeah, because you're a glutton for punishment and half-idiot! my mind screams.

Finding some toothpaste in the drawer, I use my finger as a brush, rinse out my mouth, and then take care of business before washing my hands and opening the door.

Evan is no longer in bed, but up and putting on a pair of jeans. His eyes come to me, and I brace myself, running my hands down my hair in an attempt to smooth it out. I don't know what to expect from him anymore. He always seems to be in a rush to get away from me.

"Would you have breakfast with me?" he asks after a moment.

I hear the question, I know I do, but my mind is solely focused on his shirtless torso as he moves across the room to the dresser. He always had a great body, but now it's bigger, stronger. There are muscles on top of muscles, and definition that wasn't there before. I feel my face heat when he turns toward me. He's beautiful. His body is a work of art, and I want to touch him. I want to know what it feels like to have his bearded face against my delicate skin. I want to know if the rough edges I see now are smooth to the touch.

"June." My name in his coarse tone gets my attention, but when our eyes meet, it's not anger he's looking at me with. It's raw, powerful, hungry possessiveness. My legs go weak, and I'm surprised I don't topple over where I stand. He starts toward me, closing the distance between us. Realizing he's coming at me, I back up and hit the wall with nowhere else to go.

One of his arms wraps around my waist while the other rests on the wall above my head. He's still shirtless, so I feel every inch of his hot skin through the material of my thin dress as he presses me into the wall at my back.

"Back up," I breathe, turning my head away from him, feeling his warm breath against my cheek and his hand slide up my waist, burning my skin as it moves.

"I can't. You know I fucking can't." His fingers dig into my side and I squeeze my eyes tighter. "Look at me, June."

"Back up," I repeat as my pulse races, and tingles shoot through my system.

"Look at me, baby." His voice is soft again as his hand moves to lock around my jaw.

"This isn't a good idea," I whisper the God's honest truth as my eyes open to meet his. I may think he's beautiful—I may even have at some point decided he needed a friend and that I was going to be that friend to him—but this isn't a good idea. Him touching me, calling me baby, isn't smart for either of us.

His lips wisp across my jaw, and my hands that I didn't even realize were touching him turn into talons digging into his skin.

"Ev," I breathe as his hips press into mine, and as I feel his hardness against my belly, wetness surges between my legs, and I fight the moan I feel in my throat.

"Fuck, I miss that." His hand moves from the wall above me and his fingers thread through the hair at the back of my head. When his fist tightens against my scalp, I let the moan I was holding in loose. "Beautiful," he mutters, and then his teeth are on my lips, nipping hard.

I gasp, and his tongue slides into my mouth, tangling with mine. His taste explodes on my taste buds and I lose myself in the kiss, giving as good as I get, nipping his bottom lip then soothing it with my tongue as my hands roam up his arms and into his hair. Forcing my head to the side, he kisses me deeper, taking more of me. That's when I feel it happen—I feel myself crumble into a billion pieces in his hold and allow myself to do nothing, nothing but just feel him, his hands, his mouth on me.

Crying into his mouth, he yanks me away from the wall and starts moving us across the room. The backs of my knees hit the bed and I go down. His hand never leaves my hair, and his mouth never leaves mine as he shifts me higher onto the bed.

When his mouth finally does leave mine, I don't even have a second to plea for him to come back. His warm breath trails along my neck, and I memorize the way his beard feels against my skin and the way his tongue feels against the pulse of my neck. His hand travels up and curves around my ribs, close to my breast, and then his thumb sweeps over my nipple, causing my legs to lift and wrap around his hips.

When his hand drags down the top of my dress and bra, I lift my head to watch his mouth lower over my nipple. The first tug from his mouth has me coming out of my skin. His hand in my hair tightens then moves to cup my other breast over my dress. I'm drenched as his weight presses into me, his mouth devours my breast, and his beard drags roughly against my skin. I'm close—so close I know I'm going to come from just this. Shifting to the side, his hand at my breast travels down, and I feel the cotton of my dress slide up my thigh as his fingers trail up higher until their warmth is close to my core.

"Ev," I breathe, running my fingers through his hair as his fingers slide over my panties.

"Soaked through," he grunts, releasing my nipple, trailing his lips back up and taking my mouth again. My hips lift, my hands moving to hold on to his biceps as he pushes my panties to the side and his fingers circle my clit. That's all I need. My head falls back and an orgasm washes over me, lighting everything up with its intensity. I float off to outer space, completely lost in its vastness. Coming slowly back to my body, I feel my dress roughly pulled off before I'm moved again. My head hits the pillow, my panties ripped down my legs.

Watching him tear open a condom, I whisper, "Evan."

When his eyes lock on mine, I see something familiar looking back at me, something I can't even begin to understand, something damaged and raw, and it has my legs lifting to wrap around his hips and my arms sliding around his back, wanting to hold him. At my touch, his jaw locks and his forehead drops to mine, pushing into me. My breath leaves on a whoosh and my eyes slide closed. He's so big—not just long, but thick—and it's been so long that the stretch of pain I felt the first time comes rushing back.

"Beautiful," he murmurs.

My eyes open, and I watch as he watches where we are connected. "Oh, God," I whisper, dragging my nails up his back.

"Look at me, June," he demands roughly, and my eyes I didn't realize were closed slide open and lock on his as he slides in and out of me slowly, so slowly I feel every inch of him, every single centimeter, as he possesses me. "I could die right here, right fucking here, and know I felt heaven at least once," he snarls as his nostrils flare.

Feeling tears begin to gather in my eyes, I lift my head, bury my face in the crook of his neck, and wrap myself around him. My orgasm hits me suddenly, stealing the air from my lungs and my heart from my body. Filling me one last time, he plants himself deep inside me and groans against my neck as his arms wrap around my back, holding on to me so tight it's hard to breathe. So tight, it makes me feel as if he is trying to fuse us together.

A loud sob rips from my throat, and he rolls us to our sides and rubs his hand over my back, talking softly as I cry into his chest.

Chapter 5

Evan

PULLING THE BLANKET up over us from the end of the bed, I hold June against me, feeling each one of her tears soak into my skin. It kills me that she's crying. I hate even more that I'm the reason for her tears. I shouldn't have taken her. I should have done things differently, taken my time with her, slowly built back what we once had. But when I saw the look in her eyes from across the room, the same look that was in her eyes the other day when I was on my bike, I couldn't stop myself.

Hearing her sobs die down, I jerk back my chin and notice her eyes are closed and her body has gone soft. Pulling away, I go to the bathroom and take care of the condom, wash my hands and face, and then go back to her and pull her right back into my arms. Her words from last night have been playing through my head since the moment she hightailed it away from me. Her telling me I was always good enough for her really hit home.

When I left last night, I went for a ride to give myself some time to think. By the time I got back, I knew one thing for sure—I needed to find a way to get her back, to get *us* back to what we once had. She was the best thing that ever happened to me, the reason I fought to live and to get better after I got back stateside.

Pressing my lips to the warm skin of her forehead, I rest them there. I know I'm going to have a battle on my hands. I hurt her, I know I did. I also know it's going to take a lot for her to trust me. She's strong, and stubborn as hell, but I'm banking on the fact that she feels the same pull I do, like I can only breathe right when we're together. My men and I used to joke that you never appreciate the beauty of what's under your own feet until you're walking through a minefield. This thing between us is a minefield of a different kind. Between our history and what I did to her, I'm going to be working hard to make sure we get through to the other side intact.

Lying there, I soak in the feeling of her in my arms, the same thing I did last night while she slept. I missed her so goddamn much—not just her body, but her smell, her laugh, and the way she looks at me like I hold the key to heaven and have personally granted her access through the gate. I'm not stupid enough to think I can sleep with her once and be back to where we were before. I know I'm going to have to work at proving myself to her. I'm gonna have to prove that with me is the best place for her.

I've been fighting my feelings for her for so long that now that I've let them loose, they are all flooding to the surface at once. My emotions where she's involved are irrational and extreme at best, causing me to act even more possessive than I used to. I hated it when she was with that piece of shit in Alabama, but I made my bed and was determined to lie in it, even if I was miserable. I said she deserved better than me, but I can't do it again. I can't sit on the sidelines and watch her from a distance. If she fell in love with someone else because I was too fucking scared to take what I wanted, I would hate myself for the rest of my life.

Hearing a light *tap, tap, tap* on the door, I carefully extract myself from her, slip out of bed, find my jeans on the floor, drag them on, and go to see who's there, not even bothering with the buttons of my pants.

"Is June in there with you?" July asks quietly as soon as I have the door opened up a crack.

"Yeah." I nod then lift my chin at Wes, who's standing behind her.

"Can I see her?" she asks, and I look over my shoulder at the bed.

"She's asleep."

"So your saying I can't see her?" she prompts.

"You can see her when she's awake."

"I can see her when she's awake?" she repeats in disbelief.

"Babe," Wes mutters from behind her, and her head swings toward him, giving him a glare, then back to me just as fast, the glare still in place.

"If you fuck her over, I'll cut off your balls and use them as cat toys," she hisses, and I see Wes flinch behind her as I fight my own, but I don't respond. I just raise a brow and wait for her to finish. "Just so you know, I think my dad has a feeling something is going on between you two, so you better understand that if you're with her, you're with all of us."

Feeling my jaw clench, I mutter, "Right."

Her face goes soft and her head tilts to the side as she whispers, "Please take care of her," and takes off before I can reply.

Closing the door, I kick off my jeans and get back into bed. As soon as I'm settled, June burrows her way into my chest and whispers, "Ev."

"I'm here, beautiful," I tell her, kissing her forehead.

"Hmm…" she breathes, wrapping her arm around my waist, so I bury my face in her hair and breathe her in, listening to her sleep.

"ARE YOU GOING to eat, or are you going to pout and stare at your breakfast?" I ask, feeling my lips twitch as I watch June debate with herself across from me.

When she woke up in my arms, she immediately tried to get away, but figuring I needed to put my plan into action sooner rather than later, I didn't let her go far. I pinned her to the bed and kissed her until she was panting. It took everything in me not to slide right back into the heaven I knew she held between her legs. The only thing that stopped me was knowing the walls she built between us wouldn't be coming down if I did that, if I used her own body against her, she'd resent me.

So instead, I kissed her neck and rolled off her, pulling her along with me to the bathroom, where I pushed her into the shower ahead of me then got in with her. She was a hissing cat throughout the whole shower, but I wasn't going to let her out of my sight, not even for a moment. It may have been awhile since we were together, but knowing her, she would have taken off the first chance she got and disappeared. After we got out of the shower and got dressed, I confiscated her key and drove us in her car to the diner down the street from her house.

"I'm going to eat, because it's stuffed French toast, but I'm not going to enjoy it," she mutters under her breath, and I throw my head back and laugh. At the noise, her head flies up and her face softens, making my heart clench.

"I haven't seen you laugh in a long time," she whispers, studying me from across the table.

Her serious tone sets a pause to my humor. "Tell me about your new job. Are you excited?" I change the subject before taking a bite of my omelet.

"Yes, well, I'm not excited to work the whole summer, but I'm excited to start my career and get settled," she says to her plate, and I nudge her foot under the table, urging her to give me her eyes.

"I'm proud of you. I know how important graduating was to you, and I know how excited you were to start teaching."

Her eyes stay locked on mine, and I see the wheels in her head turning as she asks softly, "What's going on?"

"We're having breakfast," I point out, and her eyes narrow.

"You... you..." She throws her hands up in the air. "And then...then I wake up in bed with you...and we...we had sex!" she shouts at the end, sending her eyes flying around the restaurant.

"Baby, calm down."

"No, no way." She leans across the table, pointing her fork at me.

Letting out an aggravated breath, I feel my nostrils flare as my eyes roam over her. "Do you know what it's like to stand in front of something you want, but know you shouldn't have, to wish you had the ability to turn off your feelings so life for the both of you would be easier?" I ask, and she flinches like I struck her. "No, beautiful, not for the reason you think. You were the best thing to ever happen to me, the one good thing I had in my life."

"Until you left me," she says quietly, and a sharp pain shoots through my chest.

"I didn't want to get you dirty," I tell her softly, honestly.

"What?" she whispers, but I see the tears in her eyes about to spill over. I don't want her to cry. Her tears fucking kill me every time.

"Let's talk about that another time," I suggest gently.

"Ev—"

"Baby, please, let's just have breakfast,"

"I don't know?" She closes her eyes. Reaching across the table, I take her hand and bring it to my mouth, and her eyes open as my lips touch her skin.

"One day, I'll explain everything."

"I don't know what's going on. I don't know if I'm strong enough to do this with you." She swallows, looking conflicted. Even with the struggle she's feeling, she's not telling me to fuck off.

"One day at a time. I've been fighting this, and I can't fight it any-more. I miss you. I miss us."

"Please don't do this." Her chin wobbles, and I kiss her fingers again.

"Just breakfast today, this moment today. We'll think about tomor-row when it gets here." Watching tears fill her eyes again, I stand and move around to sit next to her then wrap my arm around her shoulders to hold her. "I hate when you cry."

"I don't like it much either," she concedes, sounding miserable, and I smile at her tone.

"Why are you smiling?" She frowns, tilting her head back to look at me.

Leaning in, I whisper into her ear the truth—or part of it. "This morning, I took a trip to heaven. Not too much could piss me off right now."

"You didn't just say that."

"I did." I kiss her nose then grab my plate from across the table and set it in front of me. "Eat," I tell her, gaining an eye roll, but she starts to eat and doesn't pull away.

"What are your plans for the day?" I ask halfway through my omelet.

"I need to run some errands. What are you doing?"

"I need to drive up to Nashville for Jax. I'll be back around five. Do you want to have dinner?"

"Dinner?" she repeats, looking like she's never heard of it before.

"Yeah, dinner." I lean in, licking off a speck of powdered sugar from the side of her mouth.

Clearing her throat when I lean back, she mutters, "Dinner...uh...sounds good."

"Good, I'll be by your place around five."

"Okay," she agrees, and her eyes drop to my mouth, so I give her what she wants, only this time when I'm finished, her hands are woven into my shirt, holding me closer giving me hope.

"SORRY, MAN."

"It's not your fault she's a fucking bitch," Julian says, tucking the pictures of his wife I just had the unfortunate job of showing him back into the envelope. He places them in the inside pocket of his suit jacket as I pick my coffee up off the table. "If this goes to court and I need more, can I count on you guys to get me what I need?"

"I'm sure we can work something out." I detest this part of the job. There is nothing, absolutely *nothing,* worse than telling someone the person they chose to share their life with isn't who they thought they were.

"Good, my boy needs better than this shit." He taps the front of his jacket, where the pictures are. "I know I'm gonna have a war on my hands when I ask for a divorce, and I don't want that bitch to get anything."

"Let us know what you need." I pull out my personal business card and slide it across the table to him. "If something comes up and you can't reach anyone at the office, use that," I say, standing and taking my coffee with me.

"Thanks," he mutters, picking up his coffee and turning his head to look out the window. Pushing the door open and walking out of the restaurant, I head toward my bike and pull my cell out to look at the time. Shoving my cell back in my pocket, I throw one leg over my bike, back out of the space, and head for the office.

"You do the drop-off to Julian?" Jax asks as soon as I step into his office and close the door behind me.

"Yep," I reply, taking a seat across from him.

"How'd he take the news?"

"He asked if he needed more for court, if we could help him out. I told him we could."

"He thinks he'll need more than what you got?" He frowns.

"Not sure. Dude has money, but he's been married for years. I doubt he has a pre-nup, and he sounded like he wanted full custody of his boy. My guess is he's gonna hold on to this and see what his lawyer has to say before he makes his play."

"Christ, I can't imagine having to sleep next to the woman I knew was fucking around on me, so I could get my kid." Jax shakes his head and I do the same. "I think we can lay off June's place. There hasn't even been chatter about her, and I doubt there will be."

"I'll still keep an eye on her," I tell him, and his eyes stay locked on mine before he shakes his head and looks away, letting out a heavy sigh.

"You wanna tell me why you'd do that?"

"Because I'm in love with her."

His eyes narrow, and I realize Sage obviously has not talked to him about me and June's past, or the fact we have a past, period.

"You're in love with her?" he repeats in disbelief.

"I could lie to you about it, but yeah, I'm in love with her. Have been since the moment we met."

"What the fuck are you talking about?" He stands from his chair and puts his fist to the desk in front of him, leaning across it toward me.

"I met her in Alabama, before I went to Afghanistan," I say calmly, keeping my position.

"You've got to be shitting me."

"Nope."

"Did you know she was my cousin when you started working for me?" he asks.

"No, not until Sage asked me to look into Lane."

His eyes narrow before he drops his forehead. "This is fucked. How did I not know about this?" he asks the top of the desk.

"It doesn't matter now."

"You don't think so? You fuck up with her, and I'm down one man, 'cause I'm gonna have to take you out."

My spine stiffens and I growl "I'm not gonna fuck up with her."

"You were with her, and then you weren't. My guess is you've already fucked up with her."

He had a point—one I didn't like, but a point nonetheless. Still, I continued on, "Can't predict the future, but I know I regret everything

53

I did to us. I also know how it feels to live without her, and I won't do that again."

"I should've seen this coming."

"I'm not gonna say sorry."

"Jesus, Evan, you're fucking locked up tight. No one knows shit about you, and then you come to tell me this shit, and expect me to just fucking deal with it, without questioning the shit you're sayin'?"

"I don't expect anything. One: me and June are none of your concern. Two: no disrespect, but I don't really give a fuck what you think about the two of us."

"You don't give a fuck?" he asks low, cutting me off and leaning closer. Jax is a big dude, but I still have about two inches and thirty pounds on him. I'm not afraid of him, or anyone else for that matter. Once you've seen what I've seen, watched people die, and been up close and personal with death yourself, you know what real fear is. "What the fuck am I supposed to do with this, Barrister?" he asks on a growl, leaning even farther across the desk.

"Nothing, let the cards fall where they're gonna fall."

Shaking his head, he stands, taking his hands from the desk. "This goes bad, and I'm gonna have no choice but to kick your ass." He sighs, and I shrug. "This is fucked," he mutters, taking a seat and rubbing his face.

"I gotta get to June. You need anything else?" I ask, standing up.

His head turns to the side, and he lets out a breath then asks, "Does my uncle know about the two of you?"

"No, but he will."

"You may wanna wait to inform him of this shit until you and her are solid," he suggests, looking at me.

"I'm not waiting again. I should have forced her to be honest about us before, but I didn't. That was my bad. This time around, I'm doing shit differently," I tell him, and he roars with laughter, doubling over with the force of it.

"Oh, shit. I need to be there when you tell him this," he says through his cackles as I head for the door.

"I'll get you a front row seat," I mutter, before shutting the door behind me.

Once out of the office, I back my bike out of my spot and head for the compound to exchange my bike for my truck. Pulling into June's driveway twenty minutes later, I look at the dash, seeing it's ten 'til five. I park behind her bug, shut down The Beast, and hop out. Making my way down the sidewalk, the front door opens, and I notice she's dressed, but not dressed to go out. Her hair is up, and she's wearing a plain, peach-colored tank and short jean shorts with bare feet.

"You change your mind?" I ask as I make my way up to the front door.

"Um…no, I…" She looks up at me, seeming uncomfortable. "I thought we could eat dinner here?"

"Yeah?" I ask, wrapping my hand around her hip, pressing her into the house before shutting the door closed behind me.

"I kinda had a hangover and—"

"I'm good with us having dinner here," I mutter, cutting her off, and she smiles, taking my hand and leading me down the hall. "Do you want me to go out and pick something up, or do you want to order in?" I ask, and she looks at me over her shoulder.

Smiling tentatively, she murmurs, "I already cooked."

"You didn't have to do that, 'specially if you're not feeling well."

"I wanted to," she says, and I follow her into the kitchen. As soon as we reach the threshold between the kitchen and living room, I'm hit by the overwhelming smell of rosemary chicken. It's one of the things she used to make for me when she came to my place on the weekends, something I told her I loved on our first date.

"Baby," I whisper, feeling my chest tighten when she drops my hand and grabs a set of potholders off the counter to open the oven. Pulling out the baking dish holding the chicken, she sets it on the stovetop then pulls out a pan I know holds scalloped potatoes. As soon as she has the pan with the potatoes on the stove, I shut the oven, mold my front to her back, press my mouth to her neck, and breathe her in.

"Evan."

"Yeah, baby?" I ask against her skin, feeling her pulse beat against my lips.

"Um…are you okay?" she asks, her tone filled with uncertainty.

"Fuck yeah," I mutter against her neck and I feel the tension drain from her muscles.

"Are you hungry?" she inquires quietly, placing her hands over mine on her waist.

"Definitely," I rumble, feeling her shiver.

"We should eat," she whispers after a long moment.

"Give me a second," I whisper back, needing this moment, her in my arms, her scent in my lungs, proving I'm alive and here with her.

"Ev." She turns in my arms, placing her hands on either side of my neck. "Talk to me," she prompts quietly, searching my eyes.

"I'm good." I lean forward and run my nose along hers. "Great, actually."

"You seemed like you were somewhere else."

"I'm right here," I assure her quietly, because it's the fucking truth. I just had no clue we'd be here again. I never thought we had a shot, didn't dare to even dream she would welcome me into her house and prove once more how fucking stupid I was by letting her go, when she is the kind of woman to remember something as small as what my favorite meal is.

Searching my eyes again, she lets out a deep breath then looks away. "I got some beer. Find something to drink and I'll get our plates ready." I know from her tone that she's annoyed or disappointed, but I have no clue what she's searching for or what answer she wants. I'm being as honest as I can be right now.

"Kiss me, and then I'll get a beer," I pull her closer until her tits are pressed into my chest and her hands are forced to slide around the back of my neck.

"I don't remember you being this bossy."

"I probably wasn't," I tell her, leaving out the fact that I know what it's like to live without something—something I liked a fuck'uva lot—and since I don't have to be without it anymore, I'm going to enjoy it when I can get it, even if I have to demand it.

"Ev." Her forehead comes to rest against my chest as her head drops forward and her hands slide down my chest and around my back. "This…" She lets out a breath then continues quietly, "I dreamt of you…" She pauses, pressing deeper into my chest. "You used to haunt me, and I…" My gut gets tight as she pauses again. "I don't know if this is real. It can't be real."

"It's real," I rumble.

"How can it be?"

"You just have to believe that it is, beautiful." Wrapping her hair around my fist, I pull her face out of my chest and tilt her head back, taking the kiss I asked her for.

"HARDER," I COMMAND, wrapping my hands around her hips.

"No," she whispers, sliding down slowly, so fucking slow I feel my balls draw up.

"Harder, June," I repeat, ready to lose it, not wanting to come until she does. After we ate her really fucking good food, we settled in front of the TV, cuddling. I had my hand up the back of her tank, my fingers roaming across her smooth skin as we watched some TV show she swore I needed to watch. It was about a detective in New York and a woman who was covered in tattoos, which happened to be clues to cases they were working on. My mind wasn't on the show, even though I had to agree the premise was cool. Instead, my mind was on her body, lying against mine, on her couch, in her living room, in her house, doing something normal, something I knew we would have had if I hadn't fucked us up.

But when she started squirming on me, her legs fidgeting, I knew she wasn't thinking about the show anymore either. I didn't plan on taking her. I would have been happy holding her on her couch, in her living room, in her house, but my beautiful girl had other plans, and I knew this when her warm, soft hand wrapped around my cock, and making out turned into me fingering her until she came and then her straddling my lap, which brings us to now.

"I want to feel you," she breathes, dropping again and again, doing it slow.

Torturous.

"Fuck." I buck up into her then lift her up with my hands under her ass, hearing her squeak as her limbs wind around me. Moving across the house to her bedroom, I push the door open, move to the bed, put one knee into the mattress and then the other, never losing our connection as I settle her on the bed. "Hands above your head."

"What?" she whimpers as I slam into her once.

"Hands above your head," I repeat, sitting back on my knees. Her hands tentatively move above her head, and I put mine behind my neck to pull my shirt off then pull her tank off. Dropping my head, I pull her breast into my mouth and cup the other one.

Her hands move to my head, and I pull from her touch and growl, "Hands above your head, June. I tell you again and I'm spanking you." Her walls contract, and her already erratic breathing turns choppy, but still, her hands move above her, this time wrapping into the blanket. Dropping my face again, I pull her other nipple into my mouth and tug hard. I love her breasts, they're small but so fucking sensitive. I know from experience she can come from me just playing with her tits.

"Ev," she whimpers, wrapping her long legs around my hips.

Letting go of her nipple with a pop, I settle myself over her. "You wanted to play, you got me worked up." I flick her clit. "I'm gonna give you what you want, but this time, we're doing things my way." Her eyes flare and her hands clench into the blanket above her head again as her tongue swipes across her bottom lip. Rising to my knees, I hold on to her hips and slide into her slowly, slower than she was going, then skim my hands up to her breasts, watching her back arch. "Fucking beautiful." Roaming my hand from her breast and down her stomach, I circle her clit with my thumb, keeping the pressure light.

"Please," she hisses, putting her feet to the mattress raising her hips.

"I want to feel you," I use her words against her, keeping my strokes gentle and my thumb even lighter. Her walls tighten around my cock, and I bite my lip against the exquisite beauty then roll my thumb over her clit. Her hips buck on an inward thrust, and I fight the urge to pound into her.

"I…" Her head jerks side-to-side against the bed and her back arches, her toes and head the only thing on the mattress as she comes hard. Her pussy clenching, pulling me deeper into her. Bending over her, I pull her nipple into my mouth and roll my thumb in tighter circles around her clit, dragging out her orgasm until she's screaming my name and soaking my cock.

Flipping her to her stomach, I pull her hips high then slide back in. Moving my hand to the back of her neck, I hold her shoulders down to the bed then fuck her like a mad man, so hard that the headboard bangs loudly against the wall and the picture above the bed rattles. Lifting her with an arm around her chest, I impale her on my length. Hearing her whimper, I wrap my hand around her jaw and turn her face toward me, thrusting my tongue into her mouth, while I work my cock slowly deep inside of her. Her hands move up cupping her breasts. I pull my mouth from hers so I can watch her hands work her tits and her face as she pants.

"Do you love my cock, baby?" I thrust in slowly. Her dazed eyes meet mine and her head dips to the side as her bottom lip disappears between her teeth. "Answer my question." I slide one hand between her legs over her clit.

Her teeth release her lip and the word *yes* leaves her mouth breathlessly as I slide back in deep, moving my fingers faster over her. "Oh, God." Her head drops back to my shoulder as her fingers cover mine then push lower to our connection.

"Jesus." My mouth drops to her shoulder and my teeth lock onto her skin as she comes again, taking me with her this time. Planting myself deep inside her, I squeeze my eyes tight, never having felt what I'm feeling right now, not even with her the first time, which happened to be the best I ever had. Releasing her skin from my teeth, I kiss the spot then roll us to the bed and adjust her against me as I try to get my breathing back under control, along with my heart.

"That...I don't even have words for that," she mutters, pressing her sweat-soaked skin deeper into mine.

"Yeah," I agree, wrapping my hand into her hair, tipping her head back and placing a kiss to her mouth then forehead before tucking her face against my chest.

"Will you stay the night?" she asks after a long moment.

Dipping my face to hers, I use my fingers under her chin to make myself clear. "You couldn't make me leave, beautiful."

Her eyes search mine for a long time. Finally, she puts pressure against my fingers and dips her chin, whispering, "Okay."

We lie there for a while longer, so long I feel myself doze off, and then I feel her move and I roll her to her back.

"I'm gonna take care of the condom. Stay here."

"I wanna clean up."

"Stay," I repeat, kissing her softly. At her nod, I roll from the bed and go to the bathroom. Opening cabinets, I find her washcloths and toss one into the sink under the hot water while I dispose of the condom. Heading back to the room, I see she moved to bury under the covers. Pulling them away from her, I ignore her startled gasp then slide her legs apart, cleaning her up gently. Taking the rag back to the bathroom, I toss it in the sink then head right back to bed, getting in and pulling her back into my arms.

"I should go turn out the lights and stuff," she mutters sleepily against my chest as her arm slides over my abs.

"I'll get them in a bit. Sleep, baby," I whisper, kissing the top of her head. Her answer is to cuddle closer. I don't sleep. I listen until her breathing turns even then slide out from under her. I head to the living room, grab our clothes from there, shut down the house, and then fold our stuff and set them on the bench at the end of her bed. When I get back into bed, her body burrows into mine and she whispers, "Ev," like she did earlier that day when she was asleep.

"I'm here, beautiful."

"Yeah," she sighs, and then her body goes soft. I adjust us so she's half under me and follow her off to sleep, not realizing she only calls me *Ev* when she's asleep or when I'm deep inside of her. Any other time, she calls me Evan.

Chapter 6

June

"THIS TASTES LIKE strawberry milk," I mutter to JJ, taking another shot of the creamy pink-colored tequila.

"It's Tequila Rose, bitch, not strawberry milk." She laughs, pouring herself a shot.

"Still tastes like strawberry milk." I grin.

"Yeah, except the fact you're drunk proves it's tequila."

She wasn't wrong. I was drunk. Actually, I wasn't really drunk, but I was on my way there.

"You have a point," I mutter, and she rolls her eyes, releasing a breath, and I know what's coming. I knew the second I stepped out of my car when she yelled at me from her porch that she was coming over to "talk." Then she showed up twenty minutes ago with a bottle of tequila and told me to drink.

"So tell me what the fuck happened. Last time we had tequila, you told me you and Hot Guy's history, how you two got together, how it was when he joined the military, and what happened since you moved here. You seemed pretty firm in the idea you wanted nothing to do with him. Obviously, that didn't pan out, 'cause his tongue was down your throat and his hand on your bare ass this morning when I was leaving for work," she states, pouring me another shot.

I frowned. "My ass wasn't bare." And it wasn't. I put on panties and a shirt when Evan pulled me from bed and told me to walk him to the door this morning before he left.

"Whatever, that's besides the point," she mutters then continues on. "The point is he *obviously* stayed the night and you *obviously* gave him the cookie. What happened? Spill it, bitch."

"I'm stupid." I close my eyes, dropping my forehead to the granite countertop in front of me. Even knowing that, knowing I was being stupid, I was still doing it. I couldn't help myself. The second he touched me, I knew I would give him anything he asked for.

Totally stupid.

The positive: I knew what the outcome would be. I knew he wouldn't stick around, so while I had him, I would attempt to help him get past whatever it is I saw in his eyes. That raw anguish he tried to hide. And while I did that, I would have as much amazing sex as I could get, while carefully guarding my heart so it wouldn't be crushed anymore than it already had been.

"Honey, love is never stupid," JJ whispers, bringing me out of my thoughts, and my head lifts, my eyes meeting her soft ones.

"I don't love him."

Her eyes close briefly then a small smile turns up her lips. "Don't lie to yourself, honey, and please don't lie to me either."

"Wouldn't it…" I swallow and pull my eyes from her to look out the window at the back yard. "Wouldn't that be stupid?"

"Love is never stupid. It's beautiful and consuming, and we don't always have the ability to fight it when it happens."

"I don't want to love him. I don't want to get hurt again," I tell her honestly, dropping my eyes to the counter in front of me.

"I hear you. It's never easy putting yourself out there, putting yourself in a situation that leaves you vulnerable, open for hurt or pain."

"Exactly," I agree, taking the shot she scoots across the counter toward me.

"But then again, if you don't put yourself out there, don't let your guard down, don't open yourself up to the chance of love, then you will never have the experience of someone proving to you they are worthy of the gift you're giving them. You won't have a shot at happiness, not real happiness, which comes from sharing your life with someone."

"I don't need anyone—especially not a man—to be happy," I grumble, and her hand reaches out, taking mine and squeezing it tight.

"Everyone needs someone. Even people who think they're happy on their own know they were wrong the first time they have someone to come home to at the end of the night. Someone to share their sorrow with, someone to lean on when they can't stand on their own anymore. I'm not saying another person will ever make you whole, but having someone who wants the best for you, loves you, cares about your future and your well-being, is far from a bad thing."

Swallowing hard, I close my eyes against the pain in my chest, because I know she's right. I just don't know if Evan's that person. I did know before; I knew it with every fiber of my being. Now? *Now I'm not so sure.*

"What did he say that got him back in?" she asks, and it takes me a moment to understand she's asking why he was suddenly in my house after, as she put it, I made it clear I wanted nothing to do with him.

"He didn't say anything to me. My sister's husband heard him say he wasn't good enough for me." I shake my head, pulling a chunk of hair away from my face. "I... I wanted him to know that wasn't the case, that he was always good enough, so I told him that."

Nodding, her eyes go softer and she mutters, "Selfless."

"What?"

"When you love someone, *really* love them, you will do whatever is necessary to protect that person, even if you're protecting them from you."

"I didn't need him protecting me from him."

"You think that, but my guess is he didn't feel the same way."

"I don't know. We haven't talked about it. When I ask him, he says 'later.' I don't even know what the hell that means."

"Later means just that—later. I'm sure he's not looking forward to sharing his burden with you. I also doubt he wants to do that after he's just gotten you back."

"We're having sex, JJ. I don't think that qualifies as us getting back together."

"Did you tell him that?" She raises her brows.

"No," I mutter.

"Exactly." She grins then jumps off her stool. "I gotta get home. My man is cool, but if I don't feed him before he heads out, we got problems." She must read my face, because her smile turns wicked when she confides, "Honey, trust me when I tell you the punishments he doles out are always a win for me."

"Oh," I whisper, and she tosses her head back laughing then picks up the bottle of tequila and heads for the door. I walk behind her and she stops and turns to me. "Take the chance, girl. I know you're scared, and I know he fucked up before, but I got a good feeling about this and I'm rarely ever wrong."

"Thanks for the talk and the drinks." I lean in, giving her a hug but not an answer. Shaking her head, she opens the door and walks out on her heels, down the sidewalk, then across our lawns. Stopping on her front porch, she waves once and disappears from sight when she goes into her house.

Closing the door behind me, I lean back against it. I don't feel better after that talk. If anything, I feel more conflicted. Rather than thinking about it anymore, since I had been doing nothing but that all day, I head for my bathroom and turn on the tub's faucet. One of the reasons I bought my house was because of the bathtub. Three people could fit comfortably in it, and it has six powerful jets that turn it into an indoor hot tub.

Starting the water, I wander into my room to find my cell phone. I turn it on airplane mode, so that it won't annoy me, and then find my headphones and start up Adele. Going back into the bathroom, I turn on my electric candles and shut off the light. I close the door then gather my hair on top of my head, strip out of my clothes, dump a ton of peach-scented bubble bath under the running water, and climb in. It doesn't take me long to find peace and for the sound of Adele to take me away.

Blinking at the sudden bright light that fills the bathroom, it takes a second for my eyes to adjust. As soon as they do, a scream rips up the back of my throat and I scramble back in the tub, losing Adele as my ear buds fall from my ears. Sloshing water onto the floor, I stand as a man wearing a ski mask watches me from across the room.

Reaching my hand out blindly, I find a towel and cover myself, not taking the chance of pulling my eyes from him to look for something to use as a weapon. Panting, blood sings loudly though my veins as I keep my eyes on him, waiting to see what he does so I can counter his movement. He doesn't move, doesn't breathe or even make a noise. He just stares at me, his bright green eyes surrounded by black fabric fixed on mine.

I don't know how long we stand there staring at each other. It could be seconds, or minutes, but without a word or a backward glance, he walks out. Hurrying from the tub, I stumble to the door, slam it closed, and click the lock in place. Searching the room for my cell phone, I see it at the bottom of the tub. I move to the vanity and pull out the drawers, dumping the contents onto the floor.

Coming up with a pair of cheap, black-handled scissors in the last drawer, I move to the door, press my ear to it, and adjust my towel. I can't hear anything, nothing; it's silent. It takes everything in me to open the door, my scissors my only weapon, and as soon as I do, I run through the house without stopping and head for the front door. As soon as I'm there, I swing it open and run as fast as I can across my lawn and up JJ's porch, pounding on the door. It doesn't take long for it to open, and as soon as it does, I fall inside.

"What the fuck?" Brew, JJ's husband, hisses, shutting the door.

"Th—" I pant, dropping to my knees and clutching the scissors to my chest.

"June," I hear JJ whisper, but I can't answer. I can't even breathe.

"Get my phone, baby," Brew calls, and I try to catch my breath to tell them that someone was in my house, but I can't do either. "I'm gonna get you off the floor, darlin'," I hear muttered, before I'm pulled up and being moved and settled onto a couch.

"June, honey, you need to calm down and breathe for me," JJ soothes as her hands wrap around my jaw and she pulls my eyes to meet hers. Nodding, I try, I really do, and then a large hand pushes down on my back, forcing my face low toward my lap. I absently hear Brew on the phone, but I can't really make out what he's saying, because JJ is whispering in my ear to breathe. Eventually, my breath comes back, and I lift my head and meet her gaze.

"Thank fucking God." JJ wraps her arms around me, and I feel tears gather in my eyes as she hugs me. "What the fuck happened?"

"I... I took a... a bath. There... there was a guy... a guy," I whimper, burying my face against her neck. Her body goes solid, and I feel a current of something dangerous weave itself through the room. Lifting my head away from her neck, my gaze collides with Evan's. His big body is statue still, his eyes enraged, his energy so dangerous I feel it seeping into my pores from across the room.

"Brother, cool it," Brew growls, stepping between Evan and me, cutting off our connection.

"Let's get you some clothes," JJ says, and I nod. Clothes are good. Actually, they're great.

"Move out of my fucking way, Brew, before I move you myself,"

Evan rumbles, and then he's in front of me, his hands holding my face gently as his eyes scan me. "Are you hurt?" he asks, moving his hands from my face, running them over me. As I shake my head, he pulls my hands from my chest and pries the scissors from me, tosses them away, and then gathers me against him. He buries his face in my neck, holding me so tight that my breath leaves on a strangled whoosh.

"Ev," I breathe against the skin of his neck.

"Fuck, baby. Jesus…" His hold on me tightens. I feel tears sting my nose for an altogether different reason. There is no way, not right now, that I can deny my love for him, that in his arms, I feel safe.

"Let me get some clothes on her. The cops are pulling up," JJ says softly, and Evan's arms loosen as he leans back, looks over his shoulder at JJ, and nods once. Then his eyes come back to me. Panic starts to creep through my system at the idea of Evan leaving me, and without even thinking, my hands latch on to the front of his shirt in a death grip. His eyes drop to my hands then move up to meet mine and his face goes soft.

"I'll be right here, baby. I'm not going anywhere. Go with JJ and get somethin' on."

"I'm okay. I don't need to," I whisper, feeling my hands start to shake.

"He can come with us, honey," JJ says, placing her hand against my cheek and gaining my attention. Looking back at Evan, he nods at me then takes my hands from his shirt, kissing both before helping me up.

JJ's house is a completely different layout from mine. Her living room opens up to the kitchen, and all of the bedrooms are down a hall in the back of the house—two on one side with a bathroom in-between, and one on the other. Leading me into the master bedroom with Evan at my back, I follow her into the closet.

"Take your pick, honey, then come back out front. I'm gonna make sure Brew doesn't scare the cops away."

"Thanks," I whisper, and her hand comes up once more, holding my cheek, then she's gone, leaving Evan and me in her closet.

Finding a pair of sweats on one of the shelves, I hold them out in front of me shakily. "Let me," Evan mutters, taking them from my hands, dropping to his knees in front of me, and holding them open like a parent would for a child.

Placing my hand on his shoulder, he slips them up my legs under the towel, ties the waist tight, and then stands. I grab the biggest sweatshirt I can find—regardless of the fact that even being after eight, the night air is humid and hot—because I want to be covered. Taking the towel from around me, he holds the sweatshirt over my head, using the same parental technique, helping me put my arms through the sleeves.

Once I'm dressed, his fingers slide under my chin and he puts pressure there until my eyes meet his. He looks at me for a long time then leans in, running his nose across mine before dropping his mouth briefly and touching his lips to mine. "I'll be with you." Swallowing, I nod and drop my eyes to the ground. "Tell me he didn't touch you," he rumbles quietly, and my eyes fly up to meet his. His are pissed and anguished as they hold mine.

"He didn't. He didn't do anything. I... I don't... I don't... He just stared at me. I don't... don't even know what he was doing there," I tell him, placing my hand against his chest. His heart is beating so hard that I can feel it against my palm, even as it trembles.

"Did you get a look at his face?"

"No, he had a mask on." I swallow, closing my eyes. His green eyes are burned into my brain. "He had green eyes, unusual green eye—"

"June!" is roared, cutting me off, and I step out of the closet, feeling Evan at my back. My eyes slide to the door as my dad barrels into the room. The second he sees me, relief flashes across his face.

"Dad," I whisper as his arms engulf me.

"June Bug," he whispers, sounding pained as his arms squeeze me.

"I'm okay," I assure him quietly.

"What the fuck happened?" he asks, pulling back to look at me.

"Let's let her tell the cops. You can listen in while she does it so she doesn't have to repeat it," Evan says, and my dad's eyes move from me to him and his lips press tight.

Shit.

"There a reason you're here?" Dad asks Evan, and I feel my muscles tense.

"Yeah," Evan mutters but doesn't continue as he holds my dad's gaze.

"Dad, I should—"

"You wanna tell me what that reason is?" Dad asks, ignoring me, and I look at Evan, willing him to leave it.

"Me and June are seeing each other," he says, ignoring my look. My dad's eyes come to me then back to Evan's when he speaks. "We don't have time to do this right now. June needs to speak with the cops and then she needs to rest. She's shook up."

My dad's face flashes with something, but he turns, muttering over his shoulder, "Come on out. Your mom needs to see for herself that you're okay, and you need to talk to the cops, so let's get this done."

He's gone before I can say anything to him.

"Evan—"

"Not now, baby. Later. Right now, you need to tell the cops what happened."

Clenching my teeth, I let out a breath then nod. Taking my hand, he leads me out of JJ's room and down the hall.

"WHAT THE FUCK, June Bug?" my dad asks, stepping out onto his back porch and sliding the door closed behind him.

I knew this was coming, but I was honestly trying to put it off.

Which is why, as soon as we got into my parents house, I went out the back door hoping to have some time to come up with an explanation.

Earlier, Evan walked me to the living room, where three uniformed police officers greeted us along with my mom, who was more freaked than I was. I took a seat on JJ's couch with Evan sitting close, his arm wrapped around my waist, and told the cops what happened. It didn't take long, and not surprisingly, there is nothing they could do. My jewelry box was missing, along with my laptop, but my door wasn't locked, and whoever came in did just that, walked right in and took my stuff.

My dad growled when he heard I didn't lock the door or set the alarm, and Evan had much the same response, except his arm got super tight—so tight that I knew I would have five small bruises at my ribcage from his fingers. When the cops left, JJ and Brew, who had been kind enough to let us use their house, offered everyone a beer. To my surprise, my dad and mom both accepted their offer, while Evan left behind the cops, telling me he would be back and kissing me softly before he went.

I couldn't tell you how long we were there before Evan, Jax, and Sage came inside, and when they did, I didn't get the vibe that they were happy. That's when Evan told my dad straight out to take me home with him, and that he would be by in the morning to pick me up to take me home then to work.

One could say I was in a state of shock. First, my dad isn't an easy man. He's soft for his girls, those girls being my mom, me, and my sisters, but other than that, he doesn't hold much back. He sure as heck wouldn't—even when I was younger—allow a guy to tell him what to do in regards to his girls. But he did with Evan, and I swore I saw his lips twitch when he did. Now, looking at my dad, I can see he's not pissed, but annoyed, and honestly, I'm too worried about what Evan is doing to be concerned with my father's reaction to the news that I have a boyfriend. Something I haven't even come to terms with yet.

"Dad, please don't."

"Don't?" he repeats, leaning back against the railing that runs the length of the porch.

"I already know what you're gonna say."

"Yeah, what's that?" he asks, and I look at him, really unsure of what he's gonna say.

His reaction to Evan's declaration was seriously surprising, so I'm at a loss. I just know whatever he's got to say isn't going to be what I want to hear right now.

"That boy has demons," he says quietly, and I pull my bottom lip between my teeth while wrapping my arms around my waist. I'm not surprised he knows, but at the same time, I am. "That's a lot to take on, June Bug, and I don't want you to get hurt."

It's a little late for that, I think but don't say as I stare at him.

"Do you love him?" he questions, crossing his arms over his chest. Shrugging at his question, too afraid to admit it to him or myself, I watch as his eyes close then open back up. "I'm worried about you. Like I said before, Evan is a good man, but I see in him the same thing I've seen in a few of my brothers from the military. A monster lives in him, honey, and I don't know if he's strong enough to fight that monster back."

"I'm going to help him with his demons," I whisper, feeling my throat close up. I know I need to do that for him. Yes, what he did to me was horrible, but I know him—or knew him—and the kind of man he is. He deserves to have some good, to understand there is nothing wrong with him. "There... there's a lot you don't know, Dad."

"So tell me."

Licking my lips, I move over to one of the loungers and take a seat, dropping my head into my hands. I feel Dad come close, his weight hits my side, and his arm wraps around my shoulders, pulling me into him.

"The first time I looked into his eyes, I swear my world stopped," I whisper, dropping my hands to my lap and locking them together. "That was about three years ago." I look out at the back yard. "We were inseparable. Every free moment I had, we were together." I smile, remembering our quiet times alone, just him and me, talking, laughing, cuddling. Just being us.

"What happened?"

"You're gonna be mad," I tell him honestly, 'cause I know he will be. No dad wants to learn their child, especially their daughter, got married and didn't even mention they were dating anyone.

"Maybe, but I think you know I love you. Nothing you could do will change that."

"We got married," I confess quietly, feeling his body quickly go tight. "He was going into the marines. He wanted us to start a life, wanted to go to school, so he joined, wanting a good life for himself and to provide one for me. The day before he left, we went to the courthouse and got married."

"Jesus, June."

"I know." I squeeze my eyes closed. "I don't know what happened. At first, everything was fine. When he was in boot camp, we connected regularly with letters, and when he could call, he did. He was supposed to come home for leave right after boot camp, and I planned on bringing him home then."

"That didn't happen," Dad points out on a squeeze.

"No, it didn't," I agree. "They sent him to Afghanistan. Phone calls stopped soon after that. I tried to find out from his mom what was going on, but she didn't really know, or she wasn't willing to tell me anything. Then I heard he was home in Alabama. He didn't come to me, and his mom found me and gave me divorce papers."

"What the fuck?" Dad clips, and I tug on his hand, making him sit back down when he goes to stand.

"I was hurt, so fucking hurt. I signed the papers. Then I found out from Ashlyn that he got a job with Jax, and heard from her what happened to him when he was away."

"No fucking excuses, June Bug."

"You're right, but you're wrong," I tell him quietly, squeezing his hand. "There was a lot I didn't know, a lot of stuff he didn't tell me. His dad was abusive, his mom was an alcoholic, his brother was in prison, and then his friends died. I don't know the details of what happened when he was away, since we just started seeing each other again, but I can't help but think all those things messed him up, and that monster you see is a result of those things."

"Don't give a fuck, baby girl. That man doesn't deserve a second chance."

"He said he didn't want to get me dirty." That sentence had stuck with me over the last couple days. There was something about it that is wrong, so wrong. I don't... I can't even begin to understand it.

"What?"

"He said I was too good for him, that he didn't want to get me dirty. I don't know what any of that means. I don't fully understand what happened to us, but I know he loved me. I *know* he did, and I would scratch someone's eyes out if they tried to tell me that wasn't true."

"Simmer down, June Bug," Dad mutters, pulling me closer to his side, and I feel his lips at the top of my head. "I can't say I'm happy about this."

"I didn't think you would be," I murmur, wrapping my arms around his waist.

"I'm pissed you didn't talk to me about him. I'm so fucking disappointed in you."

Gahhh! Why is the whole *I'm disappointed in you* statement so much worse than your parents just being pissed at you?

"I know."

"Your ma isn't gonna be happy either, baby girl."

Squeezing my eyes closed, I drop my temple to his shoulder and nod, because I know he's right. My mom isn't just my mom—she's a friend, and I normally tell her everything. I know she's gonna be even more disappointed in me than Dad is that I didn't trust them with what was going on.

"We love you, always have and always will. One day when you have kids of your own, you'll understand that. With that said, we can still be upset about your decisions, but it doesn't mean you don't always have our support."

"I know," I agree, and we sit in silence for a few more minutes.

"Do you want to tell your mom, or do you want me to?"

I wanted to ask if she really needs to know, but I know without asking the answer to that is yes. "I'll tell her," I mumble.

"Good call. I'll get you guys some wine, and you can tell her once she's had a couple glasses."

"Thanks, Dad."

"Anything," he mutters, kissing the top of my head, then stands.

"You know I love you too, Dad, right?" I ask, tilting my head back to look at him.

"Yeah." He grins before heading out the door.

"That went okay," I whisper to the yard, hoping the talk with my mom won't end with her in tears.

Unfortunately, I'm not that lucky. By the time I get around to telling my mom that Evan and I were married, she'd only had one glass of wine. She cried for an hour then told me—just like my dad—that she was disappointed in me. By the time we were done talking and I got up to go to sleep, she was so drunk, my dad had to carry her to bed.

Though, she did tell me drunkenly that Evan is hot.

"UH... WHAT ARE we doing here?" I ask, looking through the windshield at my sister's vet clinic then over at Evan as he shuts down his truck.

"We're getting you a dog," he says, and my head jerks back as to him. "What?"

"You have the best alarm system on the market, but an alarm system only works if you turn it on."

"Seriously?" I run my hands down my face. My dad lectured me about the alarm system last night and this morning. "I agreed to turn the alarm on." I sigh.

"You'll still set the alarm, but your also getting a dog."

"What about a cat?"

"A dog will be on guard 24-7, a dog will tell you if someone is trying to get into the house, and a dog will protect you if someone does make it inside, now let's go." He hops out of the truck and slams the door then comes around to my side.

"I don't know about this," I tell him as soon as he opens my door, reaches around me, unhooks my belt, and helps me out.

"That's all right. I do," he replies, taking my hand and leading me toward the clinic.

As soon as we reach the front door, July is there pushing it open with a smile on her face, looking between me and Evan. "You said you would be here twenty minutes ago."

"Had to pick up my truck," is Evan's reply as he tugs me through the door.

When I got off work and went home, I expected to have to face my house alone, but Evan was there, outside in his truck waiting for me. He didn't even let me go inside, just took my hand and helped me into his truck. A truck that was just as cool on the inside as it was on the outside. Black leather seats with white stitching, black wood paneling, chrome everywhere there could be chrome, a killer sound system, and all the bells and whistles you could possibly ask for. I didn't ask him what we were doing or where we were going. I was honestly just happy I didn't have to be home alone, and even though I wouldn't admit it out loud, I was happy to be spending time with him.

"Are you okay?" my sister asks, sweeping her eyes over me as we step through the door.

"Yeah, well, I was. Now, I don't know."

"What?" she asks, and her eyebrows pull tight as she studies me.

"Apparently, I need a dog." I pause then turn to look at Evan, who is talking to Kayan at the reception desk. "A big one," I mutter, and her eyes light up and a smile graces her lips.

"Ah." Her gaze moves over my face and goes soft, and then she takes a step closer to me. "Are you sure you're okay?"

Letting out a breath, I nod. "I'm fine. I was freaked yesterday. I probably won't want to stay alone for a while, but I'll be okay."

"I tried to call you."

"My cell is still in the bottom of my bathtub."

"What?"

"It fell in the tub. I need to get a new one. I'll probably try to do that today."

"When I called Mom and Dad's last night, Dad said you and Mom were talking."

"Yeah," I reply quietly.

"You told them?" she whispers, looking over at Evan then back at me.

"I did," I admit, and even though it sucked telling them, I'm happy to have that weight gone.

"How'd that go?"

"As expected. Dad was disappointed in me, and Mom was Mom:

disappointed and hurt."

"Did Dad talk to Evan?" she asks, and I shake my head. When Evan came to pick me up from my parents' house this morning to take me home so I could get ready for work, I was expecting my dad to take him aside and have a talk with him. That didn't happen. All my dad said was, "Know what you have, son, and don't fuck up again." To that, Evan jerked up his chin. My mom looked like she wanted to say more, but my dad held her close to his side, not letting her have a chance to do that. The whole thing was strange, but I had a feeling my dad heard me last night, and understood in his fatherly way what I said about Evan—or at least I hope he heard me.

"Dad likes Evan, or he did," she mutters then continues, "I had an emergency surgery, but Wes called to tell me what was going on."

"How did Wes know?" I ask, but it's Evan who answers as he wraps his arm around my shoulders.

"I called the guys when I called Jax and Sage, and told them to rally."

"What?" I ask, tilting my head back to look at him.

"Wasn't sure if the guy was still in the area and wanted them to do a sweep."

"Isn't that a job for the police?"

"The cops in town are mostly good, but they're undermanned. Town's growing faster than the department. More drugs and petty crimes are happening daily, so they're spread thin."

That's true. Our town, which used to be on the smaller side, had started sprawling out over the last ten years, ever since a big automotive factory moved in. There were now more jobs, more people, more homes, and more crime. "The guy was on foot. It's easy to steer clear of a cop car, not as easy to steer clear of a guy on a Harley, or a man in a truck that looks like the rest that drive by."

"How do you know he was on foot?"

"Baby, your next-door neighbor is Brew. He has two brothers who live on your block, and all of them keep an eye out."

Okay, I didn't know that either. Then again, I just moved in, so it wasn't like I had a chance to invite people over and introduce myself to them.

"Oh," was all I could say, and when I did, I watched Evan smile then his face bent and he touched his mouth to mine softly.

"Kayan said there are a couple dogs here we can look at. If one of them isn't the one, there's another shelter a few towns over we can go to."

"I want a cat," I repeat and he shakes his head.

"You're not getting a cat."

"Remember when I said you're more annoying?" I glare.

"I remember," he says with a smile.

"Well, it's even more true now."

His eyes scan my face and his smile turns into a grin. "As cute as you're being right now, we don't have all day to argue."

"Annoying," I mutter, and July laughs while leading us down the hall into the back of the clinic to look at dogs.

Chapter 7

Evan

"HE'S KINDA SCARY looking, right?" June asks, as I open the back door to my truck. "I mean, he's white as snow, but it looks like he just killed someone."

Chuckling, I shut the door after the dog jumps in the back then turn, pressing her against the side of the truck.

"His food stained his coat. He didn't kill anyone." I smile, and her eyes drop to my mouth then lift to meet mine.

"I know, but it still looks like he did." She's right. The one-hundred-and-thirty-pound dog is pure white, but around his mouth is stained a deep red, making it look like he just ripped someone's throat out. Hopefully, that, his size, and his bark will have someone second-guessing stepping foot in June's house without being invited in. June, who had been against the idea of getting a dog, took one look at the large Akita and started cooing at him like he was a baby the moment July showed him to us.

"He needs a name." I wrap my hands around the sides of her neck and tilt her head back.

"T-bone." She smiles, placing her hands against my chest then tilts her head to the side, putting pressure on one of my hands while I laugh. And I notice, not for the first time, that she always stops to watch me laugh. She didn't do it before, but something about it hits my chest in a not-unpleasant way every time she does it now.

"T-bone?" I repeat, and she smiles and shrugs.

"T-bone, or maybe Snow. I like both, but I think T-bone is cooler."

"I think you should think about this for a while." I smile, touching my mouth to hers.

"He's already going to have a hard time settling in, since he's going to a new home. If he has to have a new name too, that's just going to make it harder on him. I don't want to call him 'dog' for a week and have him answering to that, only to figure out a name for him later," she says in one long breath, and by the time she's done, I'm pressing my lips tighter together to keep from laughing.

"T-bone, though? You really think that's a good name?" I ask, and she looks to the sky like she's thinking about it then meets my gaze once more.

"What about Fuzzy or Harry?"

"Now you're just being cute." I shake my head and ask, "What about Killer?"

"What?" her nose scrunches up.

"We'll call him Killer."

"How about a name that doesn't scare everyone, like Ninja?"

"Ninja?"

"Well, he's an Akita. I think they're Japanese dogs, so Ninja fits."

"It's better than, T-bone, Snow, Fuzzy, or Harry," I mutter, and she leans in, giving me a blinding smile.

"Ninja it is." She presses up on her tiptoes, kissing the underside of my jaw, then leans back grinning.

"Ninja it is, baby," I agree and with a press of my thumbs to the underside of her jaw, and a tilt of her head, I kiss her once more softly.

Dropping one hand to her hip, I lean her to the side, open the door, and help her in. I hear her say, "Ninja boy, you're such a good boy," to the dog, which barks once as I shut the door. Jogging around to the driver side and sliding behind the wheel, I start up The Beast, back out of the parking spot, and head out of the lot.

"Can we stop at the cell phone store in town?" she asks, as I make sure the road's clear and coast into traffic on the highway. "I don't think the rice trick will work on my phone since it was submerged in water over night," she continues and I look over at her, nabbing her hand from her lap and dragging it to mine.

"You're probably right. We'll stop on the way back to your place, then pick up dog food and supplies for Ninja while were out."

"I told my parents we were married," she says like she didn't mean to say it then moves to take her hand from my thigh, but I hold it tighter.

"I'm glad you told them," I say gently squeezing her hand. I already knew she had. Her dad was waiting at the compound for me when I got back from dropping her at work this morning. He told me he would be watching me and that he hopes I have what it takes to fight whatever it is that made me leave his girl behind the first time. He didn't give me his stamp of approval, but that didn't surprise me either. I'm going to have to earn his respect, and I have a feeling that isn't going to be easy. "I should have told them about you, about us, before," she whispers after a moment of silence and I shake my head.

"We both should have done things differently."

Her hand turns over under mine and she laces our fingers together. "I wasn't ashamed of you, and I didn't think you weren't good enough for me. I don't know what I was thinking back then, but that wasn't it."

"I know, baby," I agree just as quietly, then listen to her laugh when Ninja sticks his head between us and rests his jaw on her shoulder, where it stays until we pull up in front of the cell phone store.

"I need to make a phone call. You go on in and I'll be there in a minute," I tell her, finding a spot in front of the double doors so I can watch her while I'm on the cell.

"You don't need to come in. This shouldn't take long," she says, unhooking her belt and picking up her purse from the floorboard.

"I'll be in," I repeat, and she rolls her eyes as she exits the truck and heads into the store.

Picking up my cell, I press Send and put it to my ear. My brother called yesterday. We're not close, we haven't been for a long time. The year before I went into the military, he went to prison for possession of drugs with the intent to sell. His life was starting to look like my parents', and I knew I wanted nothing to do with that shit. A month ago, he was released after serving his time. When we spoke a few days ago, he told me he was trying to figure out his life, and I told him if he stayed clean, he could stay with me.

Hearing the ringing go to voicemail, I watch June through the glass windows then mutter, "Fuck no," when a guy moves from behind the counter with his eyes on her ass. I'm out of my truck telling Ninja to stay, and walking into the store before my brain even has a moment to catch up with where my feet are taking me.

"So the only difference is the front-facing camera?" I hear June ask, while inspecting the phone in her hand, flipping it back over, and studying the screen.

"No." The fuckwad next to her smiles like she's adorable and leans closer. "There are a lot of different features. The front-facing camera is just one of them."

"I don't know." She bites her lip studying the phone. "I don't really want to pay four hundred dollars for a phone that is basically the same one I had before, a phone I got for free when I signed my contract," she states as I move to her side, and I watch the guy's eyes move from the phone in her hand to her chest. I hear a growl and soon realize it's *me* who's growling.

His eyes fly to me and his Adam's apple bobs. "Um…" He clears his throat, while I wrap my hand around June's waist and pull her against me, keeping my stare locked on his.

"We'll take the phone," I declare, and I feel June looking at me, but I ignore her and grab my wallet out of my pocket, drop my hand from her waist, pull out my card, and hand it to him.

"You're not paying for my phone," she hisses, but I continue to ignore her, keeping my eyes on the man in front of me.

"Get one from the back and set it up. We'll be here."

"Um…" He swallows, looks between us, and then whispers, "Sure," before disappearing, without another word, to the back of the store.

"Seriously, Evan?" Her hand goes to mine at her waist and attempts to pry my fingers free. "I may as well just get you a club to hit me over the head with."

"Do you want me to be charged with assault?" I ask, dropping my eyes to meet hers.

"What?" She frowns, and I dip my face toward her then drop my eyes to her shirt.

"He checked out your ass when you walked in, your tits when I was standing next to you."

"That's not true," she gripes, leaning forward.

"Baby, he fucking did, and that shit is not okay, especially when I'm standing right fucking next to you."

"You're being ridiculous. He was doing his job." She waves me off.

Grabbing her wrist, I tug, forcing her to fall into me, then wrap my arms around her waist, hauling her even closer before dipping my mouth to her ear.

"I'm glad you don't notice when a man is checking you out. I'm fucking thankful that you're not the kind of woman who seeks out a man's attention, but it doesn't change the fact he was flirting with you and"—I give her a squeeze—"checking you out while I was standing right next to you."

"The whole cave man act you got going on is annoying," she whispers, leaning back and looking up at me.

"You're mine." I lean forward, growling, "*Mine*," then lean back and catch her gaze again. "Your tits are mine. Your ass is mine. Call me whatever you like."

Her eyes hold mine for a long time before moving to the left when the guy stutters out, "I… um… I have the phone all set up."

I give June one more squeeze then take the bag from him and hand it to her. Taking my card, I sign the iPad in his hand before putting my arm around her shoulders and lead her out of the store. The whole time, she is muttering under her breath about annoying alpha men.

"NOPE," I STATE, stopping at the end of the bed, shaking my head, and crossing my arms over my chest.

"What?" June asks, looking at me from under her dark lashes, trying to appear innocent, but she knows exactly what I'm talking about.

"No way, baby. He's not sleeping in the bed with us."

"But he's gonna be lonely." She pouts, and I shake my head again then look at Ninja.

"Off." I snap my fingers, and he looks at June then back to me, lets out an annoyed huff before he hops off the bed, stops at my side so I can give him a pet, and heads out the door.

"The bed is big enough for all of us," she says, and I step toward her, putting one hand on each side of her in the bed, and force her to lean back.

"Do you want him to watch me eat you?" I ask, and her eyes get big and she whispers, "No," breathlessly.

"Didn't think so." I lean in and kiss her then lean back. "If I'm in the bed with you, he's not."

"Do you really think it's necessary for you to stay?"

"Yes, you may have a security system and a dog now, but I have a gun, and you're safer with my head on the pillow next to yours."

"Do you know how to use a gun?" she asks, and I study her face for a moment, trying to decide how much to tell her, how much to let her in. Knowing I want this to work, I climb over, settle myself between her legs, and place my face close to hers.

"I do. I was the best in my class, and when I went overseas, I was one of the best in my unit."

"Did… did you ever get shot at?" she asks quietly, placing one hand over my heart and the other against my jaw.

"Yeah." Watching tears fill her eyes, I feel a pain in my chest, because I know those tears are for me, tears I don't deserve.

"Did…" She pauses, searching my face. "Did you ever shoot at anyone?" Her tone is tentative as she watches my eyes.

"Yeah, baby," I say just above a whisper.

Her face raises and she tucks it against my neck, where she whispers, "I'm sorry."

"Me too, beautiful." I roll us so she's lying on top of me then bunch up her shirt and run my fingers down her back.

"Why didn't you come home to me?" she asks after a moment, and my body goes tight. I make myself to relax, forcing myself to be honest.

Running one hand up her back, I hold her face close as I tell her the truth. "I couldn't look you in the eye. I fucked up so much. I kept so much shit from you. I didn't want anything to touch you, anything to soil what we were building before that. I didn't let you see how fucked up my family was, how my mom drank herself to sleep only to wake up and have a beer, how my dad would get pissed and take his anger out on me, just because I was standing there. I thought if I could build a life for us, a life I earned, one where I made it good for you, good for our kids, then none of that would matter. Then I went overseas and…" I stop talking, not wanting her to know how I fucked up.

"What?" she asks, putting pressure on my hand and pulling her face back. "What happened to you?"

I close my eyes. I can still see their lifeless faces in my head, while I relive the notion that I couldn't bring them back.

"Please talk to me," she begs gently.

"We were searching for a target. We went into one of the houses he'd been seen in. We did a search and came up empty. I knew we were missing something, so I went back in. We didn't know that while we were doing our search that someone put a bomb under our Humvee. I lost everyone."

"You would have died too," she whispers, covering her mouth with shaky fingers.

"I could have helped them. I would have made sure the check was done."

"You would have died," she repeats, dropping her forehead to my chest.

Holding her, I whisper, "Daralee's wife just gave birth to a little girl. The way he talked about her, you would think he was the first man to ever make a girl. Jabson had a girl back home he was planning on asking to marry him. He'd been with her since he was twelve. Denson had just lost his mom to cancer, and his dad was barely holding on. He was going home in three days. They all died, and I was the only one to make it out. Why should I get to live my life, when theirs all ended?" I ask the question I've asked myself a million times.

"Would they have wanted you to stop living?" she asks after a long moment, and I hear the tears in her voice.

"I don't know," I tell her on a squeeze, holding her closer, then roll to the side and bury my face in her neck. "I hated myself for being thankful that I was able to come home to you, and then the more I thought about it, the more I knew I couldn't look you in the eye, not when my boys would never be able to see their families or the women they loved again." Her body bucks against mine and her tears flow harder. "I'm sorry I left you, beautiful, so fucking sorry."

"I'm sorry too," she whimpers as her tears soak into my skin. "Sorry that you've been fighting this alone, sorry I didn't fight for you."

"Jesus." I squeeze my eyes closed and hold her tighter. Feeling weight hit the bed, I lift my head and watch Ninja as he presses his body to June's back. It takes awhile for her to calm. When she pulls her face out of my neck, her red, wet eyes meet mine. Neither of us says anything, but I see love there in the open, shining back at me. Leaning in, I kiss her softly then roll to my back.

"Can Ninja sleep with us?" she asks after a few minutes. Instead of answering, I reach over, shut off the lamp, and pull her closer to me. "Night," she whispers, cuddling closer.

"Night, baby," I murmur, knowing I won't sleep. Not for a long fucking time.

"HURRY, BABY," I grunt, slamming into her again and again, each stroke pulling me closer to the edge.

"Ev," she whimpers, locking her legs behind my back as her nails dig into my shoulders.

"Hurry, beautiful," I demand, tweaking her nipple, then roam my hand down the wet skin of her stomach, zeroing in on her clit.

"Oh, God," she moans, and I move my hand quickly to the back of her head before it can hit the tile wall as her pussy clamps hard around my cock. Moving both hands to her ass, I hold her in place as I come hard, burying my face in her neck when I do.

"I'm so gonna be late," she whispers, and I smile against the skin of her neck then pull my face away and lock my eyes on hers.

"Baby," I mutter, and her bottom lip disappears between her teeth. Laughing, I heft her up, pulling her off my dick and drop her to her feet.

"I didn't want to get my hair wet. Now I have to dry it, and that's gonna take a year," she murmurs, grabbing her body wash.

"You saying it wasn't worth it?" I ask, kissing the side of her neck, taking the bottle from her, dumping some of the liquid soap in my hands, and cupping her breasts.

"I didn't say it wasn't worth it," she breathes.

I grin then mutter, "So stop bitchin' about it."

"I'm not bitching. I'm just saying now I'm gonna be late."

"You won't be late," I tell her, running my hands over her stomach then down between her legs.

"You said quick, but then you did that thing with your mouth then you had me against the wall. You weren't quick," she complains, but then whimpers when my fingers flick over her clit.

"Still bitchin', baby." I nip her ear, thrust two fingers inside of her, and use my thumb to roll her clit again.

"Oh, my God," she breathes, coming on my fingers a few seconds later. Kissing the side of her neck, I wait for her orgasm to pass then finish washing her up. I push her out of the shower, ignoring the glare she sends my way. Getting out a couple minutes later, I grin as she stomps around naked with the blow dryer in her hand.

"You want me to get you coffee?" I ask, watching her tits bounce as she tosses her hair from one side to the other.

Grumbling a "Yes," she watches in the mirror as I wrap the towel around my waist then move in to stand behind her.

Sliding my hands up her waist, I palm her breasts, kiss her ear, and then demand, "Stop being mad," while tugging her nipples.

"Ev." She inhales sharply, and my eyes meet hers in the mirror.

"And don't look at me like that unless you want me to bend you over the counter and actually make you late." Her eyes heat, and I fight my smile, lean in to kiss her neck, muttering there, "I'll be back with coffee."

Heading toward the kitchen, with Ninja following behind me, I let him out the back door, fill his bowl with food, make sure his water's good, and start up the coffee pot. Leaning back against the island, waiting for the pot to fill, my eyes catch on an envelope on the counter, stacked with the rest of the mail June brought in yesterday. Picking it up, I flip it over and see the letter was forwarded from her old apartment and that the return address is a prison in Alabama, the same prison Lane is serving time in while his trial is in progress.

Opening the envelope, I pull out the thick stack of papers and grit my teeth as I read. Most of the letter is an apology for getting her involved. The other part is him explaining that he made it so that she would break up with him because he knew he didn't want her to be swept up in his mess, that he was attempting to protect her. But the last page has me seeing red. Him telling her that he's in love with her and that he knows she felt the same is *not* something I want to think about. Crumpling the paper in my hands, I go to the back door, let Ninja inside, and head for the bathroom, taking the letter with me.

"I thought you were bringing me coffee," she says, shutting off the blow dryer. Going to her side, I set the letter down on the vanity. Her eyes drop to it, scan the first page, narrow, and then lift to mine. "Did you open my mail?" She frowns, studying me.

"I did." I lean back against the wall, crossing my arms over my chest.

"Why?"

"I wanted to see what he had to say. He shouldn't be in contact with you at all, so I thought it might be important. It's not."

She scans my face, and she asks, "Are you pissed?"

"Fuck yeah."

"Why?" she questions, sounding baffled.

"A man telling my woman that he's in love with her is the kind of shit that pisses me off."

"Maybe we should talk about the status of our relationship," she murmurs, setting the blow dryer down on the counter next to the sink, then leans back, crossing her arms over her breasts.

"You're mine, there is nothing to discuss when it comes to who you belong to."

"I wasn't yours, for a long time, Evan. You left me. I didn't have a choice. I had to move on."

"You were always mine," I growl, leaning forward. "You know you were mine."

"How many women were you with while I was 'yours'?" she asks quietly, and I narrow my eyes and lean back.

"None." I run my hands over my head and growl, "Jesus, you think if I couldn't have you, I would have someone else? To what, pass time? Get off? Fuck no."

Her enormous eyes stare up at me and her lips part before she whispers, "What?"

"Baby, I wouldn't settle for someone else if I couldn't have you," I say, trying to gentle my voice.

"You..." She pauses, then points at my chest. "You haven't been with anyone since me?" she asks, pointing at herself, and I close my eyes then open them back up.

Reaching out, I wrap my hand around her waist, and drag her into me. "I love you, only you," I state firmly, dropping my forehead to hers.

"But—"

"No buts. Fuck, I may not have been married to you anymore, but that didn't change my feelings for you."

"Oh, my God," she breathes, placing her hands against my chest leaning forward.

"Were you in love with him?" I ask through gritted teeth, not really wanting to know the answer but needing it all the same.

"What?" She blinks, leaning back.

"Were you in love with *HIM*?"

"No." Her head shakes and she tilts farther back as her hands slide up my chest and wrap around the sides of my neck. "How could I love someone else, when you still had my heart?" she asks softly, running her fingers across my jaw.

"You were with him for a while," I remind her, and her face softens.

"I was trying to move on, but he wasn't you."

"Fuck." I squeeze her to me.

"Don't be mad at me."

"I'm pissed at myself that he ever had a shot at you, so fucking mad that my actions meant a man like him was able to breathe your air," I growl, gritting my teeth.

"Ev," she whispers, and my eyes focus on hers. "We can't go back." She shakes her head, pressing her tits harder against my chest. "If we spend all our time going back, we'll miss the fact that for the first time in a long time, we're both going forward and doing it together."

"Yeah." I drop my forehead to hers.

"I wish that things had been different."

"Me too, beautiful," I agree, leaning back to place a kiss to her forehead, nose, and then mouth. I remind her, "You need to get ready for work."

"Are you okay?" she asks, ignoring her reminder.

"Yeah, baby." She searches my face for a long time before whispering.

"Good." Leaning up she kisses my jaw then pulls away and heads for the closet. Going to the room, I pull on my jeans and tee then head back to the kitchen to fix her a cup of coffee. I take it to her then grab my cell and call Jax, letting him know Lane's been in contact before heading back to the kitchen to get my own cup of coffee, and wait for June to finish getting ready so I can take her to work.

"DO YOU THINK the person who broke into my house will come back?" June asks, and I glance over at her before turning when the light switches to green.

"I don't think so baby," I say softly, giving her hand a squeeze.

I spent the night of her break-in putting out feelers and talking to anyone I could get my hands on. No one knew anything. No one saw anything. No one heard anything. It was dead end after dead end. As it stands, we're moving blind. None of us knows why someone would show up in a mask at her house, see her vulnerable, naked in a bath, and not make a move and if they were there just to rob her they could have taken so much more. It didn't make sense...*still* doesn't make sense.

"It was just so weird," she whispers after a moment, and I give her hand another squeeze and stop in front of the school.

Putting The Beast in park, I lean over and wrap my hand around the side of her neck and tug her closer to me. "Put it out of your head, okay?" Her eyes study me for a minute, and then she nods and looks over my shoulder. Running my fingers up through her hair, I pull her even closer and her gaze comes back to mine. "I'll be here at four to pick you up."

"Okay," she agrees, and I nip her bottom lip.

"Tonight, we're going out to dinner."

"Okay," she repeats, this time smiling.

"See you at four, baby." I lean forward, kissing her softly, then un-hook her belt and let her go. Putting her hand to the door handle behind her, she fumbles then falls back into me, sliding her hands through my hair. Her lips hit mine and I let her lead for a second before I take over the kiss, and do it thoroughly, with tongue. When I pull my mouth from hers, I watch her eyes flutter open and she smiles.

"Have a good day at work."

"You too." I smile back then watch her reach for the handle again. It takes her a couple tries, but she eventually gets the door open and hops out, and I wait until she's in the building to take off and head for the office.

"YOU'RE STILL ALIVE," Sage states as I push through the door to the office.

Ignoring him, I look at Jax and ask, "You call you're uncle and tell him about the letter?"

"Called after I got off the phone with you. He's sending a message to Lane's attorney," he informs, pouring some coffee into a cup and stirring, and then he looks at Sage and me. "I'm thinking about hiring someone to run the office. I don't have time to do callbacks and run checks. You guys cool with that?"

"'Bout time," Sage mutters, taking a seat in one of the chairs. "You have someone in mind?"

"Not yet, and do not mention it to my mom. The last thing we need is her coming in here and taking over."

"I love Aunt Lilly."

"You want my mom up in your business all the time?" he asks Sage, who looks at me and grins. He mutters, "She'll make sure we always have coffee, and I have no doubt she'll make us cookies."

"My mom's out. I'm gonna put the word out and see if I can come up with someone."

"Whatever," Sage grumbles, leaning back. "What's on schedule for today?"

"I need the paperwork from the purchase of June's house," I say, going to the fridge and grabbing a premade shake.

"Why?" Sage asks, and I look between him and Jax.

"I want to know who she bought the house from. The situation isn't sitting right with me. I'm wondering if the intruder wasn't looking for someone else when they came across June, were surprised, and took off."

"Have you had a chance to talk to Brew?" Jax asks, and I close the fridge and move my gaze to him.

"That's my next stop."

"Could still be Lane trying to scare her," Jax says, studying me.

"No, he wouldn't do that. He's not going to do anything to risk not having her back in his life. I read the letter he wrote her, and he believes he's doing what he can to protect her. He said he broke up with her so she wouldn't get swept up in his mess, and as much as that shit pisses me off, I believe him."

"Does June know you read the letter?" Sage asks, and I pull my eyes from Jax and look at him.

"What do you think?"

"I don't know. You seem to keep a lot of shit to yourself."

"Sage," Jax rumbles, and Sage moves his gaze from me to focus on his cousin.

"You know as well as I do that he"—he jerks his chin towards me—"hasn't been honest. Who's to say he's not the one who sent someone to June's to make a play at getting her back?"

"Seriously?" I ask.

"Just sayin'. It's the perfect fucking play. Weeks ago, she wanted nothing to do with you, and now you're suddenly sleeping in her bed, buying a dog, and getting domesticated."

"Fuck you."

"No, man, fuck you," he says, coming off his chair, and Jax moves between us as I push forward.

"Stand down," Jax orders, looking between the two of us.

"We've known Evan for over a year, and still don't know shit about him," Sage growls, and I move toward him, stopping when Jax's hand hits my chest.

"You're right. You don't know me," I say quietly. "You don't know what the fuck I've seen or done. You've got no fucking clue." I lean forward. "And I don't need to prove shit to you." I turn and leave the office, slamming the door behind me when I go.

Getting in my truck, I head for June's block. Seeing Brew's bike in his driveway, I shut down The Beast, hop out, and head across the yard so I can ask about the previous owner of June's house, when what I really want to do is trade my truck for my bike and ride out.

Chapter 8

June

LOOKING AT THE bedroom door, I pull my legs under me to sit Indian-style and grab my lotion from the side table. As I squeeze some into my hands and rub them together, I let my mind run away with me while waiting for Evan to come into the room. Something is wrong. I don't know what it is, and I don't know what to do about it, but the second Evan picked me up from work, I felt it. I knew, without him saying anything, just from the look on his face, that something had happened.

When I asked him if he was okay, he just said, "Yeah," then put his truck in drive and drove me home. I figured we could talk about whatever it was that was bothering him when we went to dinner, but when we got back to my house, he told me Wes and July were coming over to keep me company while he went to take care of business. When he said that, I asked him about dinner, and he told me we were going to have to reschedule.

It wasn't long after that July and Wes showed up, and the second they arrived, Evan took off, giving me a short kiss before leaving. I didn't like that. Since he pushed his way back into my life, he's been just that, in my life and in my space, but I could feel the distance he was putting between us like a physical thing.

My sister noticed, but didn't bring it up. Wes noticed too, and also, thankfully, kept his mouth closed, but I could tell they wanted to ask.

Now, sitting on my bed, I feel my heart start to pound in my chest and nausea fill my stomach. I never imagined Evan and I would be together again, but since the moment he came back, my feelings for him came back with a vengeance—or maybe they were never gone to begin with.

Feeling the bed shift and Ninja nuzzle my hand, looking to where he's lying near my hip, I run my fingers through his soft coat and sigh. I didn't want a dog, but I can't lie and say I don't like having one. Ninja has stuck to me like glue since I got home, and his constant presence has made me feel not so alone. Looking from Ninja to the door, I see the lights in the living room go out then hear soft footfalls coming toward the room. Feeling myself brace for what's to come, I sit up a little taller.

"Hey," I whisper, relaxing minutely, studying Evan as he comes to stand in the doorway.

"Hey," he whispers back, then moves toward me and stops at the end of the bed as he drops his eyes to my hip. "Ninja, off," he commands, and Ninja lets out a huff but hops off the bed, stopping to get a rub before wandering out of the room.

"Um…" I pause, watching him drop his gun to the nightstand then take off his shirt before he tosses it to the chair in the corner of the room. I watch him unloop his belt and unbutton the four buttons of his jeans, exposing a pair of form-fitting black boxers that look really good on him.

"Evan," I say quietly, watching his jeans fly across the room and land in the chair.

"Fucking tired," he mutters, dropping to the bed, reaching over, and turning out the light.

"Um…" I repeat, blinking into the dark.

"Sleep, June."

Okay, one could say Evan and I had our fair share of arguments when we first started out. Some were heated, others were just bickering, but we never just went to sleep without figuring shit out.

Not once.

"What's going on?" I ask, still sitting up in bed.

"Tired," he mutters, and at his words, I feel my fear start to turn into anger.

Flipping on the light on my side, I watch his eyes come to me, and then I straddle his waist and lean my face toward his. "What the hell is going on?"

"Nothing, go to sleep," he says, as his hands wrap around my waist.

"Go to sleep?" I repeat, studying him, and his eyes narrow in a way that sets my teeth on edge.

"Baby, we've been up since six. It's after midnight. I'm fucking beat."

"Maybe you need to get out of my bed and go to sleep in your own," I suggest in a way that doesn't sound like a mere suggestion at all.

"Don't start your shit," he growls, sitting up taking me with him as he twists and puts me in the bed at his side.

Getting up on my knees in the bed, I push against his chest and yell, "You don't start *your* shit. This morning, you were all over me. Then you cancel dinner, and come home tonight barely looking at me?" I lean forward. "I don't need this kind of heartache in my life. I don't need games and back-and-forth."

"I had a fucking shit day," he roars, and I shake my head. I don't care, not even a little.

"You left me! You married me, promised me that our lives would be intertwined until the end of time, and then you fucking left me. So, I'm sorry, but I don't give a fuck if you've had a bad day. I don't care, not even a single bit, because I'm here. Stupidly, I'm here, so if you have a shit day, we talk about it. You don't shut me out!" I shout.

"Baby," he says gently, and I watch his face soften and his hands come toward me.

"You don't get to do this to me again," I whisper. "You don't get to come back, make me fall in love with you again, and then decide that because you're having a bad day, you can't handle being with me."

"June." He tries reaching for me again, but I lean back out of his reach.

"I hated you," I whisper, scrambling off the bed. "Or at least I was able to make myself believe I did enough that I was able to move on. I won't do this again, Evan, and I won't lose you again. Not with you right in front of me," I whimper, fighting back tears.

"My brother broke into your house," he says, and my lungs freeze, my lips part, and my heart topples over inside my chest.

"What?" I whisper after a moment.

"Fuck." He snarls, running his hands down his face. "Last time we spoke, he was trying to get his shit straight. I told him he could come to Tennessee, but that he had to be ready to move on in a way that would mean he would be clean and actually find a job and get his shit together."

"Ev," I whisper, taking a step toward him, then pause when his eyes lock on mine. "Today, he showed up at the compound, telling me he was ready to make a fresh start and work his shit out."

"Honey." I move closer.

"Ten minutes after I left him in my room to settle in, I get a call from one of the local cops letting me know your shit showed up in one of the pawn shops in town. I went to check it out and watched the tapes. Lo and behold, my fucking brother was on the tape, selling your shit."

"Oh no," I whisper, slumping back to sit on the side of the bed.

"All fucking day, I've been living with the knowledge that, because of me, you've been fucking violated again."

"This isn't your fault."

"He followed me to your house!" he roars, tearing his hand through his hair. "My fucking brother broke into your house and scared you."

"I'm fine, and it's just stuff. It's not a big deal," I tell him quietly, as I stand and move within reach of him but stop when his eyes darken.

"Not a big deal," he repeats in a tone I've never heard from him before, one that has me thinking I should have chosen my words more wisely.

"You ran out of your house in a towel, clutching a pair of scissors to your chest scared out of your fucking mind."

"Okay, that was bad, but I was okay, and what happened is not your fault. You didn't tell him to break in to my house, and you didn't help him do it." I rest my hands against his chest and press closer to him. "Stop beating yourself up." His eyes move over my face and his arms wrap tight, holding me close. "You should have talked to me," I scold him softly.

"I didn't want this to affect you."

"Yeah, well, when you act like a jerk, that kinda has an effect on me," I point out the obvious, watching his lips twitch, but then all humor leaves his face and he closes the scant distance between us until his breath is mingled with mine.

"You're falling in love with me again?" he asks, and I feel my body tighten.

"Evan." I press against his chest, not ready to go there again, not even close.

"It's okay, baby. I'll wait," he says quietly, holding me more firmly.

"E—" I don't even get his name out before his mouth is on mine and his hands are on my ass, lifting me up. My legs automatically twine around his hips, right before the bed is under me and his body is covering mine. "I thought you were tired," I breathe, as his hands move from my ass, up the back of my nightie, ripping it over my head.

"Not anymore," he mutters, right before his mouth is back on mine, his tongue sweeping in as one of his hands roams over my stomach and down between my legs. The first touch of his fingers to my clit has my mouth pulling from his, my back arching off the bed, and my head pressing deeper into the mattress.

"Give me your eyes, beautiful."

Dipping my chin toward my chest, our eyes lock and I watch him kiss his way down my body. His wide shoulders push my thighs apart, and then his mouth is a breath away from my pussy. Raising my hips toward him, I see him grin then drop his face lower and bury his tongue inside of me. I lose his eyes when mine close and a moan climbs up my throat.

"Is this why you didn't wear panties to bed, June?" he asks against me. "Did you want my mouth between your legs? Did you want me to eat you, baby?"

Pressing my core closer to his mouth, I hear him chuckle before he latches on to my clit, and I move my hands from the sheets to his hair, and my legs attempt to tighten.

"Look at me," he commands, and I mewl in disappointment at the loss of his sweet torture. "Eyes."

My eyes shoot open and my head lifts when two thick fingers plunge into me and curve up, hitting my g-spot. Moaning, I move up to my elbows and watch his mouth go back to work.

"I'm so close," I whisper. My legs start to shake and my eyes start to slide closed. His free hand slides up my inner thigh, over my belly, and then his thumb and middle finger tug my nipple hard. Just like that, I'm done. The orgasm that was building explodes, rushing through my blood stream like wildfire, burning every part of me from the inside out. Falling to my back, I hold on to the sheets and try to catch my breath as my body comes back to itself.

"You taste good," he growls, as my eyes slide open and the fingers of his right hand wrap around my calf, curving it around his waist. "So fucking good."

His fingers, wet with my essence, swipe across my lips.

His mouth comes down on mine.

His tongue slips between my lips, his taste mingled with mine coursing over my taste buds, as he thrusts deep inside of me.

Ripping my mouth from his, my fingers dig into the muscles of his biceps and I gasp from the feeling of being full of him, stretched by him, and surrounded by him in every way.

Taking my hands from his biceps, he laces our fingers together, placing them above my head as his thrusts slow. His face moves to my neck, where he whispers softly, "I'll always love you enough for the both of us. *Always.*" The sincerity in his tone has unexpected tears climbing up my throat and, doing the only thing I can do, I wrap my legs tighter around his hips, hold his hands more firmly in his grasp, and turn my head toward him, opening my mouth when his covers my own. I may be too scared to tell him how I feel out loud, but my body is his, just like my heart. His mouth leaves mine as he rolls to his back. "Ride me, baby."

Blinking at our new position, I bite my lip and move my hands to rest against his chest.

"Ev," I breathe, lifting ever so slightly.

"Fuck, baby." His hips buck up into mine, making me gasp again. In this position, he's so deep I can feel him against my cervix. Leaning back, I roll my hips, panting when his hands move, one to cup my breast, and the other down between my legs, where his thumb circles my clit. My head falls back, my eyes close, and my hands move behind me to hold on to his thighs.

"Jesus," he groans, rolling his thumb faster. "Look at me." My head dips forward, and I pull my eyes open to meet his. "You look beautiful taking my cock, baby."

Moaning, I fight to keep his gaze, but I feel it building and I know it's going to be huge. "Come for me, June. Come on my cock."

Whimpering, "Ev," my eyes slide closed and my body falls forward.

His hands move to hold my hips tight and his hips thrust hard into me, making my orgasm take on a life of its own. Moving me to my back, his hips piston into mine hard and fast. I cry out and lose my breath. My head lifts and I latch on to his chest with my teeth. His roar fills the room as his thrusts slow to a glide for one…two…three…four…five strokes, and then he plants himself deep inside of me. My mouth releases his flesh as I fall back onto the bed exhausted, out of breath, and completely sated.

"Fuck, but I could seriously live in your pussy, baby," he growls, pressing his hips deeper into mine.

"I love your penis," I mutter, and I feel him shaking. My eyes fight to open, and when they do, I see he's fighting laughter. "What's so funny?" I ask with a frown. His head shakes and his face dips, so he can place a quick kiss to my lips.

"You love my penis?" he asks, and I scrunch up my nose, because I can see he's trying not to laugh. "No one calls it a penis, baby."

"Um, that's what it is," I tell him, putting pressure against his chest, which he ignores as he drops to his elbow and pushes my hair away from my forehead.

"Cock. You love my cock." He grins.

"Whatever," I mutter, rolling my eyes and pushing at his chest to no avail.

"Only medical professionals call it a penis."

"Fine, I love your cock."

His grin turns smug. He slides his cock out of me, only to push right back in. "Fuck yeah, you do. You're soaked."

"You're so full of yourself," I mutter.

"Wrong, you're so full of me." He presses his hips farther into me while running his nose along mine.

"This is about the time I stop talking to you," I grumble, and the bed and I shake as he buries his face in my neck and laughs. Feeling him laughing while still inside of me is something I've never felt, yet something I love immediately. "It's late," I remind him, and his face moves back to hover over mine.

"I love you," he says gently, running his fingers along my hairline. "Never going to stop loving you, baby."

"Ev," I breathe, feeling tears burn my throat.

"I'll wait for you to find it again. I'd wait forever for you." He leans in, covering my mouth with his before I can reply. When his mouth leaves mine, he pulls out of me slowly then rolls, taking me with him. He adjusts us in the bed, with my cheek to his chest and his arms wrapped tight around me. Closing my eyes, I wonder why his brother did what he did, and then wonder where he is now.

"Ev," I call quietly, as he reaches over to turn out the light.

"Yeah, baby?"

"Is…" I pause, not wanting to set him off again after his reaction earlier.

"What is it?" he asks on a squeeze, rolling back into me.

"Is your brother okay?"

"He's sitting in jail," he says, not sounding upset about that at all. In fact, there is no emotion in his tone.

"I'm sorry," I whisper, pressing closer to him.

His body turns toward mine and his arms go tight enough that the air rushes out of my lungs. "Do not," he growls, getting close enough for me to feel his breath against my skin, "feel bad for him." Okay, there was definitely emotion there. His arms loosen, but his face stays close as he continues, "He fucked up. This isn't the first time he's fucked up either. Me and him are done. He's going back to prison, where he's likely going to spend a few more years. He's had the opportunity to get his shit together, but he continues to squander that shit."

"But he's your brother," I say softly. My sisters and I are close. The rest of my family and I are close too, and I can't imagine ever cutting any one of them out.

Growing quiet his fingers shift through my hair then run down my back. "My family isn't like your family, baby, and my brother and I don't have a relationship like you and your sisters have. I've tried with him, tried over and over throughout the years. I knew he was fucked up from how we grew up, understood the reasons why he did the shit he did before, but he's not a kid anymore, and I won't make excuses for him. I won't allow you to feel bad for him."

"Maybe—"

"I want you to listen," he cuts me off before I can suggest that maybe his brother needs help, real help, and not the kind prison offers. "I want you to hear me when I say this. It's going to sound cold, but this is the truth. He's never going to change. He's going to use our childhood as an excuse for his fucked-up behavior for the rest of his life, and that shit is on him."

"But—"

His thumb presses over my lips and his face dips even closer to mine. "Don't. I love you, baby, and I know you. I know you see your family and the way they are, and you think that's the way it is for everyone, but it is not. Some people have the same blood running through their veins, but that blood doesn't mean shit at the end of the day. When shit went down for you, I didn't once think of calling my blood. I called my *brothers*. And the minute I did, they rolled out. *That's* loyalty. *That's* love and respect. *That's* a bond stronger than blood. You get me?" he asks, and I nod in the dark. "Good." He removes his thumb.

"How did you meet up with Wes and the guys?" I ask, referring to my sister July's husband, who also happens to be the president of The Broken Eagles MC club. The men Evan obviously considers his brothers. July explained to me that Wes and his boys were all in the military together. They ride on weekends, work on their own bikes and cars, and do the same for friends. Wes came here to visit his mom, who lives in Nashville, took one look at the beautiful state of Tennessee, and decided once they were all free from the service, they'd move here, settle down, and start their own bike and car repair business.

"Soon as I got back stateside and discharged, I looked up a friend of mine, Colton. He was in our unit, but had gotten sent back stateside for surgery after being shot once in the chest and once in the back two weeks before we lost our unit. Colton was in New York at a rehabilitation center, but he put me in contact with his dad. Their family owns a biker bar near Chattanooga. I didn't know what I was going to do. I just knew that whatever I did, I needed to be away from Alabama, my mom, and my dad," he says, holding me a little closer. "I also didn't want to risk seeing you."

That stung. I understood why, but it still hurt. I can still remember the pain I felt when I found out he was in Alabama and hadn't come to me. I remember it so accurately, it feels like it was just yesterday.

"We're moving forward, baby," he whispers, and I squeeze my eyes closed and nod. "I had been working at the bar for a week when Harlen came in. We talked the whole time he was on the stool. Before he left, he gave me his number, and we talked some more. During one of our calls, he explained that he was part of an MC, and that most of the members were Vets. He invited me to come out for the weekend and I took him up on his offer. It wasn't long after that, that Wes introduced me to Jax."

"I'm glad you have them," I say softly. I'm glad that after his messed-up childhood and what happened to him when he was in Afghanistan, he has guys he considers brothers, people to depend on and lean on.

"Me too, baby."

"And Colton, is he okay now?" I ask, wondering if his friend realizes his life was also spared because of what happened to him.

"He is now, but wasn't before. He may have been gone, but he also lost men he thought of as brothers. Had to learn how to walk again, spent a year in rehab. His longtime fiancée broke up with him while he was going through that shit, so he wasn't good, but he's back home, settling in, and working at his dad's bar. Last time we spoke, he sounded happy."

"His longtime fiancée broke up with him while he was learning how to walk again?" I breathe, not even beginning to comprehend that.

"She's a cunt and proved that shit. I don't know the details. We don't talk about her. I just know he's done with her in a way that there will never be any fixing that shit. I can't say I blame him. She should have stuck by her man or waited until he was on his feet, literally, before dropping that kind of bomb on him. They weren't just dating, they were engaged and talking about starting a family. That shit proves the kind of woman she is."

"Wow, what a bitch," I murmur, and his arms give me a squeeze.

"Yep."

"Good for him, getting over her, though."

"Yeah, baby, good for him. He's a good guy, has a solid family, so I think he'll be all right."

"Good," I whisper.

"You'll meet him. We'll take a day and ride out to see him and his parents one day."

"On your bike?" I ask hopefully.

"You wanna go on my bike?" he asks, and I put my hand to his chest and drape my body over his.

"Do you remember when you rode down my block on your bike?" I inquire, and I feel him go solid, but he still replies with a quiet, "Yeah."

"That night, I spent forever getting myself off. I was so turned on I couldn't even get to sle—" Before I can say more, he rolls me to my back and covers my mouth with his, and then he does more things to me. Things that end with me screaming out his name, and him groaning mine down my throat, proving the reality of him is much better than the fantasy.

WAKING, I FEEL warmth down my back, knees bent in toward mine, and a hand I know is Evan's tucked close to my chest. It's Saturday, and all I want to do is sleep, but I know I need to get up to let Ninja out and feed him, so I carefully unlace my fingers from Evan's and scoot out of the bed. Once I'm free, I go to the bathroom and take care of business, brush my teeth, and grab a hoodie from my closet, along with a pair of cutoff sweats, putting both on before leaving the bathroom.

I take a second to appreciate Evan in my bed—the sheet down to his waist, his strong arms and wide chest on display, along with his tattoos. Fighting the urge to go back to bed and curl my body into his, I leave the bedroom, shutting the door softly behind me. "Hey, Pup-Pup," I whisper when Ninja looks at me from his position on the couch and yawns. "Come on outside." I walk past the couch and push the double glass doors open.

His eyes stay on me as he lets out an annoyed huff, which I'm sure means, *It's too early to get up.* His body stretches out, his front paws hitting the floor first, before he slowly slides off the couch like he has all the time in the world. Laughing at him, I give him a cuddle when he reaches me before leaving the door open for him to come back in, and then head for the kitchen to start some coffee.

Sitting out on my back deck in a foldup chair, with my feet resting on the wood railing and a cup of coffee in my hands, I look over my shoulder when the door slides open, and watch Evan step out wearing nothing but a pair of loose shorts and holding a cup of coffee.

"Hey," he greets, his hair rumpled and his face still soft from sleep.

"Hey." My eyes rake down his chest and abs, taking in all that is him, and there is a whole lot more than there used to be—all of it seriously hot. Coming toward me, he bends at the waist, touching his mouth to mine, saying softly against my lips, "I don't like waking without you."

"I wanted to let you sleep," I reply just as softly, and then laugh when Ninja nudges between us and leans against Evan, so he's forced to take a step away from me.

"I see we're gonna have problems." He chuckles, running his hands over Ninja's head.

"He's my Pup-Pup." I smile, rubbing Ninja's snout, and he instantly forgets about Evan and moves closer to me.

"Pup-Pup?" Evan asks.

I look at Ninja then grin, and chirp, "Yep."

His eyes drop to my mouth and he shakes his head, then mutters to Ninja, "Go get your ball." As he sets his cup of coffee on the edge of the deck and grabs one of the chairs that are folded up against the side of the house, he unfolds it next to mine then fits his big body into it, causing the cheap metal to groan and squeak under his weight.

"I'm not sure my chairs are built for you," I tell him, as he leans forward to grab his coffee, causing the chair to groan again.

"We'll take my truck today, get some deck chairs that won't give out, and pick my shit up from the compound," he says almost to himself, taking the ball from Ninja when he brings it over.

"We will?" I ask, and his eyes move to me and scan my face, and then he transfers his coffee to his other hand and nabs me from behind my neck, pulling me closer until we're sharing the same breath.

"We're moving forward, and we're doing that together. I know you still have doubts about us, but I don't. We'll work through your shit and settle in, baby."

"My shit?" I whisper, and his eyes scan my face again.

"Do you want me to leave?" he prompts, and I feel my heart lodge itself in my throat at the idea of him leaving. His eyes lock on mine, and his voice drops as his fingers flex against my skin. "I have enough love for the both of us. Doesn't matter if you love me back. I'm not giving you space or room. You're mine, June. You have been for a long fucking time and I want what we could have had to start now."

"Do..." I pause, licking my lips, and his eyes drop to my mouth. "Do you think we should slow down a little?"

"What's going to change if we slow down?" he asks, which is a good question, and it's a good question that annoys me, since I know by the determination in his eyes that nothing is going to change. Besides, since he's been back, I can't imagine it any other way.

"My dad's going to kill me," I mumble. He grins and leans closer, brushing his lips against mine, and then leans back to take a sip of coffee.

"He'll adjust," he says, pulling the ball from Ninja's mouth and tossing it again. "Hell, he doesn't like me anyway, so fuck it."

"He likes you," I tell him, or at least he *did* like him. Now, I'm not so sure, but seeing how he's alive, I'm sure that means Dad doesn't exactly hate him.

"Baby," he murmurs, sounding amused. "He told me that if I fucked up again, he was going to cut off my dick and feed it to me."

"Oh." I cringe then listen to him laugh. Taking a sip of coffee, I wonder how long it will take for my dad to come around.

"He'll come around," he assures, reading my mind.

"My family is a little overprotective." I sigh.

"I get it. I'll be the same when we have girls."

"Ev," I whisper, holding my cup tighter. When Evan and I were together, we talked about starting a family sooner, rather than later. I wanted to be a mom while I was still young, and I wanted at least three kids, if not more. Evan wanted the same as me.

"We got delayed, baby, but I already searched your shit and couldn't find any birth control. We didn't use any kind of protection last night." His words stun me, and I'm not prepared when his hand nabs me again, pulling me close once more. "When I said we're moving forward, I meant with everything."

My breathing starts to turn ragged and my stomach rolls into a knot. I don't know what I'm feeling, but it's not panic or fear; it's something different, something unexpected. Finally, I get the word, "What," out, but that's all I'm able to say before he kisses me again and leans back, taking another sip of his coffee.

"It'll all work out," he says casually, picking up the ball Ninja drops at his side, tossing it out into the yard.

"Are you crazy?" I ask when I find my voice.

"Was crazy for a while, baby. I also couldn't breathe. I couldn't even fucking take a breath. Three days ago, I finally took a breath, and since then, I've been breathing easy. So no, baby, I'm not crazy."

Okay. I can feel it happening. I know it's coming, so I turn my face away from his and pull in a breath through my nose to fight the tears back, but it doesn't work. I hiccup on a sob, and then before I have a chance to cover it, my coffee cup is removed from my hand and Evan is picking me up, placing me in his lap. Crying into his neck, I cling to him tighter, and then scream when the chair under us gives out and we both fall to the deck below us.

"Are you okay?" he asks, rolling me to my back, away from the broken chair.

"I'm fine." I giggle, and then giggle louder as I push Ninja away when he licks my face. "I told you my chairs weren't built for you," I say softly, as his eyes change and his hips press into mine.

"You're so fucking beautiful, baby, the most beautiful woman I've ever seen," he whispers, catching me off guard. His hands move and hold each side of my face, and his thumbs swipe over my cheeks, where the tears had fallen moments before. "Even crying, you're fucking gorgeous." His lips brush over mine, and then I pull my head back and cover my face when Ninja licks between our faces.

"I think we need to get up." I laugh.

"Let's go. We have a busy day ahead of us, and that day is starting in the shower." He stands, pulling me up along with him, and leads me into the house by my hand, shutting the door once Ninja is back inside.

"I'll shower alone. I don't want to get my hair wet," I tell him, and his fingers flex between mine as his eyes move from my hair, down my body.

"Sorry, baby, but more than just your hair is gonna get wet."

"Evan, I'm serious," I scold, trying to get him to release my hand.

"So am I, baby," he mutters, dragging me behind him down the hall, through the bedroom, and straight into the bathroom.

As much as it annoys me to admit it, having to blow dry my hair after our shower was totally worth it.

Chapter 9

June

WALKING INTO THE bar, my hand held tightly in Evan's, I wait for my eyes to adjust to the dim light. Evan kept his word from last Saturday about taking me for a ride to meet his friend Colton in Chattanooga. Well, really, he's taken me on a lot of rides over the last week, but honestly, I think it's because every time he's given me a ride on the back of his bike, he's gotten a ride of a different variety when we get home.

I don't ride a bike like my sister July and I don't want to learn, but being snug to Evan's back, the feel of power between my legs, the wind in my hair, and the warm sun beating down on us is something I have come to crave.

So much has happened over the last two weeks. Evan moved in that first Saturday we had together. We went to the compound and picked up his stuff, not that he had a lot of anything really. All he had was some clothes, a few guns, which I ignored as he packed them away, and two pictures that were not framed and were worn around the edges.

The first picture was of him and me, which he took on his cell phone one day when we were together at his apartment in Alabama. I didn't have my shirt on, because we had been making out hot and heavy in his bed. My body was pressed to his back, my chin on his shoulder. I was smiling at the camera, with flushed cheeks and swollen lips. He had told me I looked beautiful and that he needed to capture the moment. So he rolled to his side to grab his cell off his side table, and I followed him, pressing close. I forgot about that moment until I saw the picture.

The other was a picture from the day we got married. I was wearing a simple white summer dress with a pair of strappy taupe sandals on my feet, and he was wearing a pair of dark jeans and a dark blue button-up shirt. We were both in profile, his face dipping toward mine, his hand on my waist, mine at his back, with our marriage certificate in my hand.

When I saw those pictures, I cried. I knew he said he was always mine, but seeing those photos, the worn edges and crinkles in the paper from being handled often, I knew he *always* kept me with him. After I finally pulled myself together, we dropped his stuff at my house then went to the local gardening store and bought furniture for the deck, all dark wood with bright cushions, along with a simple table, chairs, and a grill, because "we needed a grill"—or *Evan* needed a grill, since I don't have any luck with barbequing. Every time I tried in the past, the meat was overcooked or burnt to a crisp, and completely inedible.

After we got home that day, we spent time together just us, and did the same for the last week—being lazy, being a couple, and arguing and bickering about what to watch or what to cook for dinner, but we did it all together. Things between us have been falling back into place, and everything about that feels good. No…it feels amazing, while still being a little scary.

Feeling Evan's hand give mine a squeeze, I come out of my thoughts and tilt my head back toward him. His eyes search my face for a moment, and I know he sees it there when he grins then dips his face closer to mine, and whispers, "We'll get a room for the night and ride home tomorrow afternoon."

Shivering at that, I lick my bottom lip and whisper back, "Sounds good to me."

His face lowers so he can kiss me, and when he pulls away, I turn my head when a deep rumbly voice says, "Fuck me. Jesus Christ, fuck me, Evan?"

Looking toward the back bar, I watch a very handsome man step out from behind the counter and come toward us, smiling huge with his arms out at his sides.

"Colton." Evan smiles, and my eyes go back to Colton.

Holy hotness.

I mean, I have my very own hot guy, a man that is the definition of hot, but this guy is gorgeous. Tall and lean with dark hair and even darker eyes, surrounded by thick lashes, his jaw is square and shadowed with stubble accentuating his full lips and straight white smile. Seeing him and his smile, I do not even understand how his bitch of an ex could stand to walk away from him.

"Good to see you, man," Evan mutters, letting me go so he can hug his friend.

"Fuck, man, it's been too long," Colton rumbles, patting Evan's back hard as they embrace. When they release each other, Evan's arm goes around my shoulders, tucking me close to his side.

"Want you to meet June," Evan says in introduction, and Colton's eyes move between Evan and me.

"Nice to meet you." I smile, and then his smile broadens and he tugs me from Evan's grasp, picks me up, and hugs me so tight that my sides hurt from the pressure.

"Shit, man, you did not fucking lie. She's pretty as hell."

Okay, that was sweet and felt really good.

"You can stop touching her now," Evan grumbles, and I bite my lip, trying not to laugh.

"Aw, I see you're still a selfish bastard." Colton laughs, setting me on my feet.

"With her, always," he says, tucking me back to his side. "You got time for a beer, or are you working?"

"I got time." He grins, patting Evan's back once more and shaking his head before turning toward the bar, where we follow him. "What do you guys want to drink?" he asks, as we take a seat on two barstools.

"Whatever's cold for me," Evan says. "June'll have a Miller Lite." Giving his waist a squeeze, I lean deeper into him. I know it's not huge, but I love that he remembers what I drink, how I take my coffee, what foods I do or don't like, all of those unimportant things that end up being important in the end, because they tell you the person you're with cares enough to pay attention to the small things about you.

"Gia, baby, come here," Colton calls, looking to his right, and I follow his gaze toward the open door to an office, where a very pretty, petite girl with loads of curves, long, dark, wavy hair, olive-toned skin, and startling green eyes is standing next to an older woman who looks a lot like Colton.

"One day, I'm going to kill your son," I hear the girl, who must be Gia, mutter. The woman she's standing next to laughs loudly, saying something I can't hear before shoving her our way.

"You rang," Gia says when she's close, and Colton grins at her.

"Gia, this is Evan. We were in the marines together, and this is his wife, June," Colton says, and my heart contracts, and not in a good way. I'm not his wife anymore, and even though I've known that for a very long time and felt like I came to terms with it ages ago, hearing what once was kills me.

"Nice to meet you guys." She smiles, showing off two dimples, one in each cheek.

"You too." I smile back, as Evan lifts his chin and asks, "This your girl?"

"Yeah," Colton says, smiling as Gia states, "No," turning and tilting her head way back to frown up at him.

Giggling, I look between the two of them then watch Colton smirk down at her, as he mutters, "Babe, we've been through this."

"That's my point!" she cries, tossing her arms in the air. "We've been through this, and you're still not listening." In a flash, his hand is on the back of her neck, pulling her close, and then his mouth is on hers and he's kissing her deeply, with tongue. By the time he rips his mouth from hers, her hands have moved from pushing him away to holding him closer.

"Oh my," I whisper, once again wondering what the hell his ex was thinking.

"I told you to stop kissing me," she breathes, blinking up at him, as her cheeks turn pink.

"And I told you, baby, that's never gonna happen," he whispers back, kissing her once more, this one swift and just a touch of his mouth to hers.

"Don't mind them," the woman who looks like Colton says, coming to block our view of them as she leans over the bar and pats Evan's cheek. "I miss you, kid."

"Miss you too, Ma Rose," Evan says, sliding his arm around my shoulders. "I want you to meet June."

"June," she speaks quietly, moving her gaze to me.

"Nice to meet you." I smile, and her eyes move between us before she focuses on Evan once more.

"You got your girl back?" She smiles a soft motherly smile that makes me like her even more.

"Pulled my head out of my ass," Evan replies, and she laughs then shakes her head.

"Kirk's gonna be happy," she mumbles, still smiling.

"Where is the old man?"

"Home, he was at the bar late. He should be here in a couple hours, if you two want to stick around. If not, you can ride over to the house. I'm sure he's up puttering around the garage, working on his bike."

"We'll be here for a while," Evan says, and she smiles and pats his cheek again. I know he and his mom are closer than he is with the rest of his family, and by close, I mean they talk, but his mom isn't around unless she wants something. So, I'm happy to see he's built relationships with people who are healthy and normal, relationships that are two-sided, where he's not the only person doing all the work.

"Here." Colton slides a beer bottle in front of me and mug of beer in front of Evan, and then leans against the bar, crossing his arms over his chest.

"So, I take it you're good?" Evan asks, looking back toward the office, where Gia has disappeared along with Colton's mom.

"Couldn't be better. Well, it could be, but Rome wasn't built in a day." He shrugs, grinning, and Evan laughs, shaking his head.

"That, I understand." Evan looks at me, and Colton's grin turns into a small smile.

"Man, it's really fucking good to see you," Colton says quietly, the words spoken with a deeper meaning than just seeing his friend after so long. They're spoken in a way to where I know he understands, more than most, that had Evan not gone back to check in the house, he wouldn't be sitting here right now.

"You too, brother." They hold each other's gaze for a long time before each of them clears their throat and looks away. Leaning into Evan, I press a kiss to the underside of his jaw that is clenched. His eyes drop to mine and his face softens, along with his jaw.

Are you okay? I mouth, and he nods then presses a kiss to my fore-head. The words *I love you* are stuck in the back of my throat as I sit back and take a sip of my beer. I feel so torn between the need to tell him how I feel and the need to hold on to those words. My gut actually aches every time I think about saying the three words out loud, as though by saying them, I'll wake up and realize all of this was just a dream.

"You okay, baby?" Evan asks against my ear, pulling me from my thoughts.

"Yeah, sorry, I spaced out," I mutter, then my eyes go to Colton and I notice him watching me closely. I give him a smile, and he returns one, but it doesn't quite reach his eyes this time.

Oh well.

Taking another sip of beer, I lean closer to Evan and listen to him and Colton talk, and occasionally laugh or smile when they tell me stories about things they did together or things that happened when they were deployed. When Colton's dad arrives and introduces himself, I look around. I didn't even notice how much time had passed or how full the bar had gotten. There must be at least a hundred people here now, if not more.

"I'll be back," I tell Evan, sliding off my barstool.

"'Kay, baby, come right back."

Rolling my eyes at that, I mutter, "Yes, sir," under my breath, and his eyes darken at my words. Before I know what's happening, I'm back in his grasp and his mouth is close to my ear.

"I'll be sure to put that into play tonight." His words vibrate against my ear, sending a shiver down my spine and a tingle between my legs.

"Ev." My eyes slide closed when his teeth nip my earlobe, making me clutch onto his shirt at his ribs so I don't fall on my face.

"Go and come back to me." He grins, looking smug.

"Tease," I whisper, leaving his side, hearing his laugher behind me as I head toward the restroom. Walking into the girls' bathroom, I find Gia is standing and waiting for the one and only stall with her arms crossed over her chest, glaring at a tall brunette who's washing her hands.

"Hey." I smile when her eyes come to me.

"Hey." Her face softens, and then she moves back as the stall opens up and a girl with long blonde hair stumbles out, giggling when she bumps into Gia.

"We really need an employee bathroom," she mumbles, looking between the girl at the sink and the girl who just came out of the stall.

"So you and Colton?" I ask, bumping her shoulder with a grin on my face, blaming the question on the five beers I've had since I've been here.

Gia's eyes meet mine, but before she can reply, one of the girls at the sink whispers to her friend loud enough for us to hear, "Did you know Lisa and Colton had lunch yesterday?"

Turning to look at them, I blink then feel my jaw clench when the other one answers, "I know. Lisa said she's so happy to be wearing the ring he gave her again."

"No," I mutter to myself. I feel completely invested in Colton's life, like it's a daytime TV show and he's the leading man, and Lisa is the conniving bitch who is secretly sleeping with his brother. Not that he has a brother, or that I know him at all, but after hearing his story from Evan, I know if he gets back with his ex, I'm going to kick his ass myself.

"Who are you?" the brunette asks, sliding her eyes from her lips, which she's applying lip-gloss to, to mine in the mirror.

"Colton did not have lunch with her," I say, not answering her question and really having no idea if he did have lunch with her yesterday or not. For all I know, he could have, but judging by the way his eyes followed Gia all around the bar, I didn't think that was true.

"He did. Lisa told us," the blonde says, turning to face me.

"Well, Lisa is a liar and a dumbass," I tell her, looking to my side and seeing Gia glaring at both girls.

"Who are you?" the blonde asks again, turning to face me and crossing her arms over her obviously fake boobs.

"Who I am doesn't matter."

"Yeah, if you're calling Lisa a liar, it does matter," the brunette states, turning to stand by her friend.

"Why are you guys even here?" Gia asks, looking between the two of them. "This isn't your normal hangout, and last I heard, you weren't even supposed to be in the bar."

"I doubt Colton's going to kick out his fiancée's friends." The blonde rolls her eyes.

Okay, I'm officially crazy, or maybe I had one too many beers—not that I feel even a little drunk—but these chicks are seriously pissing me off.

"He is not her fiancé," I growl.

"He is." The blonde leans forward, pushing me in the chest with a finger.

Um, hell to the no.

"Did you just touch me?" I ask in disbelief.

"Yeah, what are you gonna do about it?" she snaps, taking a step closer to me.

Leaning forward, I open my mouth to reply, but jump back when—"What the fuck is going on?" echoes through the room. Putting Gia behind me, my eyes fly to the door, where Colton is standing, looking pissed.

"Thank God you're here. This crazy girl was just telling us that you and Lisa aren't together!" the brunette cries, dramatically pointing at me.

Hearing a rumbled, "June, come here," my eyes skate past Colton's shoulder and meet Evan's cold gaze.

Crap.

"I told you once, and this is the last time I'm saying it. Get the fuck out and stay the fuck out. You are not welcome at my bar," Colton grits out though his teeth, and I fight the urge to stick my tongue out at the girls and say "I told you so."

"But—" one of the girls whispers, as Colton roars, "Now!" making them jump and move quickly through the small space Colton and Evan allow them.

"Gia, baby, are you okay?" Colton asks, and I turn to look at Gia, seeing her face is set in annoyance, but her eyes look watery.

"I'm fine." She moves, turning her back on him, going into the stall, and shutting the door.

"June," Evan repeats, and my eyes move to him.

"Give me five and I'll be out."

"You don't come out and I have to come back in, we're gonna have problems."

"And where exactly am I going to go?" I ask him, which probably isn't the right thing to say, since his jaw ticks at my question. "I'll be out." I sigh then look at Colton, and whisper, "I'll make sure she's okay," pushing the door and effectively moving him out of the bathroom.

"Is he gone?" Gia asks after a moment from the other side of the stall door.

"Yeah."

"God, I hate those girls," she says, opening the door and moving to the sink.

"They're liars," I tell her, hoping it is something she knows herself.

"I know," she agrees softly, washing her hands. "I shouldn't let them get to me, but I can't help it. Lisa is constantly showing up or calling. I have so much going on that I can't even focus on her and Colton. Not that I want to, but…" She shrugs.

"I get it," I say softly, giving her shoulder a squeeze as I move past her into the stall, taking care of business quickly.

"How did you know they were lying?" she asks, when I'm out of the stall and washing my hands.

"Um… I'm not sure if you noticed, but Colton doesn't exactly let you out of his sight. I can't imagine that a man who's trying to get back with his ex would be so invested in someone else," I point out the obvious, and her cheeks darken as her face drops.

"He makes me crazy." She shakes her head, closing her eyes before opening them back up and meeting my gaze.

"He's hot." I grin, and she tries to fight it, but she can't. She tries to cover her smile by hiding her face behind her hands and laughing, but I know it's there.

When she pulls her hands away, I see why Colton is obsessed with her. She's fragile; something in her needs protecting. And for a guy who put his life on the line for his country, I bet her soft spot isn't something he can resist wanting to protect.

"Thanks for taking my back."

"Oh, please. That was fun, and seriously, I don't know much about Colton, but my guess is he isn't the kind of guy you let go of. Only, his ex is an idiot and did it in a big way. Now, she's realized her stupidity, and her loss is definitely your gain, sister."

"You should see her," Gia whispers, and my brows draw together.

"Who?"

"His ex. She's like a walking Victoria's Secret model."

"Have you looked in the mirror?" I question. I mean, seriously, Gia is gorgeous, and honestly, she fits Colton perfectly.

"I'm serious! She's, like, perfect, and I'm—well…" She pauses. "Me. I don't get it. Plus, there is all kinds of stuff going on, and I hate having Colton and his family involved in it."

"One thing I know about men," I start, gently grabbing her hand, "is they don't do anything they don't want to do. And honey, for real, you are gorgeous. You have nothing to worry about."

"I guess," she mutters, then looks at the door when it opens and a woman walks in. "I better get back out on the floor."

"Wait, let me get your number. If you ever want to talk, you can call me. Anytime."

"Really?"

"Of course. Us girls need to stick together." I smile again, taking my phone out of my pocket. I add her number to my contacts, and we leave the restroom together. Once I'm back at the bar, I go directly to Evan's side and take a seat on the barstool next to his.

"What the hell happened?" he asks, leaning closer to me, but my eyes are on Colton's, which are filled with concern as he looks behind us, where I'm sure Gia is waiting tables like she was doing earlier.

Pulling my attention from Colton, I turn to meet Evan's gaze. "I'll tell you later," I murmur, and his eyes search my face before he nods and wraps his warm hand around the back of my neck, so he can tug me closer and place his lips to my forehead.

"You okay?" he asks when he pulls back.

Grinning, I answer, "Absolutely."

"You're a pain in the ass." He smiles, and I lean closer, pressing my mouth to his ignoring his statement.

"OH, MY GOD," I hiss, holding on to Evan's hair as his mouth devours me, my naked back pressed to the wall just inside the hotel room's door, with him on his knees in front of me, still fully clothed. As soon as we got into the room, he made quick work of stripping me naked, and then made even quicker work of giving me an orgasm. Now, I was working toward the second.

"Fuck, baby, get there. I need inside of you," he growls, thrusting two fingers deep, sending me to my toes.

"I'm close." I moan, "So close."

"Fuck," he snarls, tossing my leg over his shoulder, opening me up more. My head bangs back against the wall and I cry out as another orgasm slices through me, sending me reeling. Before I'm even back to earth, my body bounces against the bed and Evan is towering over me. Ripping his shirt off over his head, my hands go to his chest then down to his abs.

"I need you in me," I tell him, fumbling with his belt buckle, while his lips close around my nipple, sucking deep. "Oh, God," I whimper, when his fingers pull on my neglected nipple, tugging the tip, causing my hands to lose purchase on his belt and my back to arch.

Releasing my breast, he rolls to his back. His hands finish unhooking his belt and the button of his jeans. "Mouth around my cock, baby," he growls, sending a thrill down my spine as his hips lift, exposing everything that is him. Helping him get his boots and jeans off, his knees lift and his hand wraps around the base of his cock, stroking once. Moving between his spread thighs, I wrap my hand over his and glide down his length, holding his gaze. "Give me that mouth."

Leaning over him, his hand and mine move together as I lick across his lips. His free hand tangles in the hair at the back of my head, bringing me closer so he can kiss me deeper before his hand tightens and he forces me back an inch, then more pressure as he guides my face down. The dominance in his move has wetness spreading between my legs.

Licking around the tip, I slide my mouth down, meeting our hands. His hand moves from under mine to over it as I swirl my tongue and take him deep. "Jesus, your fucking mouth," he mutters, and my free hand moves up his thigh, cupping his balls gently as I twist my other hand up with every downward glide of my mouth. Working him over, I feel him tense, and then his hand in my hair tightens once more as he pulls me away from his cock.

"I wasn't done," I tell him.

"You can do it again later," he mutters, wrapping his arm around my back.

"I was doing it now," I complain, as he moves me to my back, tosses my legs around his hips, and slams into me hard.

"You can do it again later," he repeats, sliding out.

"Later," I agree, pulling his mouth down to mine. His tongue slides in as his hand moves between us, zeroing in on my clit.

God, yes.

"You're soaked, baby," he groans, going deeper as I lift my hips higher off the bed.

"I know," I agree, running my hands down his back and grabbing on to his ass, feeling his muscles contract as he plows into me. "I'm going to come," I whisper, shoving my face into his neck, while he circles my clit faster and his hips buck into mine so hard that my breath catches.

"Hold it."

"I can't," I whimper, digging my nails into his skin.

"Hold it, baby."

"Ev, I can't!" I cry out, trying, really trying, to hold it off, but the way it's building, I know there is no way I will be able to hold the orgasm back once it takes over.

No way at all.

"Fuck, baby, come," he growls, and I do. I come hard as his fingers pinch my clit, tugging once. My body arches and my legs tighten as he rides me out, thrusting twice more before planting himself deep inside of me.

Breathing heavily, my arms and legs tighten around him farther and my face moves to his shoulder, pressing there as waves of pleasure course though me. My skin feels undone and my limbs feel like jelly. "You okay?" he asks, pressing a kiss to my neck, dropping his elbow to the bed, while his hand sifts through my hair.

"Yeah," I whisper, leaning back to look at him.

"Good," he whispers back, and his face goes soft as the next words leave his mouth. "I saw it, baby,"

"Saw what?" I question, studying him and thinking he is beautiful.

"What you're afraid to say. What you're afraid to admit to your-self…to me."

"Ev…" Tears fill my eyes as my heart speeds up.

"I know it's there already. Maybe it never left, but I saw it, and I want it."

"I…" I close my eyes, wishing I could make him understand what I'm feeling, why I'm so afraid.

"I'm not going anywhere. I'm not letting you go anywhere either." His fingers sift through my hair again, and my eyes open to meet his.

"I believe you." And I do. I see it in the way he looks at me, feel it in the way he touches me. I know deep in my gut he's telling the truth, but I'm still afraid.

"I hate that you don't have my last name anymore. It killed me when Colton introduced you as my wife and I knew it wasn't true."

"I didn't like it either," I say, as he rolls us to our sides, effectively severing our connection, and then adjusting me so I'm draped over him.

"He didn't know. His mom and dad knew, because I worked the bar with them, and they eventually dug it out of me. But he didn't know."

"It sucked, but it's okay. He's nice. I can see why you two are friends."

"He's a good guy," he agrees, running his fingers down my spine. My eyes start to drift closed. The three orgasms I had, his touch, and the sound of his heartbeat against my ear lull me close to sleep. "Gonna marry you again, baby," he says quietly, and with those words ringing in my ears, I fall asleep smiling.

Chapter 10

Evan

TOSSING THE BALL for Ninja into the backyard, I pull my cell out of my back pocket when it rings, and sigh once I get a look at the caller ID. I've been avoiding this phone call for the last week, but I know I need to get it over with.

"Hello," I answer, picking up the ball once more, watching Ninja take off before it is even out of my hand.

"I've been calling," my mother says, and I can hear the drunken twinge in her tone even over the phone.

"Been busy."

"Too busy for your family?" she asks snidely, and I grit my teeth. There was a time I wanted nothing more than to help my family, to fix what was broken between us, but I learned early on that shit was impossible. "Your brother is in jail," she informs me, and that anger I felt when I watched the tapes of him pawning June's shit comes back, coursing through my veins.

Seeing her sitting on JJ's couch, wrapped in nothing but a towel, holding a pair of scissors in a death grip—it's a vision that will haunt me for a long fucking time.

"And?" I ask, as Ninja bumps my leg with his nose then looks at the ball he dropped at my feet, telling me to pick it up.

"You don't care?" she asks.

"He broke into June's house, stole her shit, and pawned it. So, no, I don't give a fuck."

I hear her enraged huff on the other end of the line. "He's your brother, your blood!" she cries, and I imagine her pacing the small living room of her house, ripping her hand through her hair in aggravation, or going to the kitchen and pulling down the bottle of vodka from the cupboard.

"He's my blood, but he's not my brother," I say low.

Silence from her, and then, "He's had a hard time. You… you were gone. And your dad is hard on him. He's always been hard on you boys."

"Stop making excuses for him," I grit out. "Yeah, I know Dad can be hard. I know he's mostly an asshole, but I also see *why*."

"You're agreeing with the things he's done, how he's treated your brother and me?" she asks in quiet disbelief.

"You're a drunk," I whisper, hearing her sharp intake of breath over the line. None of us has ever said it out loud, but we all know it's true. A dirty secret. Something everyone's been denying or avoids talking about since I can remember. "Jay's a drug addict, and you denying your problems along with his isn't helping. I don't agree with Dad taking a hand to us in anger when we were younger, but you're a part of the problem, part of his problem, part of Jay's problem. You guys are all toxic, and together, you're a fuckin' deadly combination."

"Oh, now you're too good for us? June took you back, so now you don't care about your family?"

Fuck. For as long as I can remember, it's always been the same shit—guilt, and manipulation until they get what they want, whatever that might be.

"I'm starting my family with June," I say quietly.

"I can't believe you would do this," she whispers. "I can't believe you're turning your back on us."

"I don't want my kids around your mess. You, as my mother,

should have protected me from Dad, and Dad should have protected me from you and your drinking. Neither of you did that, but *I'm* going to protect *my* kids from all of you."

"I'm not a drunk."

"You drink every fucking day, *every* fucking day. You don't even know what it's like to be sober."

"If I was a drunk, how would I keep the same job for the last fifteen years?"

"Why the fuck am I even doing this shit right now? I'm not debating this shit with you, and honestly, Mom, you need to admit that shit to yourself. You need help."

"So this is it? You're just done with us?" she asks, and fuck me, but I wish it didn't come to this. I can't have their kind of poison in my life, though. I may not've been able to do anything growing up to shield myself from them, but I won't let June or any kids we have, have contact with their toxic way of life. I won't let them suffer the way I did, believing it's okay for people to show up only when they need something, and then disappearing until they need something else.

"You get your shit together and we'll talk, but I'm not helping you bail Jay out, and if you're smart, you won't help him either. He needs to grow the fuck up."

"I liked June, but now I'm seeing I shouldn't have," she hisses, and my stomach knots.

"She's the best thing that ever happened to me, the one fucking thing I have in my life that's good and pure. You should want that for me," I say, then pull the phone from my ear and press End.

Fuck.

Putting my hand to the back of my neck, my eyes drop to my boots, and then I feel hands slide around my waist and June's warm body press to my back. Dropping my hand from my neck, I cover hers.

"Are you okay?" she asks softly. My answer is an immediate, "Fuck yeah." Having her back in my life, knowing the future we're building together, makes everything else seem really fucking unimportant.

Her body moves to the front of mine and my hands settle on her hips as she searches my gaze. "That phone call seemed…" She pauses, looking up before meeting my gaze again. "Kinda sad."

"The only thing sad about it is how in denial my mother is when it comes to the fact that her family is in shambles and the role she plays in that. *That*, baby, is sad," I agree, giving her a squeeze.

"I'm sorry," she whispers, dropping her forehead to my chest, and that alone is enough to make me fall in love with her all over again.

"It was going to happen. I've been putting that phone call and that conversation off for awhile."

"I only caught the last part," she confides quietly, like I'm gonna be pissed she was eavesdropping, when she absolutely wasn't.

"Then you heard the most important part. Unless a miracle occurs and my mother gets help, she's out of my life for good."

Her head tips back at that and her eyes meet mine, looking confused. "I… when we were together…" She pauses again. "You didn't seem to have a problem with her."

"I didn't have contact with her often, baby." I give her a squeeze then move us toward one of the chairs and tug her down into my lap. "I had my own place," I say, wrapping my arms around her waist. "Jay was in jail, and my dad was doing what he's always done, meaning he took off for parts unknown. When she's not surrounded by them, she's not sober, but she doesn't drink as much," I say, as she tucks her head under my chin and pulls her legs up, so her knees are pressed to my side and her arms are around my waist.

"Has she ever tried to get help?" she asks, and I run my hands along her smooth skin from the edge of her shorts to her knees.

"No one's ever told her, as far as I know, that they know she has a problem."

"How can that be?" she asks quietly, putting her hand against my chest, sitting up, and turning in my lap to study me.

"At first, she hid it well, but then it became our norm to find empty vodka bottles shoved under the sink in the kitchen or the bathroom behind things or full ones tucked away carefully, where she thought we wouldn't find them. We knew she was hiding it, and I'm guessing, like me, my dad and my brother didn't want to be the ones to bring it to her attention that they knew what she was doing."

"Until now," she says, leaning in and running her finger over my bottom lip.

"Until now," I agree, grabbing her hand, kissing her fingers, and then wrapping my hand around her neck. I pull her close, kiss her forehead, and tuck her head back under my chin to hold her against my chest.

"Do you think you bringing it to her attention will wake her up?" she asks softly after a few moments.

"Probably not, but I learned awhile back to never say never," I answer just as quietly, and her body goes tight before melting further into mine. "What do you want to do for dinner, beautiful?" I ask, wanting to take her mind off of her thoughts. I know she's scared. I can feel her fear. See it seeping into her eyes or her body on occasion, but I know there is nothing I can do but wait her out and let her see I'm not going anywhere.

"I don't know. What do you want to do?" she answers, then sits up when her cell phone rings in the house. "I was looking for that earlier." She kisses my chin, climbing off my lap. Shaking my head, I know she's talking about her cell phone; she never has it, or is always leaving it someplace she can't remember.

Whistling for Ninja, who's walking the fence and sniffing the ground, his head comes up and he runs full tilt toward the house then in through the open backdoor. Walking into the house, I slide the door closed behind me and watch June stroll toward me through the kitchen, holding her cell phone to her ear.

"Um, sure, we can do that," she murmurs and then asks, "What time?" She nods. "Okay, see you then." She ends the call, taking the cell from her ear and tossing it in the vicinity of the couch to be lost once more.

Feeling my brows draw together, I ask, "What's up?"

"Mom and Dad are having everyone over to their place in an hour, so they want us to come by," she says quickly then bites her lip. "I guess now we don't need to worry about dinner."

Fuck!

I knew this was bound to happen. The Maysons are close. I knew this before, from stories June would tell me when we first got together, and then learned it firsthand when I moved to town. The difference between those times and now is that before, I had to suffer hearing about June and what she was up to secondhand from her uncles and cousins, and even her dad a couple times. Now, they know we're together, and know we had been very fucking together, as in married, before. I don't expect tonight to go well. The men in her family, just like her cousin Sage, who I'm still pissed at, are protective. I know this isn't just a get-together. This is them wanting to see first hand June and I together.

"Do you want me to tell them we can't go?" Feeling her hands on my chest, my gaze moves to her. I was so caught up in my thoughts, I didn't even realize she had closed the distance between us.

"No, baby," I mutter, wrapping my fingers around her hips.

"Are you sure? I don't mind."

"I'm sure," I say on a squeeze. Her eyes search my face. Her mouth opens and closes, as if she wants to say something before thinking better of it, and then she lays her cheek to my chest, wrapping her arms tighter around my waist.

"It will be fun, I promise."

"Not sure about that, baby."

Her head tilts back and her bottom lip disappears between her teeth once more. "We don't have to go."

"Do you love your family?" I ask, and her face softens when she nods. "Then we do. I'm not going to let us have them between us." I know she knows what I'm saying. I should have done so much shit differently before, but this time, I'm not going to make the same mistakes.

"We can leave early if it becomes..." She pauses, giving me a small smile. "Intense."

Ignoring her comment, I pull her closer, until her body is pressed the length of mine, and breathe against her mouth "You can make it up to me tonight."

"I can do that," she replies, leaning even closer.

"What do you want, baby?" I smile down at her, watching her eyes slide half-mast.

"You to kiss me," she murmurs, pressing closer, rolling up onto her toes, but still not close enough to reach my mouth. Sliding my arm around her waist, I haul her up and drop my mouth to hers, kissing her until I hear her moan then rip my mouth away and rest my forehead against hers, breathing in through my nose in an attempt to get myself under control.

"Let's cancel," she says, and my eyes open, meeting hers.

"Go get ready," I say with a laugh, standing to my full height. "I'm gonna feed Ninja."

"I'm really okay with not going," she insists, sliding her hands up my chest to the back of my neck, putting pressure there.

"Baby, as much as I want to fuck you—and I really do want to fuck you right now—I can't," I mutter, clasping her wrists and pulling them from behind my neck.

"But—"

"Go get ready." I kiss her swiftly then move away a step before I toss her over my shoulder and take her to bed, which is what I really fucking want to do, especially when she's looking at me with heavy eyes, her nipples hard through her thin tank, and her lips swollen from my kiss. "Baby," I growl.

Her eyes widen, as she says, "I'm gonna go get ready."

"Good idea." I grin, watching her ass sway as she takes off toward the bedroom.

"HERE," SAGE SAYS, holding out a beer to me while folding his body into the chair next to mine. Since our blow up, we haven't spoken unless it has had to do with work. I'm still pissed about the shit he spewed, even if I do understand it.

Taking the beer, I mumble, "Thanks," and move my eyes to where June is standing with her mom.

"Look," Sage starts, and my eyes move from June to him. I watch him sit forward, putting his elbows to his knees. "I know you love her, and you're still breathing, which means we *all* know you love her," he says, and I raise a brow and his eyes narrow. "I'm trying to apologize."

"Is that what that was?"

"I'm not going to say sorry for worrying about her."

"You accused me of setting her up in order to get her back," I remind him quietly, working to hold my temper in check. I don't need to get into a fistfight with him in June's parents' backyard with her family in attendance.

"Yeah, that was fucked. I didn't mean it, but seriously, you're so fucking secretive with everything."

"Have I ever left you hanging or put you in danger?" I ask, and he shakes his head. "I'm not the kind of guy to sit around and spew out my life story to anyone."

"We've known each other for awhile, man," he says, his tone also quiet.

"We have," I agree, taking a pull from my beer. "So do you want to start the heart-to-heart, or would you like me to?" I ask, raising a brow.

"Don't be a dick," he says low, sitting closer.

"Tell me about Kim." His eyes narrow and he sits back. He may think I keep shit to myself, but he does the same. Kim is a woman who works at the hair salon next to our office. She's also the woman he slept with once then dismissed. Now, she's the woman who has a man, the woman who every time she's around, his eyes move to her and his jaw goes tight. And she's the woman he wants but can't have.

"Is it really that obvious?" he asks, surprising me with the question.

"If by 'obvious' you mean can I see that you're pissed you let her get away, then yeah, it's obvious."

"Fuck," he mutters, running his hand over his head, looking annoyed that anyone could tell he's hung up on her.

"She'll come around, man. You may not see it, but she still looks for you every time we leave the office."

Shrugging off my statement, he leans forward once more and his eyes meet mine before he speaks in a hushed tone. "You look settled. In the time I've known you, you've never looked settled, so I'm happy to see that. And my cousin's happy. That's all because of you. You're it for her, and I now see she's it for you."

"She is," I agree, looking across the pool toward June, and her head turns and her eyes meet mine as I watch her smile.

"Are we cool now?" he asks, and I pull my gaze from June and look at him again.

"We're good."

"Good, now I need to warn you as your friend. Uncle Asher is on his way over," he says then stands and walks away.

Jesus.

"Didn't think you'd show," Asher says, taking the seat Sage just vacated.

"Like I told you when you came to the compound, I'm not giving her up, and she loves you guys, so I'm not going to make her feel like she has to choose between me and her family," I tell him, holding his stare. Do I want to be here, right now? Fuck no, but I know June would be disappointed if we didn't come, and I want her happy. So if I have to sit in her parents' backyard for a few hours to accomplish that task, I'll do it.

"As a little girl, she was always moving," he says, sitting back in the chair and placing his beer on the armrest.

"Pardon?" I ask, confused by his statement.

"June, as a little girl, she was always up to something. She couldn't sit still for more than a few minutes at a time. Where the other girls would happily sit and watch a movie, June had to be doing something, experiencing something new. Her mom and I worried about her. We didn't think she would ever be content in one place for long. Her first year of college was the same. There wasn't a week that went by that she didn't call home, saying she wanted to change her major or move to a different school. But then that stopped. We didn't know what happened or what helped her settle. We just knew something did," he says, and then sits forward, putting his elbows to his knees.

"That was you. I didn't realize it until the other day, but you help her settle, bring her peace, keep her grounded. My grandmother used to say, 'Don't take a moment for granted, just because you think you'll have a thousand more.' I think you get that more than most," he mutters, and a deep burn hits my chest before coursing through my body, making it hard to breathe.

"I love her."

"That's good, since she loves you," he grumbles, sounding annoyed which makes me fight back a smile. Closing his eyes, he rubs his forehead then sits back and pins me in place. "One day, when you're a father, you'll understand how painful it is to be replaced by another man."

And with that, he gets up and wanders around the outer edge of the pool toward June and her mom. As soon as he reaches them, he pulls June into his side and places a kiss to her temple. Watching her mouth move, I can't tell what she's saying, but his chin jerks in my direction. Her eyes come to me and her face softens before looking back up at her dad and leaning deeper into him.

"What's up?"

Pulling my eyes from June, I look up at her Uncle Nico and mutter, "Nothing. How's it going, man?" I put out my hand, shaking his.

"Good." He cracks his neck, taking a seat. "I was gonna call you tomorrow, but since we're here, I figured we could talk now."

"What's going on?"

"I need some help on a case."

"Have you talked to Jax?" I ask, and he shakes his head then drops his voice.

"Can't have too many people in on this, and he doesn't have the connection I need."

"What's that?" I prompt, taking a pull from my beer then sitting back down.

"The Broken Eagles," he says.

I growl, "Fuck no," jerking my head back.

His body moves closer to mine and his voice dips. "It's one of their new recruits. I can't go to Wes with this. He will lose his fucking mind and blow my case."

"Ask someone else." I shake my head and pull my eyes from him. No way am I going to go behind the backs of men who have taken my back at every turn.

"You know there's no one else to ask," he replies easily, and I let out a breath, because I know he's right. "I can't risk anyone knowing about this until I have a solid case, and in order to build that case, I need to keep this guy right where he is."

"You know you're putting me in a really fucked-up spot with my brothers, right?" I clarify, and his eyes go to where June and her parents are standing.

"Two of my nieces are involved with men connected to this guy. That shit doesn't sit well with me."

"Who is it?"

"Are you in or not?" he asks, and I close my eyes in frustration.

"If shit starts to go south, I'm filling the brothers in, and we'll handle if from the inside."

"I'm gonna ignore that statement," he mutters, then grins a wicked-looking scary grin. "Told Asher my niece is safe with your crazy ass." He sounds proud as he pats my shoulder.

"Who is it?" I repeat, and his eyes hold mine.

"Jordan."

"Why doesn't that shit surprise me?" I mutter. I didn't like the prick, even before he cornered June. There always seemed to be something off about him, something I noticed from the first moment he came into our circle, something I couldn't put my finger on.

"What's he into?"

"He's connected with a club in Nashville, the Southern Stars. They have their fingers in just about everything—pussy, guns, drugs. You name it, they deal in it. From what I've found out so far, he was sent to town to look for a club to take over so they could expand their business."

"Jesus," I hiss, feeling rage course through me. Unlike some of the other clubs in the area, the Broken Eagles are clean. They don't deal in drugs, pussy, or guns, and would flip if they knew that shit was touching the club in any way.

"We'll meet after the weekend and discuss the details," he says looking over my shoulder with a smile. I turn my head and watch June strut toward us.

"Is everything okay?" she asks, looking between her uncle and me.

Reaching out, I take her hand, pulling her down into my lap, ignoring the tightness in her body. "It's all good," I assure her, giving her middle a squeeze.

"We're at my parents' house," she says, scolding me over her shoulder.

"Yep," I agree, kissing her shoulder.

"Seriously, my—"

"Relax." I give her another squeeze and hold her gaze as her eyes narrow.

"You're so bossy," she grumbles, relaxing back into me and making me grin.

"I gotta head out," Nico says, standing and clasping my shoulder. He leans over, kissing June's head, and mutters, "Be good, kid," before wandering off.

"What was my dad saying?" she asks, tipping her head back to look at me once her uncle is gone.

"Nothing."

"Hm," she murmurs. "And my uncle, what did he say?"

"Nothing, baby."

"So you're not going to tell me?" she surmises, and I put my fingers to her chin, pulling her gaze to mine.

"There's nothing to tell. It's all good."

Her eyes search my face before she nods once then leans back farther into me. A few minutes later, July and Wes come over, taking the seat Nico vacated, and not long after that, we call it a night and head home.

"Ev," June whimpers, pushing her pussy into my mouth as I slide my hands up her thighs, holding her legs open.

"Come for me, beautiful," I growl, sliding my thumb inside of her. Her back arches off the bed and the heels of her feet press into my back as she comes loud. The white dress she wore to her parents' had tormented me since the moment she walked out of the bedroom wearing it. On the way home, she didn't help any when her hand wandered continuously over the bulge in my jeans. As soon as we pulled up to the house, I went around to her side of my truck, threw her over my shoulder, listening to her giggle herself stupid, and carried her into the house. Straight to the bedroom. I tossed her on the bed, dropped to my knees, and shoved my face between her legs to pay her back for teasing me by not letting her come. Until now.

Before her, I could take or leave eating pussy. I didn't enjoy it; it was just something I did to get my partner off. But I could spend hours drinking her in—the way her body writhes, the sounds she makes, her taste, everything about it is a turn-on.

Giving her one last lick, I wipe my chin on her inner thigh then stand, pulling my shirt over my head and dropping it to the floor. I lose my boots and jeans, along with my boxers. Dragging her dress over her head, I climb between her thighs, keeping my gaze locked with hers. Her long legs wrap around my waist as my hand slides up to cup her left breast and my mouth lowers to cover her right. Cupping her breast with my hand, I pause, realizing she doesn't have a nipple.

"What the fuck?" I frown, pulling my face away from her chest, looking at some strange flesh-colored sticker covering her tip.

"Oh, I totally forgot about those," she whimpers, dipping her face down to look at me, her eyes dark with desire, her lips swollen, and her cheeks pinked, revealing just how turned on she is. "Just pull them off," she hisses, pressing her hips into mine.

"But what the fuck are they?" I repeat, taking the edge of the sticker and ripping it off like a Band-Aid. I regret it, though, when she cries out, covering her chest with her hand.

"The other one now," she says, and I look up, seeing her laugh. Doing the other one slowly, I take both stickers and attempt to flick them off my fingers, but it takes a few tries before they fly off, and by that time, her body is shaking uncontrollably under mine. "Oh, God." She giggles. "You weren't supposed to even see those."

"A little late for that," I inform her, cupping her breast. Her laughter stops immediately and her back arches, pressing her breast into my hand. Moving my mouth over the other one, I lick her nipple, pull back, and blow a breath across the surface, watching it pucker.

"No more teasing," she moans, running her fingers through my hair.

"No more teasing, baby," I agree, pulling her nipple into my mouth while pinching the opposite one. Her hiss of breath has my already hard cock turning to stone. Licking up her neck, I wrap my arm around her waist and use my other arm to toss her leg behind my back, while sliding into her warm, tight, wet heat. There is nothing better than her. Gritting my teeth, I fight back the urge to come immediately, like I do every time I enter her.

"Jesus Christ," I grate out through clenched teeth, as her walls tighten. "Open your mouth." Her eyes slide open and my fingers trace her lips before I dip my thumb into her mouth. Her lips close around it, her teeth press in, and her tongue flicks the tip, making my balls draw tight. "Release." Her lips slide open and I push back to my knees, place my thumb against her clit, and circle slowly.

"I thought you said no more teasing," she pants, wrapping her legs around my hips, circling hers in sync with my thumb. Ignoring her comment, I roam my free hand up her belly, keeping my eyes locked on our connection and the wetness coating my cock every time I slide out. Fuck, but every part of her is seriously fucking beautiful. Cupping her breast, I tug her nipple, and her already tight walls tighten further. "Ev...I..." Her hands move to my chest, down my abs, and then her fingers span my cock sliding into her. "You feel so good," she breathes, and my eyes move up her body to meet hers.

"Let it go, beautiful," I gently urge, and her teeth dig into her bottom lip as her legs tighten along with her pussy.

Dropping forward, I grind my hips into her before losing myself deep inside her. Rolling to the side to keep my weight off her, I take her with me and listen to her breathing even out, while drifting my hand down the skin of her back.

"I need to let Ninja out," she says, sounding half-asleep, and I grin at the ceiling.

"I'll get him in a minute."

"I also need to clean up," she mumbles, pressing her face into my chest.

"I'll also take care of that in a minute," I reply, kissing the top of her head.

"I also need to set the alarm," she whispers, now sounding like she's talking in her sleep.

"I'll take care of it, baby."

"I love you," she mumbles, as her body goes limp against mine. My arm tightens around her instinctively as my lungs compress with the weight of those three words.

"I love you too, beautiful," I murmur, even though I know she can't hear me in her sleep.

Chapter 11

June

"I LOVE YOU," I say, looking at myself in the mirror. "I love you," I repeat, watching my brows draw together. I can obviously say the words out loud, even though every time I've tried to say them to Evan, they get clogged in my throat. "What the hell is wrong with you?" I gain no answer from my reflection in return.

Letting out a frustrated breath, I tug the rollers out of my hair and toss them carelessly into the sink. Over the last week, Evan has been saying *I love you* more and more, and every time he says it, I beg the words to come out, but they never, ever do. Just like a few minutes ago, he came up behind me to tell me he was leaving and kissed my shoulder, whispering, "I love you," against my skin. I wanted to tell him, "I love you too," but couldn't. So instead, I stood there, like an idiot, looking at him while he smiled at me in the mirror.

"You know he's not leaving, so obviously, this is *your* issue now and not his anymore," I reprimand myself, tugging off my towel, tossing it to the sink top, and then grabbing a new set of nipple covers, smiling at the memory of Evan finding them the last time I wore them, as I put them on. Once they're stuck in place, I head into my closet and tug my little black dress off its hanger near the door. Slipping it on, I turn to look at myself in the mirror.

The dress is one I bought months ago for nights like tonight—dinner and drinks with the girls. The top of the dress is black lace with a deep *V* and a matching deep *V* in the back. The bottom is a black, sheer fabric with a black underlay, hitting mid-thigh. If I had boobs, I wouldn't be able to wear this dress, because there is no way you can possibly hide a bra in it, but unlike normally, I'm thankful for my small chest.

"Who were you talking to?"

Squeaking, I turn around and place my hand to my chest, glaring at my sister December, who is standing in the doorway of the closet, wearing a black dress of her own. Hers is so tight, it shows off every one of her curves.

"Don't sneak up on me," I snap. I completely forgot I wasn't alone in the house.

"I didn't sneak up on you. I walked right in," she says, putting her hands on her hips and studying me. "So, who are you talking to? Is your house haunted? Do you have a ghost you're trying to convince of your love?"

"Shut up," I growl, grabbing my strappy, black suede heels from the shelf and stomping past her.

"What's going on?" April asks, and I groan.

"Nothing is going on," I tell her, wondering if the dress she has on should be worn in public. The strapless black dress leaves nothing to the imagination and is so short that I know if she bends over, everyone will be getting a show.

"Uh… okay." She frowns, moving her gaze from me to December, who shrugs.

"I thought we had a reservation?" I remind them, as they look between each other.

"We do," July says, coming into the room, wearing a dress similar to mine, minus the deep *V.* "And Wes just pulled up and is waiting outside. Are you guys ready?" She looks between the three of us.

"Yep, totally ready," I lie. I don't really want to go out tonight, but my sisters and cousins are in town and we've had this night planned for months, which means it's girls' night—whether I want it to be or not. "Where's May?" I ask, slipping on my heels.

"Waiting in the living room," December says, watching me closely. Ignoring her, I move to the dresser, grab my perfume and spray it behind my ears.

"Where was Evan going?" April questions, and my eyes move to hers in the mirror while I put in my earrings.

"He's with Harlen and the guys tonight. I guess they're going to be at the compound," I say, then look at July. "Is Wes going to be with them?"

"Yeah, he's meeting up with them after he drops us off." She smiles.

"Nice, so we have free rein." April grins, and I know that grin. I also know that means we're all going to be in trouble before the night is over if we're not careful.

"I'm not getting drunk," I mutter to her, and her brows snap together.

"Yes, you are."

"No, I'm not." I shake my head, and she plants her hands on her hips and narrows her eyes further.

"Yes, you are."

"Do we really need to argue over getting drunk?" December asks, exasperated, flopping back onto my bed and grumbling at the ceiling about how annoying we are.

"We argue about everything," July points out the God's honest truth. It's like an unspoken rule in the sister handbook.

Thou shalt argue about every single thing under the sun when in the presence of your sisters.

"Are the girls meeting us at the restaurant?" I ask, changing the subject before we all start arguing about arguing, which is something we would do.

"Yep, they're already there waiting on us," July confirms, referring to Jax's fiancée, Ellie, and our cousins Ashlyn, Hannah, Willow, and Harmony, leaving out Nalia, since she's in Colorado with her mom and probably won't be home until Christmas.

"Okay, so let's go," I sigh, once I finish putting in my earrings.

"At least pretend to be excited," I hear murmured from behind me, but I ignore that and head out of the room toward the living room, where I find May, wearing a long black dress that ties at her shoulders, cuddled up on the couch with Ninja.

"I need a man in my life," she murmurs when she sees us.

"Maybe if you didn't turn every single guy down when they hit on you, you'd have a man," April says, picking up her purse from the couch.

"And maybe if you didn't sleep with every single guy you met, you wouldn't be a slut," May replies, and April glares. April and May live together and have always been more like best friends than sisters, so I'm not surprised by their constant badgering anymore.

"Can we just get along for the night?" December pleas, looking at each of us with the same glare our mom used to give us when we were little and misbehaving.

"This *is* us getting along," July says, and she's not wrong. Us not getting along consists of rolling around on the floor, pulling each other's hair—something we still do from time to time.

"Let's just go," I mumble, tucking my slim black purse under my arm as I head for the door, listening to the girls following behind me.

"Jesus," Wes growls from the end of the sidewalk, where he's waiting outside his SUV. If I didn't think he'd be pissed, I would laugh at the look on his face. "Babe, where the fuck is the rest of your dress?" he asks, and July giggles then spins in a circle.

"This is all of my dress." She smiles, and his nostrils flare and his fists clench.

"Maybe I should go with you guys."

"You are not coming with us," April puts in, opening the backdoor. "It's girls' night, not 'girl-and-hot-annoying-husband' night," she finishes, before scooting into the backseat.

"Sorry, honey, you're not invited." July grins, placing her hands against Wes's chest, pushing up to touch her mouth to his.

"You're in so much trouble when you get home," he grumbles, and I giggle then stop when his eyes slice to me. "I'm guessing Evan didn't see you in that dress."

"Evan won't care," I mutter, and he raises a brow, making me wonder if I should have worn a different dress. "He won't," I repeat, even though I'm not sure if that's true as I stomp past him to the backdoor, ignoring his chuckle as I follow December into the backseat, followed by May.

"Did you tell them the rules?" he asks July, as he slides in behind the wheel.

"The rules are there are no rules," April says, and Wes's head turns to scowl at her over his shoulder.

"There sure as fuck are rules."

"I don't know how July puts up with you," April gripes, glaring at him.

"Let's just go. I'll make sure we don't get into any trouble," December says, and Wes's eyes move to her.

"The rules," he begins, ignoring April's huff as he backs out of my driveway. "You guys do not take drinks from anyone. You don't leave your drinks unattended, and you stick to each other like glue."

"Rules two and three are acceptable, but rule number one is vetoed," April chimes in, and I start to laugh but bite my lip when Wes's eyes meet mine in the mirror and narrow.

"You can either follow the rules, or I follow you guys and babysit. Your choice."

"Whatever," April grumbles under her breath, but smartly doesn't say anything else. The rest of the ride is silent, and when we make it to the restaurant, we all pile out onto the sidewalk while we wait for July, who is talking to Wes, doing a whole lot of eye rolling and hand movements at whatever he's telling her.

"He's so bossy. How the hell does she put up with that?" April asks, as we watch Wes wrap his hand around the back of July's neck and tug her forward, until his mouth is an inch from hers.

"You do know that when you find a guy, he's probably going to be a million times worse?" May asks, and she is probably right. It's going to take a different kind of man to tame April.

"I think it's sweet," December whispers, bumping my shoulder with hers.

"You would." April rolls her eyes at me then walks over and taps on the driver's side window, yelling, "Let her up. It's time to go."

Surprisingly, Wes lets July go then rolls down the window, looking at each of us demanding, "Be good and remember the rules."

"We'll be fine."

July smiles, and Wes smiles back, muttering, "Be good, baby," before driving off.

"Finally, sheesh! I thought he would never leave," April says under her breath, threading her arm through July's and leading her inside the restaurant, followed by the rest of us.

"How are things with you and Evan?" December asks as soon as we're seated.

"We're good."

"Thank God he's not crazy like this one's man," April mumbles, jerking her thumb at July.

"Obviously, you haven't met Evan." July smiles and I shrug. I love that he's protective and possessive, and I don't care what that says about me as a woman.

"He didn't inspect her outfit, so obviously he's not psycho posses-sive like Wes."

"Is my dress that bad?" I ask, and all eyes at the table turn to look at me, each look saying the same thing: *Are you seriously asking that question?* "Okay," I grumble, looking down at my dress. I know it's a little flirty, but I really don't think it's that provocative.

"Just saying if Evan sees you in that dress, you're in for a good night." July smiles, and my eyes land on Ellie, Jax's fiancée, and I watch her smooth out her very clingy dress, blushing when her eyes meet mine.

"Now tell us why you were talking to yourself," December says, and I glare at her.

"I wasn't talking to myself."

"What do you mean talking to yourself?" May asks, and I let out a frustrated breath. I may as well get this over with.

"I can't say 'I love you' to Evan. Every time I try to tell him that I love him back, the words won't come out."

"Why not?" Harmony asks, and my eyes go to her.

"I don't know. Every time I try to say it back, I can't. The words literally won't come out of my mouth."

"You're probably holding on to some anger," July says, and I shake my head.

"I'm not. I forgave him, completely forgave him," I say, looking around for the waiter. I need wine and lots and lots of wine.

"Maybe you should just write it down and tell him that way," April chimes in.

"Don't listen to her," May frown's, looking at April like she's crazy.

"Don't tell her not to listen to me," April snaps back, glaring at her.

"It will happen when you're ready for him to know," July says, leaning into my side. I nod, even though I know now is the time. It's killing me that he doesn't know how I feel, and I don't want him to think I don't love him. Maybe I *should* just write it down on a piece of paper and give it to him.

"Enough talk about guys. Let's drink," Ashlyn demands, and April leans across the table, giving her a high-five.

"Yes! No more guy talk," she agrees.

As if on cue a young guy makes his way over to our table. "I'm Cori. I'll be your waiter tonight. What can I get you ladies to drink?" He says, coming to stand at the end of our table.

"Tequila," Ashlyn requests, and I look over at her as she shrugs then mutters, "If you knew what my day was like, you would understand."

"Is it Dillon again?" July asks, and Ellie giggles as Ashlyn looks at her and glares, and then looks at July and growls.

"We're not saying his name anymore. From this day on, he doesn't exist."

"Who's Dillon?" Willow asks, and July fans herself, whispering, "Dillon is a tall glass of hotne—"

"Dillon is a dick and doesn't exist outside of the office, where I unfortunately have to be subjected to his dickheadedness," Ashlyn says, cutting July off, and I make a mental note to ask July about Dillon, or to go by Ashlyn's office so I can get a look at Dillon myself. There is obviously more to the story than Ashlyn is letting on.

"Umm... so is everyone drinking tequila?" our waiter asks, breaking into the conversation, and we all laugh.

April exclaims, "Tequila all around!"

Leaning my head back, I look up at the ceiling, knowing exactly how this night is going to end. I just hope I don't regret it in the morning.

"MOTHERFUCKER." TURNING MY head at the sound of Evan's deep, rumbling voice, a voice I would know anywhere, I smile, listening as giggles break out around me.

"Hey, honey," I breathe, as I sway toward him on my stool.

"You wasted?" he asks, dropping his eyes from my mouth to the top of my dress, and I notice they darken when he does.

"Yep." I grin then press my lips together and lean forward even more, whispering loudly, "I only bought one drink." I hold up a finger then point to the glasses in front of me. "All of these were free." I smile. "Isn't that amazing?"

"Free?" His brows draw together and he crosses his arms over his chest while looking in front of me, where there are at least ten shot glasses, with four of them now empty.

"Free," I concur, looking around the table at my girls when I notice they have all gone quiet. I also notice the table is surrounded by men, men that include a pissed-off looking Wes and Jax. "Um… we all got free drinks," I say quietly, wanting to take the heat off of only me, when it seems I said the wrong thing.

"Girls' night is over," Jax cuts in.

I look at him and cry, throwing my hands in the air, "It can't be over! We just started having fun." And we did. The start of the night kind of sucked, because Dillon the Dick, who also happens to be Dillon the fuck hot gorgeous—like toss-your-panties-at-him gorgeous—showed up at the restaurant we were at. That wouldn't have been so bad, except for when he saw Ashlyn, he made a beeline for our table to say hi, which under any other circumstances would have been nice. But his fiancée was with him, and she is not only a bitch, but *a screaming* bitch at that. She took one look at our table and made a face like she was witnessing a group of zombies eating the last human left on planet earth then made a snide comment about Ashlyn. The only good thing about that was witnessing Dillon tell her to shut the hell up. Even though he didn't use those words exactly.

"Men bought you girls drinks?" Wes asks, cutting into my thoughts, and my eyes focus on July, who bites her lip then looks around at us for help, while April smiles and Ashlyn giggles.

"They were being nice, and as you can see, we are here alone, so technically, we're still following your rules," April chimes in unhelpfully.

I look up at Evan and ask quietly when I notice that he hasn't come any closer or touched me, "You're not mad, are you?"

"Mad, no. Pissed, yes," he says in a tone I've never heard from him before, a tone that sends goose bumps sliding across my skin.

"Why?" I frown.

"Do you want a list?" he asks, and I think about it for a second then nod like the drunk I am.

"Walking into a bar, seeing men stare at you in that dress is enough to make me mad. Those same men buying your drinks is a big fucking no."

"I like my dress," I inform him drunkenly, ignoring the rest of what he said.

"That's good, baby, and I'm glad you got to wear it once before I rip that shit to shreds and toss it in the trash."

"You're not ripping my dress to shreds," I breathe, putting my hands over the lace covering my chest. "This dress cost me almost a hundred dollars, and that was after it was marked down two times," I inform him, holding up two fingers, and watch his eyes heat further as he takes a step toward me, crowding me against the table with one hand at the back of my neck, the other on my knee.

"This dress," he murmurs just loud enough for me to hear, while sliding his hand up my thigh under the hem, "is fucking hot. You do not wear a dress like this unless you're with your man."

"Oh," I whisper, absently hearing someone say, "I told you so," from behind me.

"Oh," he replies, looking down at the top of my dress. The look in his eyes conveys he's either really, really pissed or really, really turned on, and I hope for my sake it's the latter.

"I don't want to leave!" Ellie cries, and I pull my eyes from Evan's and look across the table, where Ellie is sitting with her hands wrapped around the edge of the table, holding on like it's a life preserver.

"I don't have a problem bringing the table with us when we leave, Ellie, but one way or another, you're coming home with me now," Jax growls.

"You can't take the table. Isss not yours ta take," she slurs, glaring at him.

"Oh, Lord," December murmurs, picking up one of the shot glasses from the tabletop, shooting the creamy liquor back, and then picking up another, doing the same, before muttering, "I'll clear the table," which makes me break into a fit of giggles.

"I'll help." I giggle louder, picking up one of the shots, only to have it snatched out of my grasp. "Hey! I was going to drink that," I complain.

"You're done," Evan says, placing the shot glass down with a thud.

"You're not the boss of me."

"Baby, if you think that, then you've obviously gotten shit confused."

"No, I don't. I'm my own woman. I make my own choices."

"No, you're my woman. *Mine,* and like I said, you're done." He pulls me off my stool and into his warm chest.

"You can't just act like a caveman, Evan," I shout back, glaring up into his handsome face.

"Caveman?" He grins a wicked grin that has my girly parts tingling, then before I know what's happening, I'm up over his shoulder with his hand on the back of my thighs, thankfully keeping my dress down and me from flashing everyone my panties, as he carries me, screaming, "Put me down now!" out of the bar and down the street to his truck.

"I can't believe you," I say, crossing my arms over my chest, as I glare out the front window of The Beast. No one came to my aid when Evan carried me out of the bar and down the street yelling. No one even seemed to care that a man was carrying a woman over his shoulder, hollering into the night, as he walked casually down the sidewalk. "What kind of world do we live in that you can just carry me, an unwilling woman, around without someone stopping to ask if everything is okay?"

"Babe," he mutters. I hear the smile in his voice and turn to look at him to see if I'm right, that he thinks this is funny. "This isn't funny!" I cry when I see his grin. "I mean seriously! Why are there not police cars following us right now? For all any of those people know, you could be a crazy person! You could be taking me to your house in the hills, where you plan to hide me away in a secret room built in your basement."

"You need to stop watching so much TV," he laughs.

"You would think that, since you're the one who kidnapped me," I mutter under my breath.

"Not sure the cops will think taking the woman I live with home to the house we live in together is kidnapping."

"Tomayto, tomahto."

"How is it, one second, I'm seriously pissed at you, and the next, all I can think is how you're really fucking adorable when you're drunk?"

"First, you don't have a reason to be pissed at me. I didn't do anything wrong. And second, I *am* really adorable, so that's not surprising." I snap.

"I do have a reason to be pissed, baby."

"No, you don't."

"I do. You're not a man, so you will never get it, but I have a dick. I know what every man in that bar was thinking, and I also know that none of it was PG."

"Whatever," I sigh, refusing to admit he's right, even though he probably is.

"You're still in for it when we get home, so don't think you're off the hook," he says, and my core clenches at his tone.

"What does that mean?" I ask, as we turn onto our block.

"You'll see," he says, pulling into the driveway and putting the truck in park. His body turns toward me and his hand rests casually over the steering wheel as his eyes scan me. "You're beautiful."

"Um…" I lick my lips, wondering where he's going with this.

"The first time I saw you, I knew there was something about you that I had to have, and every moment I have spent with you since has given me a taste of something I want more of. I'll never get enough of you."

Oh, God. Once more, those three stubborn words are clogging my throat. I want to say them so badly. I want him to know I feel the same, that my feelings for him have never changed. "I want you too," I say, feeling like an idiot, because those words are not even close to the way I feel.

"No, baby." His fingers unhook my seatbelt and he drags me across the seat toward him. "You're mine. I mean that in the most fucked-up, primal way possible. If it were legal to own you, I would."

"Oh," I breathe, as he wraps his hands around the backs of my thighs and tugs me forward against the bulge in his pants.

"Now do you understand what I mean when I say you're mine?" he questions, moving his hand up my back and into the hair at the nape of my neck.

"I… I think so."

"You need to marry me again. Maybe then I won't feel as crazy as I do now," he whispers, studying me. "Then again, I'm not sure there is anything that can change how I feel."

"Evan," I whisper, searching his eyes, seeing how intense they are. I want that again. I want to be his. There is nothing I want more.

"I love you, baby."

"I—" His mouth covering mine cuts off what I was going to say, and I get lost in his kiss, so lost that I don't even realize we are out of the truck and in the house until I feel my back hit the wall and hear the front door close.

"I'm giving you a head start," he says, pulling his mouth from mine. "If you can get that dress off before we make it to the room, you can keep it. If you can't, then it's going to be used to tie you to the bed."

I gasp at his ultimatum. "I love this dress," I declare, as his mouth travels down my neck, between my breasts, and then he's moving the lace of the dress aside and his large hands cup my breasts in each of his palms.

"I fucking hate these things. They are constantly in the way of what I want," he growls, ripping the pasties off my nipples.

"Oh, God," I moan, letting my head fall back and my hands slide through his hair. His fingers work my nipples, pulling and tugging as his mouth slides between my breasts, tormenting me. "Evan."

"Go," he says, stepping back suddenly, leaving me panting against the wall.

"What?" I blink up at him, trying to understand what happened, why he stopped touching me.

"Five," he states, sliding his eyes over my face then chest.

"Wh… what?"

"Four." His jaw clenches as he growls, "Three."

"Oh, shit." I pull myself away from the wall and stumble, still half-drunk, down the hall, listening to him countdown behind me as I run into the room, trying to tug my dress up over my head as I go. Realizing that's not how I put it on, I pull one hand out of a sleeve and then the other.

"One," I hear as a hand goes to my back and I'm bent over the mattress, my dress now down around my waist. Then the bottom of the garment is up and the cool air of the room meets the bare skin of my ass.

"Evan."

"These are not even covering my pussy, June," he mutters, roughly running a finger along the edge of my lace thong from my outer hip, down between my ass cheeks, and lower, grazing my pussy. "You have a beautiful ass." His hand runs over the cheek soothingly, and my hands bunch the duvet between my fingers as I slide up on my tiptoes, tilting my backside toward him, silently begging him to do whatever he wants to me.

"Give me your hands," he commands, and my pulse speeds up as I release the duvet and put my hands behind my back. "You're being very good right now."

Oh, God, his tone is doing crazy things to my insides, making me feel like every inch of me has been somehow lit on fire, and only his touch can put the inferno out. Feeling smooth material wrap around first one wrist then the other, I start to pant.

"This dress is really fucking nice," he states, as my wrists are pulled tightly together, causing my chest to arch forward and my cheek to press deeper into the bed. "Now I have you how I want you," he mutters, as if he's talking to himself, and my thong is dragged up higher between the cheeks of my ass, causing the material to rub roughly against my clit, making me gasp. "Stay just like that."

Breathing deeply, I hold my position, listening closely to him moving around. The sound of fabric hitting the floor registers, then soon, after one thud then another, which I know are his boots, metal clinks and more fabric hits the floor and a drawer opens and closes before I feel his heat behind me. His hands on my hips slide around my waist and down over the material of the lace covering my pussy. "You're wet for me. Does being tied up and at my mercy turn you on?" he asks roughly, and I nod, breathing heavily and pressing my hips forward, needing his touch. "Tell me what you want, June."

"You! I want you," I plea, becoming desperate.

"You have me."

"No!" I cry, when his hands move back to my hips, holding me once more.

"Tell me."

"I want you to touch me," I whimper, feeling his hard length so close to where I need him.

"I am touching you." His hands move over my ass and down the back of my thighs then up between my legs, still not close enough to where I need him to be.

"Evan, please," I beg, feeling his fingers move the small piece of material covering my soaked core to the side, and my arms strain against the material of my dress as I try to gain more of his touch. My legs move farther apart and my ass tilts higher.

"Beautiful, all you have to do is tell me what you want, and I'll give it to you."

"I want you to fuck me!" I practically yell at the top of my lungs. "Please, fuck me." I feel tears of frustration prickle the back of my eyes, but then he's there. In me. Slamming so hard and so deep that my breath catches and my head arches back in ecstasy from the stretch and feeling of fullness.

"Goddamn." His fingers hold me tighter around my hips. So tight, I know I will be bruised from his touch. So tight that I can't move, can't do anything. I'm completely at his mercy. Then, my hands are grasped in his as he fucks me hard and fast, bringing on an orgasm that didn't even get a chance to build, one that makes my knees buckle and my teeth sink into my lower lip so hard that I taste copper.

I finally find my breath again, only to have it taken away when my arms are released and the feeling of pins and needles shoots down my limbs, and my body is lifted and placed onto the bed. My legs are spread wide with his hands on my ankles, holding me open, then his mouth is on me. His teeth and tongue devouring me like he's starved for my taste, like he needs my essence to survive.

"Oh, God, don't stop. I'm so close," I whisper, squeezing my eyes closed as my core contracts.

"Give it to me. Rock that pussy. Get off on my tongue." His words send me over the edge and I give him what he wants, not being able to stop myself, even if I wanted to.

"Evan," I cry his name, as my body goes limp and my eyes slide shut, only to shoot open moments later when the sound of material ripping meets my ears. "You ripped my dress."

"Told you I was going to. Now get on your knees and open your mouth. I want that pretty mouth of yours around my cock." Energy from somewhere else moves through me, as the visual of me sucking him off filters through my brain. I roll to my belly then slide up on my hands and knees, moving to where he's kneeling on the bed with his hand wrapped around his length, stroking himself. My core tightens again, and I know I want him inside me. But the need to taste him on my tongue is almost overwhelming as I crawl toward him.

"Christ, you look like a fucking wet dream. Change of plans. Sit back on your knees and cup your tits."

The look in his eyes is one I've never seen before. One that makes me want to please him. So I do what he asks and rise up on my knees and slide my hands up my thighs, over my waist, and then cup both of my breasts, letting my head fall back and my eyes slide closed.

"Spread your legs wider, baby. Let me see your pussy. Let me see what belongs to me."

Sliding my legs wide, I tilt my head back toward him and try to open my eyes, wanting to see the look on his face, wanting so badly to see that I'm pleasing him. Then a soft buzz fills the room and his hand moves toward me. My eyes drop, noticing he has my small clit stimulator in his hand. The first touch of my toy against my clit has my hips jerking back. It's too much for me to take, too much for my over-stimulated body to deal with.

"Do not fucking move." At his harsh tone, my body locks and my eyes meet his. It takes everything in me to keep my legs wide open for him, as the small vibrator runs against my clit. "Pull your nipples."

Licking my lips, I cup my breasts and tug my nipples, the sensation not as pronounced as when he is touching me, but I still feel the zing from my nipples to my core, causing a strangled cry to climb up the back of my throat.

"It's too much."

"Come for me."

"I can't. It's too much."

"I said fucking come for me." His free hand wraps around my hair, tugging me forward, and then his lips are on mine and his tongue is pushing into my mouth, as I moan my orgasm down his throat.

My hips buck, and the sound of the soft buzz disappears as his hand cups me over my pussy. My body is so loose and my eyes grow heavy as I'm laid back onto the bed. His hand is at my jaw, pulling down. "Open." Forcing my eyes open, they meet his as he leans over me, running the tip of his cock against my lips. "Open, June. Don't make me tell you again." Shivering, I open my mouth and run my tongue around the crown of his cock. "Good girl, now take me deep."

I do. I open my mouth farther and feel him bump the back of my throat with each thrust. My body, which I thought couldn't take any more, primes itself back up as his hand slide over my stomach and between my legs. His feather-light touch against my clit is giving me something, yet nothing at all, as I work him with my mouth and move my hands to cup his balls. His groans and grunts egg me on, making me want him to feel what I feel every time he touches me.

He pulls from my mouth with a pop and I cry out, "No!"

"I come inside of you." He tosses my leg over his shoulder, and then he's inside of me again, filling me, making me feel complete. His eyes lock on mine and his hands move, holding my hair away from my face, while his hips move slowly and his weight presses me into the bed.

"I love you," I breathe, wrapping my arms around his back, and my legs up high around his hips. "Oh, God, Evan." My walls contract, and his hips jerk before pressing fully into me as he comes, leaving no space between us.

"Are you still drunk?" The soft words are spoken against my mouth, causing tears to pool in my eyes.

"No. Yes." I shake my head and wrap myself tighter around him.

"Promise me that you'll remember saying it."

"I'll remember. I've wanted to..." I pause to pull in a breath. "I tried to tell you."

"You have told me. In your sleep, you tell me every night."

"What?" I breathe, pulling back to search his face.

"When you fall asleep, when I pull you into me, you tell me you love me, but even if you didn't say the words out loud, I would know."

"I was going to write it down and give it to you in a note," I tell him truthfully, and his body starts to shake above mine before he's rolling us over, so that I'm draped half across his chest.

"You were going to write that you love me down on a piece of paper and give it to me?" he asks, still laughing, and I fight my own smile, because it really does sound crazy.

"It was April's idea."

"Was she drunk when she came up with that idea?"

"Um, no actually. It was before we even had dinner or anything to drink."

"Hmm," he murmurs, running his hand up my back.

"Did you really just rip my dress?" I ask, after a long moment of lying there, feeling his fingers run over my skin.

"Yep."

"Caveman," I mutter, while smiling into the skin of his chest.

"Yep," he mumbles back then rolls toward me. "I need to go let Ninja out. Do you want me to clean you up, or do you want to take off your makeup?" he asks, while running his fingers through my hair.

"I need to take off my makeup," I whisper, then lean in and press my mouth to his in a soft touch, saying, "I love you." I need to prove to myself the words that came out earlier weren't a fluke.

"I know you do, baby," he agrees against my mouth, before kissing me deep and long and so sweet that I feel it down to my soul.

Chapter 12

Evan

LOOKING ACROSS THE open room of the compound, I watch Jordan talking to one of the new guys. Since Nico talked to me weeks ago about him, I've been keeping an eye on the guy and have noticed on more than one occasion that he has been working his way through the club, talking to recruits.

"That motherfucker is gonna end up in a ditch somewhere." Harlen comes up at my side, and I turn to look at him. "I know you've been watching him too," he mutters, taking a pull from his beer as his eyes slide to where Jordan is across the room. "I did some research and found out he was a member of another club, the Southern Stars, out of Nashville, just a few months ago. Word on the road is his dad is the vice president."

He's right. That is the exact intel I got from Nico, along with Brew, whose crew, the Wild Hogs, have had a few run-ins of their own with the Southern Stars over the last couple years. Unlike the Broken Eagles, the Wild Hogs do have dealings in the shadier side of the biker club lifestyle, but they also kept to themselves and have been known around town to do more good than bad. Or at least that's the image they've portrayed to the public.

"I don't trust him," Harlen says, cutting into my thoughts.

"I don't either," I agree, looking across the room to where June and July are playing a game of pool. My eyes constantly seek her out, not that they need to. I know where she is without even looking for her. I swear my body is in tune with hers, like there is an invisible wire connecting us.

"Wes wants him out."

Fuck. I turn on my stool to meet his gaze once more. If he's out, Nico's whole case goes under, and as much as it shits me to break my word to Nico, the only way I can keep the stupid fucker around is to talk to Wes and the rest of the guys about what's happening.

"We need to talk, and we need to do that shit now," I say, sliding off my stool. "Get the guys and meet me in the shop in five. I'm gonna get the girls out of here."

"Sure," he agrees, reading my tone.

I don't even look back. I make a beeline across the room to June who is bent over the pool table taking a shot.

"Hey." She smiles when she sees me, resting the end of her pool stick on the floor.

"Come with me," I mutter, taking the stick from her hand and setting it on the table. Looking at July, I point at the ground. "Don't move from here. She'll be right back."

"Uhh. Okay." July frowns, and I tug June's hand, lead her halfway down the hall, and press her to the wall.

"What are you doing?" she asks breathlessly, running her hands up my chest to my shoulders.

Leaning closer, I move my mouth to her ear. "Get July and take her to our house. You girls stay there until I come home," I instruct, moving my hands up the back of her shirt and running them along her smooth skin.

"Wh-what?" She leans back, running her eyes over my face.

"Get July and take her to our house. I need to talk to the guys, which means no one I trust will be able to look out for you two for a few."

"Is everything okay?"

"Everything's fine. I just want you girls out of here for a while."

"Okay." She frowns then tilts her head to the side. "Are you sure everything is okay?"

"I'm sure."

"Promise?" she asks softly, and my forehead drops to rest against hers.

"I promise, baby." I mummer and her body relaxes.

"Okay," she agrees. I touch my mouth to hers before taking her back toward the pool tables, where July is now standing with Wes.

"The girls are heading to our place," I tell him quietly, gaining a chin lift before he looks at July and leads her out the door toward the parking lot, muttering, "Stay with June, text when you get to her house."

"You know I hate it when you keep me out of the loop," she gripes, and he grins then leans in, saying something I can't hear before kissing her pouting mouth. "You're annoying," she says when he releases her, and I look at June, handing her the keys to my truck since I drove us here.

"Text when you get home and set the alarm," I tell her, kissing her forehead then her lips.

"I know, I know," she sighs, then climbs up into the truck, which looks way too big for her, as July gets into the passenger side seat.

"Drive careful."

"Maybe." She smiles, starting up The Beast, slamming the door, and then rolling down the window. "I've never driven a truck this big. Maybe we'll skip going home and take this thing off-roading and see what it can do."

"If you feel like getting spanked, have at it, baby." I smirk, and her eyes light with mischief, which makes me shake my head. My girl's a freak, and I fucking love that about her. "Be good," I mutter. I watch her wave and back out of the parking lot. As soon as the truck is out of sight, I move to Wes. "Let's go."

We head for the shop next to the compound. When we enter, all eyes come to us, and I move with Wes to the office while everyone follows.

"What's going on?" Wes asks, breaking the silence as Harlen, Everett, Zee, Mic, Blaze, and Jinx move around the room in a circle.

"Nico approached me a couple weeks ago at June's parents' house and asked me to help him out with a case he's working on," I confess, and watch the guys look around the room. They all know June's uncle. They all respect him and know what he does, so I'm sure they know exactly what I'm going to say next. "I told him I didn't feel comfortable doing shit behind your backs, but he insisted I keep this to myself, and I agreed under the circumstances that I would unless shit got out of hand." I pause and look at Wes.

"Harlen told me tonight that you want Jordan out. That shit can't happen."

"Pardon?" Wes asks, and I move my eyes through the men in the room to meet his once more.

"Jordan has been sent into the club to recruit the lower-ranking members and eventually take over by offering them a different kind of lifestyle."

"You have got to be shitting me," Wes growls.

"Nico knew you'd be pissed."

"If he knew that, then he should have fucking talked to me about it."

"He couldn't, and if you think about it, you'd agree that he couldn't. You would have lost your mind and blown his case. I know you don't want the dirt Jordan is bringing into the club, but it's already here and spreading. I know for a fact he's gotten to a few of the guys, and he's been putting feelers out to a few of you to see what you think and to test your loyalty to Wes," I say, looking around, and a few of them nod.

"He approached me and Jinx a week ago," Blaze says, and Wes frowns at him. "He didn't go into detail. He just asked a few questions about our thoughts on making more money for the club."

"You didn't think to tell me about that?" Wes asks, and Blaze cuts his eyes to him.

"No, I didn't think anything about it until right now. We didn't even take him serious."

"So what the fuck is Nico waiting for?" Harlen asks.

"I'm not sure. I only know he wanted me to keep an eye out and tell him who Jordan approached."

"This is bullshit," Z clips, looking at Wes. "Our fucking hands are tied and this motherfucker has free rein. He's been around my wife and kid. That shit is not okay with me."

"Does Jax know about this?" Wes asks, and I shake my head.

"No one does outside of this room and Nico's team."

"Fuck," he barks, running a hand over his hair. "How many clubs have they taken over?"

"Three that Nico knows of." I let out a breath then continue, "None of the other clubs put up a fight. Most of them were already leading themselves down the road the Southern Stars are traveling, and were all too happy to hand them over the reins, while keeping some control of their clubs and gaining a bigger profit in the long run."

"We need to know how many of the guys have agreed to follow Jordan," Harlen says, crossing his arms over his massive chest. "If he's spreading that shit through the club, we need to know who's willing to take him up on this offer."

"As far as I know, only a couple of new guys have seemed interested. I don't think the Stars did much research before sending Jordan into our midst. They don't know that most of the men in this club are ex-military and loyal to a brotherhood stronger than theirs. If they would have looked into us, they would know this is the wrong type of club to bring that shit to."

"We need a plan," Harlen conveys, and all eyes go to him. "Jordan's dad is Vice President. We can't just take the kid out without blowback, but we also can't let this stand. I understand Nico is working this case, but I say we give him a timeframe, and if he doesn't get this sorted within that time, we cut ties with Jordan and make a statement that won't go misunderstood."

"Harlen's right," Mic agrees, and I look over at him, surprised he's throwing in his two cents. Mic never has much to say. He's the guy who is always observing everyone, keeping his opinion to himself. "One way or another, we're going to have to make a statement about this shit, or we will have men who are wearing our patch committing crimes, using our name as a scare tactic. That shit is not okay with me, and I know it's not okay with anyone in this room."

"He's right," Wes cuts in, looking at me. "Others will think it's okay to test us if we let this shit slide and don't make a statement. We can't have that. Regardless of what Nico wants or what he thought my reaction would be, he should have brought this shit to me. This is our club, our name, and I'm not okay with being used."

"I didn't want to keep this from you guys, but I got what Nico was saying." I shrug. "I won't apologize for my actions. I did what I felt was necessary at the time, and if given the same situation again, my choice would remain the same."

"I know," Wes mutters, patting my shoulder. "I get why you did what you did, and there are no hard feelings, but this shit isn't okay with me, and I won't let our name be dragged into some fucked-up turf war just so Nico can close a case. I won't risk something happening to July or any of the brothers who wear the Broken Eagles cut."

He was correct. There could be blowback on the club if shit went sideways, and at the end of the day, protecting our families and the men who have had my back since I walked into their club is more important than helping Nico. "I'll talk to Nico, fill him in on tonight, and explain he has a limited amount of time to do what he needs to do before we step in."

"I'll also be talking to him," Wes says, crossing his arms over his chest. "He should have talked to me about what was going down and let me decide my course of action."

"You know with what happened to July, you would have shut him down," Mic retorts, pinning Wes with his gaze. "I get why he went to Evan with this. He knows Evan's loyal to us, but also knows what we stand for and that we wouldn't want Jordan or anyone not loyal to what we stand for riding with us. You would have gotten rid of Jordan and any member loyal to him without hearing Nico out, and brother, as much as I hate to say this shit, I agree with what Nico is doing. I didn't spend years fighting for what I believe in to take the easy way out when some slimy motherfucker thinks his balls are bigger than they are. He and his crew might think they found a group of men easy to turn, but they are going to learn the hard way that's not the case."

"Well, there you go," Z mutters, and the rest of the guys chuckle, while Wes lets out a sigh then looks at me.

"I want to know how long he thinks this shit is going to take. When we have that information, we'll figure out our next step," he mutters and heads for the door. I do the same, lifting my chin to the guys before stepping outside behind him.

"LANE'S FREE. ALL charges were dropped yesterday," Jax says as soon as I put the phone to my ear, before I even have a chance to say hello.

"You've got to be shitting me," I growl, and June, who is asleep, draped half over me, her leg thrown over mine with her hand across my waist, stirs. "Hold on a sec," I mutter to Jax, dropping my phone back to the nightstand.

Kissing the top of her head, I move out from under her, being careful not to wake her as I slide out of bed and pick up my sweats off the chair. Putting them on, I grab my cell and leave the room, shutting the door behind me.

"I thought they had a case against him?" I prompt, when the door is closed.

"Nothing stuck. His lawyers made it look like he was just a good, wholesome college kid with a bright future, and a fucked-up family who happens to be into bad shit."

"Fuck." I run my hands over my face, taking a seat on the edge of the couch and putting my elbows to my knees. "Is the no-contact order still in place?"

"No. Like I said, he was cleared of all charges."

"I want a restraining order against him. I don't want him anywhere near June," I say, while trying to keep from roaring or crushing my phone, which is exactly what I want to do.

"I'll see what I can do, but my guess is that won't be possible. He hasn't harassed or threatened her in anyway, so it won't be easy to convince a judge there is a need for one."

"Try," I demand.

"You know I will."

"If he shows up here, I won't be held responsible for what I do to him."

"I don't think he'd hurt her," he says quietly, and my teeth grind together. I don't think he'd hurt her either, but the fact that he's touched her is enough of a reason for me to put a bullet in him. "Evan," Jax calls, and I let out a breath, realizing I had gone quiet.

"If it were Ellie, how would you feel?"

"Point taken," he mutters. Ellie and her daughter Hope, who Jax adopted as his own, are the two most important things in his life. Jax would never let anyone he perceived as a threat anywhere near them, and knowing that, I know he understands where I'm coming from.

"I need to talk to June. See what you can do about the restraining order and get back to me. I'm sure Nico already called her dad, and with my luck, he's going to show up here, wanting to talk to his girl in person."

"You learn quick," he laughs.

"No, I just know what I would do if I had a daughter."

"Right." He sighs. "I'll get back to you on the restraining order."

"Thanks," I mutter.

"Have June call me when she's up. I need a favor."

"What's up?"

"I made reservations for Ellie and me weeks ago for Diego's in Nashville. Mom and Dad were supposed to watch Hope, but they had to go out of town, and Ashlyn's busy, so I need to see if June minds watching her."

"Bring her over."

"You sure?"

"June will probably need the distraction, and we'll be home."

"Thanks, man. I'll give you a call back," he says then hangs up.

Dropping my eyes to the carpet, I sigh. This shit is fucked up and not what we need right now. Knowing there is nothing I can do at the moment, I look at Ninja, who is lying on the chaise with his head hanging half off the side, watching me as his head lifts and tilts to the side.

"Come on. Let's go outside." I stand then move to the backdoor, turning off the alarm before sliding the door open and letting him out. I watch him for a few minutes while he wanders around the backyard, sniffing everything he comes in contact with. Leaving him out back, I head for the kitchen and start a pot of coffee then hear June's phone

173

ringing from somewhere in the house. It's not in the bedroom, but where the fuck it is, is anyone's guess. Half the time, I wonder why she even has a cell, since she never has it on her and can't find it most of the time.

Heading for the laundry room, planning to start my search for the phone there, I hear a loud thump and cry from the bedroom. I rush back in that direction then laugh when I open the door and find June on the floor, the blankets tangled around her and her hair in disarray.

"I fell off the bed." She shakes her head, looking around.

"I see that. Are you okay?"

"I haven't done that since you've been back," she mutters, looking confused and completely adorable as she blows a strand of hair out of her face.

"That's 'cause when I'm in bed with you, you're attached to me like an octopus," I explain, walking fully into the room and picking her up off the floor.

"I don't attach myself to you like an octopus!" she cries. "You attach yourself to me. I can't even move an inch in the bed without you following me and pinning me in place."

"Babe," I chuckle, "if I didn't control you in your sleep, you'd roll off the bed or knee me in the nuts."

"Whatever," she huffs, trying to unwrap the twisted sheet from around her naked body.

"Let me help you with that," I insist, taking the edge of the sheet from her grasp, giving it a tug, and making her fall into me while the sheet falls to the floor.

"Ev," she gasps, looking up at me with wide eyes.

"What's up, baby?" I run one hand up her back, wrapping my hand around the back of her neck, while the other slides down, cupping her bare ass cheek.

"Ev," she breathes against my mouth that has lowered, an inch from hers, pressing her chest into mine, while her hands slide around my waist and down the back of my sweats.

"I love that." My words are spoken against her mouth as my hand slides down farther, cupping between her legs, feeling she's already primed for me. "Hop up." I tap the back of her leg then catch her when she does, and wrap my hands around her thighs. I carry her toward the bathroom while her tongue licks up my neck, ending its ascent at my ear which she nips. The sensation obliterates all thoughts of this morning's phone call and the conversation we need to have.

"WE NEED TO talk, beautiful," I tell June, once we're out of the shower and in the kitchen. Taking the coffee pot off the heater, I pour her a cup then turn to look at her when I notice she hasn't answered me. I find her digging through a big box she brought into the kitchen a few minutes ago.

"What's up?" she asks, distracted, pulling odds and ends out of the box and setting them on the island.

"What are you looking for?" I move to her side with her cup of coffee in my hand, wondering what she's searching for.

"Found it." She grins, holding up a small, silver paper box. Opening it up, she takes whatever is in the box out, and holds it out between us, before sliding it on her finger.

It takes me a second to recognize the shiny piece of gold metal sitting around her ring finger. A piece of metal I put there years ago. A piece of metal I never thought I would see again. The ring I gave her when she became my wife. It was what I could afford at the time. I knew that one day, when we were settled and I could afford it, I would put a diamond on her finger. A ring worthy of her. But after everything that happened, I never thought I'd get the chance.

"Ev?" she whispers, and I drop her cup of coffee to the island then lift her up, planting her next to it.

"Do not move," I demand, pointing at her while speaking through the lump that has formed in my throat, as I let her go and head back to the bedroom. I dig through my bag sitting in the bottom of the closet until I find what I'm looking for, and shove it into the pocket of my sweats.

Going back to the kitchen, I find her where I left her on the counter. Her eyes are on me, but her guard is up. I can tell she doesn't know what to think. "Take that shit off your finger," I growl when I'm close. Her eyes widen and her bottom lip trembles as she drops her gaze from me to her hands. Rolling the ring around on her finger, she swallows then slowly slips it off.

"I'm sorry. It was stupid." Her head shakes. "I don't know what I was thinking."

Grabbing her knees, I open her legs wide, making room for my hips, then take the ring from her hand and hold it up between us. "Look at me."

"I should get breakfast started," she murmurs to her lap, where her eyes are still pointed. The sadness and defeat in her tone makes my gut clench.

Pressing closer, I soften my voice. "Look at me, beautiful." Her head slowly comes up and I see tears swimming in her eyes. "This ring was put on your finger by a coward," I say, and I watch anger fill her eyes, anger that catches me off guard. It's an emotion that makes me realize for the millionth time the kind of idiot I am, because I know that anger is her wanting to defend me. "It was put there by a man who wasn't strong enough for you. A man who didn't deserve you," I continue quietly, closing the ring tightly in my fist.

"No." She lifts her hands, pushing at my chest, trying to shove me away. "No!" she repeats, yelling this time.

Grabbing her wrists, I hold them to me, watching her chest rise and fall quickly. "The kind of man you deserve wouldn't have left you. He wouldn't have given up on you. He would have done everything possible to make sure you never doubted his feelings for you. I wasn't that man before."

"Stop!" she screams, and I let go of her left hand, reach into my pocket, and then drop to my knee in front of her.

"The man I was didn't deserve you. He didn't even deserve to breathe the same air as you. But I do. I'm not the man I was then, and I vow, every day until I take my last breath, to prove myself worthy of you." I hold up the ring, which I picked out weeks ago, between us. A ring worthy of being on her finger, given to her by a man worthy of her. "Will you marry me? Will you be my wife?"

"Oh, God." Her hand covers her mouth and tears fall from her eyes as she looks between the ring and me. "Oh, God," she repeats, dropping forward, wrapping her arms around my neck, shoving her face there, and sobbing, "Yes."

"Calm down, baby. You're scaring the fuck out of me," I whisper, rubbing her back while listening to her loud sobs as her body shakes.

"I can't calm down!" she cries on a hitched breath, pulling her face out of my neck. "Who could possibly calm down after that?" she asks, using her hands to wipe the tears off her face.

"Can you at least pull it together long enough for me to put the ring on your finger?" I request, picking her up and placing her back on the top of the counter.

"Yes. But only after I say something," she breathes through her tears, resting her warm hands against my chest while searching my face. "There was never a time you didn't deserve me."

"June," I warn, giving her knee a squeeze.

"No." She shakes her head. "You have always, *always* been good enough for me. I fell in love with you—all of you—not just one piece of you that I thought was perfect. There was never a time I didn't love you. You need to know that." She slides her hand up my chest to my neck and under my jaw. "I love you, Evan, all of you. Even the parts of you that you don't like."

"I don't deserve you," I get out through clenched teeth.

"And I don't deserve you either, but I'm keeping you anyway." She smiles and tilts her head to the side, smiling brightly. "Can I have my ring now?"

"Yes." I lean forward, kissing her softly, then pull back and take her hand, sliding the three-carat, cushion-cut diamond ring on her finger, transfixed by the sight of it.

"It's beautiful," she whispers, holding her hand to my chest, turning it one way then the other and watching the light catch on it before looking up at me. "But when we get married, I want my old ring sitting next to this one. I don't want something new, when my something old was perfect to begin with."

"Christ, you're killing me," I groan, wrapping my fist in her hair and taking her mouth in a kiss that shows her how much I love her, only pulling away when the doorbell rings, reminding me of the shit I needed to talk to her about. "Fuck," I clip, reluctantly ripping my mouth from hers.

"I wonder who that is," she whispers, dazedly looking toward the door.

"My bet is on your mom and dad," I grumble, looking at her mouth that is swollen and her face that is soft, wishing this moment wasn't going to be ruined by the past.

"Did they know you were going to ask me to marry you?" She frowns, hopping off the counter when I take a step back.

"No, and I need to make our talk we were supposed to have earlier a quick one before I go let them in."

"What talk?"

"Lane is out of jail. All charges were dropped and he was released this morning."

"What?" She looks toward the hall when the bell rings again, and Ninja finally jumps off the couch, barking as he heads for the door.

"He's out, and I don't want you having any kind of contact with him."

"I wouldn't. I mean, why would I?" She shakes her head while her brows dart together.

"It's not you getting into contact with him that I'm worried about," I explain, brushing her hair away from her face.

"You think he'll come looking for me?"

"You're hard to forget, beautiful, so yes. I have no doubt he will eventually show up here," I mutter, dropping a brief kiss to her lips before heading for the door which is now being pounded on. Looking out the peephole, I sigh when I see who's on the other side. Not that I didn't know they'd show up, but after what just happened with June, and the fact that she agreed to marry me again, I can think of a million and fifty other things I'd prefer to be doing with my fiancée this morning. None of them have one goddamn thing to do with spending time with her parents.

"Are you going to open it or just stand there?" she asks, coming up and placing her hand against my side, while using the other to push Ninja back a step.

"I'm trying to decide," I grouch, listening as she giggles and pushes me to the side so she can pull open the door.

"Hey, Mom. Hey, Dad," she says in greeting with a kiss and hug to each of her parents. "I know why you're here, but I have bigger news." She hops up and down then shoves her hand out toward her parents. "Evan asked me to marry him!" she yells happily, making them showing up worth the annoyance of not having my morning free, just to show her how much I love her wearing my ring.

"Oh, honey, I'm so happy for you," her mom squeals, giving her a hug as she steps into the house.

"Thanks, Mom," June whispers, then looks at her dad when her mom releases her. "Dad?" She takes a step toward him, and his eyes soften while his hand stretches out to take hers, looking at the ring there.

"I'm really happy for you, June Bug."

"Thanks, Dad." She smiles, closing the distance between them and wrapping her arms around his waist.

"I told you she'd love the ring," November says, leaning into my side while smiling at her husband and daughter.

A few days after I asked Asher for his daughter's hand, wanting to do everything right this time, I called up her mom and asked her to help me pick out the ring. She cried the whole time we were shopping, but I could tell me asking her to be involved meant everything to her. What she didn't know is it also meant a lot to me to have her approval.

"You did," I agree, placing my arm around her shoulders, giving her a squeeze, while her arm wraps around the back of my waist, doing the same.

"Now, I don't care what either of you say. We are going to have a wedding, a *real* wedding. The kind of wedding that takes planning. You are not going to run off to the courthouse or off to Vegas and get married, and you are definitely not going to give me just a few days to throw together a wedding like your sister did," November says, looking between June and me as she moves to her husband's side.

"We'll see, Mom." June grins, leaning into me.

"Oh no, we won't see. I want at least one of my girls to give me what I want, and since July is already married, she's out. We all know April is never getting married, unless there is a guy crazy enough to try and tame her. May is…" She pauses, looking at her husband and scrunching up her face. "I don't know what May is, but I doubt she will be getting married anytime soon. And December, way too picky to settle down. So that leaves you."

"Babe," Asher cuts in, shaking his head.

"Don't *babe* me. I want to plan a wedding. A *real* wedding."

"Maybe you and Dad should renew your vows. You could plan that," June suggests, leading us down the hall toward the kitchen.

"I don't want to marry your dad again," she mutters under her breath, but we still hear it, followed by a smack before she cries, "I already married you, Asher Mayson!"

"You'd think with time, you'd stop being a pain in my ass. Nothing has changed," he says, and I hear the love he has for his wife in his words, even if they are slightly annoyed.

"Whatever," she replies, dropping her purse to the counter next to the box June was looking through earlier as she reaches behind her to rub the cheek her husband obviously smacked.

"Have you had breakfast?" June asks, looking between her parents while picking up her cup of coffee and taking a sip.

"We ate earlier, honey," November tells her, taking a seat on one of the barstools. "We weren't planning on staying long. We tried to call, but as usual, you didn't pick up your phone, so we decide to just swing by."

"Oh, I don't know where my phone is." She looks around like the damn thing is going to appear out of thin air.

"You need to start keeping better track of it. I want you to keep it on you at all times," Asher says, sounding all-dad now.

"Dad." She sighs.

"No, June Bug, this is serious. I'm guessing Evan told you that Lane is out of jail."

"He did, but I really don't think I have anything to worry about. Lane nev—"

"Don't say it," I cut her off, before she can defend him. "He could have gotten you in a lot of fucking trouble, and I have no doubt he knew that shit when he was seeing you."

"I know, Ev." She sets her coffee cup on the counter, wrapping her arms around her waist. It takes everything in me not to go to her and comfort her right now, but she needs to understand the kind of man Lane really is.

"No, you don't know, baby. If you did, you wouldn't even think about defending him. You're lucky your uncle was there when they were interrogating you and stopped them from sending you back to him. That shit could have ended badly. Lane's family is crooked, and I mean that in the worst ways possible. They have no problem killing anyone, and they wouldn't have thought twice about making you disappear if they thought you knew something you shouldn't have, or that you were working with the feds."

"You need to keep an eye out for him. If he approaches you, get away and call one of us, or head for the police station," Asher instructs, and I watch her eyes widen.

"Do you guys think that's necessary? I'm sure if I told him to leave me alone, he would."

"What part of 'you're not to have contact with him' are you not understanding?" I growl, clenching my fists at my sides, and her eyes drop to them.

"Evan—"

"No, baby, this isn't a joke. You see him on the sidewalk, you turn the other way and call me. You get a phone call from him, you hang up and call me. You do not talk to him."

"Okay," she whispers, looking between her parents and me. "I won't talk to him."

"Good," I agree, closing the distance between us and taking her into my arms. "We all just want you safe. I know Lane never gave you a reason to believe he was dangerous, but he is." I kiss the top of her head, while my eyes lock with Asher's. His eyes move between his daughter and me, and his chin lifts, while his arm slides around his wife's shoulders, and seeing that, the strength of their relationship, and the love they have for their daughter, shows me what I will have with June for the rest of my life.

Chapter 13

Evan

"THREE, TWO, ONE, zero." I end my countdown and pull myself up from the couch, where I was sitting with my face covered, and then look around, pretending I don't hear the giggles coming from under the kitchen table, where Hope is hiding.

After Asher and November left, June and I ate breakfast out on the back porch. She was quiet for a while, and I could tell she was upset and reflecting on her relationship with Lane, which was like opening an old wound. If I hadn't fucked up, Lane wouldn't even exist for her—for us—but I couldn't think about that or could I continue to dredge up the past. I gave her time to think but wouldn't bring him up again. I just knew that if he did show up, I would make it clear to him that he needed to stay away for good. It wasn't until I told her that we would be babysitting Hope for a few hours that her whole mood changed. She and the rest of the family had fallen in love with the little girl, and I had to admit, I had too.

"Found ya." I smile, ripping open the shower curtain in the second bathroom, making June yell, "Dammit!"

"Babe, the house isn't that big. You couldn't have thought it would take me a year to find you." I laugh at her pouting face.

"I thought it would at least take a few minutes," she gripes, stepping out of the tub.

"Sorry, but you lose." I kiss her upturned face then take her hand

and lead her toward the living room. "I got June. Hope, I hope you're hiding better than she did," I say, hearing her giggle louder as I pass her on the way to the kitchen, where I open cupboards, pretending to look for her. "I wonder where she could be." I sigh loudly, planting my hands on my hips while looking around.

"I will never tell," June says, taking a seat on one of the chairs at the table, and Hope laughs again, making me smile. Walking back toward the living room, I stop at the table, and Hope goes quiet, so I move back toward the bedrooms, coming back out a minute later.

"I don't know where she is," I grumble to June, who grins at me. "I guess we'll just leave her here while we go get ice cream."

"Ice cream!" Hope yells, crawling out of her hiding space. "I was inbisible." She jumps up and down.

"How do you become invisible?" June asks her, and Hope holds her finger up between her eyes.

"Like this!" She laughs, and June looks around then looks at me with wide eyes.

"Where did she go? She was just right here." She moves her arms around like she's searching for Hope, who starts to giggle.

"I'm right here!" she cries, dropping her finger from between her eyes.

"Oh my, you scared me when you just disappeared," June fawns, picking her up, swinging her around, kissing her cheeks, and making her laugh.

Standing back, I watch the two of them together and feel an ache in my chest. I always knew June would be a good mom, but seeing her with Hope, I can see up close and personal the kind of mom she'd be.

There were times when my mom was affectionate, but they were few and far between when I was younger, and when I started to become a man, those times ended all together. I couldn't even tell you the last time I hugged a member of my family, but with June and the Maysons,

I see that easy affection every time they're around each other.

"Can we have ice cream now?" Hope asks, looking up at me once June places her on her feet.

"Get your shoes." I smile at her, and she throws her hands up in the air, yelling, "Yay! Ice Cream!" then takes off toward the couch, where her bag is sitting.

"Are you okay?"

Looking into June's beautiful eyes, I smile and wrap my hand around the side of her neck, tugging her closer. "Absolutely."

"You had a strange look in your eyes a minute ago," she says quietly, while scanning my face.

"You're going to be an amazing mom one day," I tell her, watching her face soften and lips part as she leans in closer, placing her hands against my chest.

"And you're going to be an amazing dad. Hope adores you." I couldn't say I would be an amazing dad. I had a shit example for one, but I knew I never wanted any kids if they had to grow up like I did. "You will be," she says softly, leaning up and kissing the underside of my jaw before turning toward the living room, stopping a few feet away and looking at me over her shoulder. "Come on. Let's go get ice cream."

Just like always, she has no idea how much her words effect me, how much she makes me want to be a better man.

"ARE YOU SURE you want Fruity Pebbles?" I ask, looking at Hope.

"Yep." She smiles brightly up at me, and I look from her cute, excited smile to the frozen yogurt cup in her hand which is overflowing with strawberry, banana, chocolate, and kiwi yogurt, topped with chocolate sprinkles, gummy worms, vanilla wafers, blueberries, and Oreo cookies.

"Okay, kiddo, but I think this is the last thing that will fit in that cup," I tell her, and she looks at me, her smile widening farther.

"That's okay." She lifts the cup higher, and I scoop out some of the fruity cereal and sprinkle it on top, and then lead her to the counter to pay, while June follows behind us with her own strange concoction of blueberries and peanut butter cups over birthday cake yogurt. After I pay the almost twenty dollars for the two cups of yogurt, we head out front to one of the tables and take a seat.

"Want a bite?" June asks, holding out a spoonful of her mixture toward me.

"No, thanks." I shake my head, opening my bottle of water.

"Your loss, more for me," she says, shoving the spoonful in her mouth and making me laugh.

"Can I be your flower girl?" Hope asks around a spoonful of yogurt, and June turns in her chair to face her. As soon as Ellie and Jax showed up to drop off Hope, June shoved her ring in their faces. Jax had clapped me on the back, while June, Ellie, and Hope all did the whole girly scream and jump around bit. I was happy June got to share this part of getting married with her family. They didn't get to before, and I could tell it meant a lot to her to be able to share her happiness with the people she loves.

"I would love that." June smiles then looks at me, and asks softly, "I know Mom wants me to have a big wedding, but do you want that?"

"As long as you are my wife at the end of the ceremony, I don't really care what we do," I tell her honestly, sitting back in the chair, and her head tilts to the side, studying me.

"Would you wear a tux?"

"If I have to." I shrug. I hate wearing suits, but for her, I would do just about anything.

"So, you don't really want to wear a tux?"

"What I want is for you to be my wife and to have my last name. All the other sh—" I pause looking at Hope. "All the other stuff doesn't really matter to me, but I will say, I'm not waiting a year. If your mom and you want to plan a wedding, then you have four months to do that, before I take you to Vegas and marry you in front of Elvis."

She rolls her eyes. "Elvis is not marrying us," she says matter-of-factly, as Hope asks, "Who's Elvis?"

"Elvis isn't alive anymore, honey, but he was a famous singer who dressed kind of crazy, and there are people who dress up like him and put on shows or sometimes marry people."

"Like Halloween?" she asks, looking confused.

"Exactly like Halloween," I confirm.

"I want to be a pirate for Halloween." She shrugs, swinging her legs back and forth while biting off the head of one of her gummy worms.

"You don't want to be a princess?" June asks, and Hope scrunches up her face and shakes her head.

"No, I want to be a pirate. They live on ships and look for treasure. Pirates are cool! I want to be a pirate when I grow up."

"Pirates are definitely cool," June agrees, not letting Hope know that pirates, or at least the kind she wants to be, don't exist anymore. By the time we leave the yogurt place, Hope is on a sugar high talking a million miles an hour—about what, I have no fucking clue—but it's cute listening to her babble from the backseat as we head home.

"Maybe we shouldn't have let her get a large cup," June mutters with a laugh, as we watch Hope dance around the living room, singing one of the songs from *Frozen,* which she insisted we watch as soon as we walked into the house.

"She's gonna crash soon," I bet, sliding my arm around her shoulders and pulling her deeper into me.

"Are you sure you still want kids now?" she asks quietly, and I turn my eyes from the TV and look at Hope, who has moved across the room to where Ninja is laying, and has her little hands holding his face while she sings to him.

Dipping my face back down toward June, I rumble, "Yes."

"Me too." She smiles softly then lays her head against my chest while draping her arm over my abs. And that's how we spend the rest of the night. June and I cuddled up, watching a movie with Hope, who eventually climbed up on the couch next to us and fell asleep, and as simple as the night was, it was one of the best I've ever had.

"IT'S SO QUIET," June mutters, coming to stand next to me at the sink in the kitchen, where I'm washing out our breakfast dishes. It's the weekend after we watched Hope. The week flew by between work, dealing with the Jordan situation, and November coming over every evening to talk about the wedding. The wedding I somehow got roped into planning with them. If I have to spend one more minute sitting at the table with them looking at wedding shit, talking venues, dresses, flowers, and cakes, I will lose my fucking mind.

"Yep," I agree, even though after this last week, I'm enjoying it just being us in the house, since I have no idea when someone will show up.

"Do you want to watch *Frozen* with me?" she asks, leaning into my side and pressing her tits to my arm.

Shaking my head, I laugh. "No."

"Do you think Ellie and Jax would notice if I kidnapped Hope?"

"Probably." I grin, watching her pout out her bottom lip.

"Darn." She sighs, hopping up on the counter next to the sink. "I'm bored, and Mom said she won't be here for a few hours."

Shutting off the faucet, I move between her legs, wrap my hands around the back of her knees, and drag her flush against me. "I'm gonna head out when she gets here, but until then, I'll entertain you." I run my wet hands up her thighs, watching her eyes heat before her brows draw together.

"You're leaving when she gets here?"

Moving my mouth to her exposed shoulder, I nip her skin and

mutter,

"Yep."

Her hands move up the skin of my back and her nails dig in as my mouth moves up her neck, licking and biting along the way to her ear. "We're planning a wedding," she breathes, as my hands glide up to cup her breasts, which are bare under her tank, allowing me to feel her nipples harden.

"No, *you're* planning a wedding with your mom." I nip her ear.

Pushing me back, her eyes search my face. "I thought you said you didn't mind having a big wedding."

"I don't, but I don't need to be here when you're planning it."

She frowns. "You don't want to be involved in planning your own wedding?"

"Nope," I confess, skimming my hands down her sides then her hips, stopping there before moving my hands in and up the loose material of her shorts, finding her bare. My fingers slide deeper, skimming over her clit, making her hips jerk.

"This isn't fair." Her head falls back and her legs spread wider, while her eyes slide to half-mast.

"All's fair in love and war, beautiful."

"This isn't war. It's planning a wedding. Our wedding," she gets out through a moan.

Ignoring her comment, I growl, "Tank off, put your hands behind you on the counter, and lean back." Moving quickly, she takes her tank off, dropping it to the floor, then leans back, arching her chest forward. Lowering my mouth to her breast, I pull the whole thing into my mouth, listening to her whimper as I circle her nipple with my tongue.

"Ev," she whispers, making my already hard cock leak.

Leaning away from her, I rip her shorts down her legs and kick off my sweats before moving in on her neglected breast, giving it the same treatment. Hearing her moan I slide my hands down the backs of her legs, I pull her forward on the counter and toss them up high around my waist.

"Lock your legs, baby." I kiss between her breasts, leaning her back until she's flat on the counter.

"I need you," she pants, rocking her wet pussy against me, and I grit my teeth, fighting the urge to slide inside of her and give her what we both want.

"You'll get me. Now, lock your legs." Feeling her legs tighten around my hips, I lean back, groaning at the sight of her. "So fucking beautiful." My hands span her hips. They move up the curve of her waist to her breast, where I tug each nipple, making her back arch. "So fucking hot. Do you know how sexy you look right now?"

I pull her nipples again, this time twisting them gently between my fingers. Her eyes slide closed and I listen to her moan so loud that I wouldn't be surprised if the neighbors heard her. "I love you, beautiful, but I'm not sitting through anymore wedding shit." I glide one hand down over her stomach, placing my thumb over her clit.

Her eyes open, meeting mine, and she pleads, "Please touch me."

"No more wedding shit," I repeat. Her hips rock forward and her hands slide up her chest, cupping her breasts.

"No more wedding shit," she breathes.

Moving one hand to her hip, I take my cock into my hand, slide it up and down her core, and use the tip to circle her clit, watching her wetness coat the head. "Fuck, but you get so goddamn wet for me every time I touch you."

"I know," she agrees, lifting her hips so the tip nudges her entrance. "Please fuck me, Ev. I need you filling me." Her words are my undoing, and I hold her hips tight and slide into her, feeling my skin prickle. Nothing feels as good as being inside of her.

"Yes," she hisses, locking her legs tighter as my pace picks up. Thumbing her clit, my eyes move from where my cock is disappearing inside of her, her breasts that her hands are cupping, her hair spread out on the counter, and her eyes closed with her lips parted.

"Fuck, you're perfect," I hiss through my teeth, grinding my hips into hers while my thumb works faster. Feeling her start to convulse, I pull her up with my hand behind her neck. Her fingers dig into my shoulders, and I cover her mouth with mine, thrusting my tongue inside, tangling it with hers while her silky walls clamp down around me, making me come hard and fast. Slowing my strokes, I glide in and out of her before planting myself deep at the root.

Our mouths never separate, even as we both pant for breath and she whispers, "I love you."

Moving my mouth from hers, I drop my forehead to her chest. "I love you too," I tell her, wrapping my arms around her back, even though those words do not even begin to define the way I feel for her.

"I won't ask you to help with the wedding anymore," she says quietly after a long moment, while her hands trail down my back.

Pulling back, I hold her face gently in my hands and kiss her, whispering, "Thank you."

"You could have said something." Her hands move to my jaw while her eyes watch her fingers glide over my beard. "I just assumed you'd want to be a part of it."

"I can't speak for all men, 'cause I'm sure some guys get off on shit like planning weddings, but that's not me, beautiful."

"I kind of know that now." She smiles, lifting her eyes to meet mine. "My mom was actually surprised by your involvement this week. She said she would have to tie my dad to the chair if she wanted to discuses flowers and stuff with him. And you made it through five days of not only flowers, but cakes, colors, and venues." She grins, moving her fingers to glide over my lips.

"I would do anything for you, baby, even sit through that shit all over again."

"So you're saying you'll be here when my mom comes over later?" she asks, biting her lip.

"Fuck no," I groan, and she drops her forehead to my chest, breaking into a fit of laughter that I feel in my dick, which is still semi-hard and deep inside of her.

"It was worth a shot." She giggles then squeaks as I lift her off the counter.

"I will, however, continue to entertain you until she gets here," I mutter, lifting her up slightly before dropping her back down on my cock, letting her feel that I'm ready to go again. It doesn't take much for her to get me hard. Hell, her fucking voice is enough to put me on edge.

"Oh," she moans, locking her arms around my neck, while I carry her back to the bedroom. Keeping my promise, I entertain her while she rides me, and then I take her into the shower and entertain her with my mouth, making her come twice more before carrying her half-asleep to the bed, where I leave her with a deep, wet kiss and a promise to see her in a few hours.

"YO," SAGE GREETS, sliding into the booth across from me, pushing a yellow folder across the table toward me before looking across the bar at the waitresses. With a lift of his chin, he calls her over.

"I'm guessing since you have this"—I hold up the envelope—"you got something."

His eyes come back to me. "Not sure," he mutters, then looks at the waitress when she comes to stand at our table.

"What can I get you?" she asks quietly, avoiding looking at him in the eyes.

"Just a beer. Whatever you have that's cold," he says, and she nods before wandering off toward the bar.

Opening the envelope when she's gone, I pull out a stack of photos and flip through them. Nico's been working on closing up the loose ends on his case, while Wes and the guys have been building theirs. We know for a fact Jordan is attempting to build up alliances within the club. What we don't know is exactly who he's convinced to follow along with him, so Wes asked me to recruit Sage to see what he could find out. Scanning the photos, I pause on one and study it.

"What is it?" Sage asks, and I flip the photo over and push it across the table.

"When was this taken?" I tap the picture of Jordan standing outside next to his bike, talking to a woman, a woman I swear I've seen before, but can't place.

Picking up the picture, his eyes scan it and he shrugs. "Last Saturday night, I followed him to a bar downtown. When he got there, he didn't go inside. He stayed on his bike, parked out back for about ten minutes, before she came out the backdoor to talk to him."

"Why does she look familiar?" I ask myself, studying the picture.

"I don't know. Did you hook up with her?" he questions, and my eyes narrow when they meet his. "Do not fucking go there," I growl.

"Just asking, man. I don't know who she is." He frowns, looking at the picture. "He gave her something. I couldn't see what it was from where I was parked. But I did notice she made sure to keep herself away from him, even when he tried to reach out and touch her. She moved away before he could make contact."

"Fuck," I clip, realizing that the woman belongs to one of the new members. I haven't seen her more than a couple times, but studying the picture, I know it's her. "That motherfucker."

"What?" Sage asks, and I pull out my cell phone, hit Harlen's number, and press Call.

"This better be good," Harlen says, answering on the third ring.

"What was the name of the bar?" I ask, looking at Sage, who is watching me closely.

"What?" Harlen asks in my ear, while Sage says, "Dakota's."

"Does Lee's woman work at a bar called Dakota's?" I ask into the phone, watching the waitress come back our way with Sage's beer, setting it on the table before taking off once more without another word.

"Yeah, why?" Harlen asks, and I grit my teeth.

"Jordan paid her a visit last weekend and gave her something. I don't know what he gave her or what they talked about, but I can fucking guess."

"You've got to be shitting me," Harlen growls, knowing exactly what I'm saying.

A few months before Lee was discharged from the marines after being injured, his daughter was diagnosed with leukemia. The insurance the military provided prior to his discharge was enough to make sure his little girl got the care she needed, but now that he's no longer in the military, his benefits have been cut. Fucking Jordan knows that shit, and my guess is he's using it to get to him.

"How many men has he gotten to using this same tactic?"

"I don't know, but I'm going to find out. I'll get back to you," Harlen clips, hanging up.

Setting my cell down, I move through the pictures again, slowly this time, and notice more than once that Jordan has met up with women. None of them are women I'm familiar with, but that doesn't mean shit, since I don't really pay attention to who the guys are spending their time with. Rubbing my hands down my face, I fight the urge to pick up my half-empty beer bottle and toss it across the bar.

"You good, man?" Sage asks quietly, settling his elbows on the table and leaning forward.

"No," I grit out.

"It—" His words cut off and his jaw tightens when his eyes move over my shoulder. "Fuck," he growls, tightening his fingers around the bottle in his hand. Turning my head, I spot Kim walking toward the bar with her boyfriend. "I'm out, man. Call me if you need anything else."

My eyes move back to him as he pulls cash from his pocket, tossing it on the table before stalking to the door without a backward glance. Looking over to where Kim is standing, I see her eyes fixed on the door that Sage just left through and shake my head. Eventually, one of them will give in to the obvious pull they feel and when they do everyone better stand back.

Chapter 14

June

"SO WE AGREE the colors are peach, taupe, and pearl?" Mom asks, looking across the cluttered table at me, and I nod.

The first week of wedding planning was exciting. The second week of wedding planning was fun. The third week of wedding planning has me wanting to jump out a window. Everyday, I'm more and more tempted to throw in the reins and tell Evan to book us a flight to Vegas and let Elvis marry us.

"And the cake. Do you still like the chocolate one with the raspberry filling?" she questions, jotting something down in her notebook. A notebook that would put the world's best wedding planner to shame. "I kind of liked the vanilla spice one, but it's your wedding," she mutters absently to herself before I can answer, and I roll my eyes. I don't even think this wedding could be defined as "mine" anymore. I love my mom, but she has lost her damn mind and gone Momzilla all over this damn ceremony.

"Mom, it's almost ten. How about we work on this again in a few days?" I yawn, looking toward the bedroom, where I know Evan is hiding away, watching TV with Ninja. Both of them are smart enough to stay out of sight when my mom's here. It's crazy, but I miss him. We live together and I see him every day, but I miss him. This wedding planning business is ruining my life. I could totally be having sex right now, but instead, I'm confirming things I've already confirmed a hundred and fifty-two billion times.

"We just need to go over a few more things," she says, dropping her pen to the table so she can move some of the swatches and things around on its surface, while muttering to herself under her breath.

"I'll be right back," I tell her, but know she is so lost in La-La Wedding Land that she doesn't hear me. Going to the living room, I look for my cell there, and then head to the laundry room to do the same, before finally finding it in the kitchen under the mail Evan brought in when he came home. Pulling up the text to my dad, I slam my fingers down on my keys in rapid, annoyed succession.

Dad, do whatever you have to do, but get the crazy woman you call your wife out of my house NOW! before I kill her.

I press Send then watch a bubble appear on the screen, letting me know he's replying.

On it, June Bug.

Sighing in relief, I move back to the table, just as my mom's cell rings, and take a seat, praying my torture is almost over. Picking up her phone, she looks at it and shakes her head then presses a button, making it go silent.

"Don't you want to answer that?" I ask in a panic, as she goes back to writing stuff down in her notebook.

"It's just your dad. He can wait until we're done."

Dropping my head to the top of the table, I debate just leaving her and heading for my room. *At this point, she might not even notice,* I think, as her phone starts to ring again.

"Mom, your phone is ringing," I point out, watching her silence it once again.

"He can wait," she repeats then glares at my phone when it starts to ring. "Do not answer that." Her tone is one I know to obey, one she's used since I was little. Biting my lip, I sit back and listen to my cell ring and ring before going to voicemail.

"Now," she continues when my phone goes silent. "I think the venue is a toss-up between Southhall Meadows and Springtree Farms. I called both, and if we book either one by the weekend, they can lock in the date."

"Both are nice," I say absently, looking at the cupboard above the fridge where I keep my tequila. Maybe if I'm drunk, this won't feel like torture. Hell, maybe I can convince her to take a few shots and she'll pass out.

"Asher called me. He said answer your phone," Evan says, scaring the crap out of me when he steps into the room, wearing a pair of loose sweats and a white shirt that fits him snug, showing off the muscles of his torso. Coming up behind me, he rests his hands on my shoulders then leans down, kissing the top of my head.

"He called you too?" Mom frowns, looking at Evan, then drops her eyes to her phone when it starts to ring again. "Hello," she answers on the second ring, then pauses, turning her body away from Evan and me. "Asher," she hisses then mutters, "Fine, but I'm not happy, so you will not be happy either."

"Is this the kind of thing I have to look forward to?" Evan asks, and I tilt my head back to look up at him, shrugging, which makes him shake his head, grin, and pull me up out of the chair so he can kiss me.

"Well, apparently I've been summoned by your father," Mom says, rolling her eyes. "I'll be over tomorrow, and we'll talk about the stuff we didn't get settled tonight, since I need to get home."

"Next week," Evan cuts in before I can say anything, and my mom looks at him with wide eyes.

"We're planning your wedding, a wedding that we only have a couple months to plan. We have so much to do. We can't stop now," Mom sputters, and Evan shakes his head, wrapping his arm around my waist and bringing me even closer.

"Next week. June needs a break. She's been running herself ragged.

You guys can get back to planning after the weekend."

Mom's eyes move from Evan to me, and whatever she sees makes her eyes go soft. "Oh, all right, next week," she agrees, surprising me. "But we really do need to get the details ironed out."

"I promise we'll sort everything out next week," I agree, and she reaches out, touching my cheek softly.

"I just want your wedding to be perfect," she whispers, making me feel like an ass for just wanting the whole thing over with.

"I know," I whisper back, stepping forward and giving her a tight hug. Leaning back, she searches my face for a moment then kisses my cheek.

"I better hurry and pack up, so I can get home before your dad calls again or shows up." She rolls her eyes, letting me go so she can drag the large suitcase she came in with back toward the table, where all the contents that were inside of it are now scattered.

"Jesus, do you really need all of this shit?" Evan asks, taking the suitcase from my mom once we have it packed and zipped. "This bag has to weigh at least thirty pounds."

"We're not planning a party. We're planning a wedding, so yes, I do need all of that shit." She glares at him, the same way she would glare at my dad when he's annoyed her.

"Just asking." Evan grins, and Mom's eyes narrow on his mouth before her head swings in my direction.

"He's just as bad as your father." She tosses her thumb over at Evan. "Your dad complained for an hour after I made him go up into the attic to get the suitcase. He said it was crazy that I needed a suitcase to haul around wedding planning stuff."

"It's a little crazy." I shrug, smiling at her, and she looks at the bag in Evan's hand. I can tell she's wondering if maybe, just maybe, she's going a wee-bit overboard. "I love your crazy, Mom. So it's okay," I say softly after a moment.

I know she's doing all of this because she loves me. I'm lucky to have a mom like her, a mom who would twist herself into knots to make me happy and to give me the perfect wedding. Both my parents could have decided they hated Evan without ever getting to know him after what happened between us, but they didn't. No, they weren't waiting with open arms to embrace him, but they did trust my judgment enough to give him a chance to prove himself.

"Love you too, honey." She smiles then leans her head back, looking at the ceiling, when her cell phone rings in her hand. Putting it to her ear, she snaps, "I'm walking out of her house as we speak, Asher Mayson."

Giggling, I turn my eyes to Evan, and the air in my lungs freezes when I see the tender look on his face pointed at me. If I weren't madly in love with him already, that one look would have sealed the deal. *I love you,* I mouth, and his eyes soften even further.

"I don't know how I put up with that man," Mom grumbles, breaking into the moment between Evan and me.

"You love Dad."

"I must," she gripes, heading for the door.

Following her out to her SUV, Evan puts her bag into the trunk, while I give her another hug and a promise to call her. Then, I watch while Evan gives her a hug of his own and a quiet thanks, that makes her smile and pat his cheek before getting in behind the wheel, slamming the door.

"Your mom's awesome," Evan mutters, while we watch her back out of the driveway.

"I know," I agree, waving back at her, while Evan wraps his arm around my shoulders.

"Are you tired?" he asks, sliding his hand down my arm and locking his fingers with mine as he leads me back into the house.

"Totally exhausted," I reply through a yawn.

"Too tired to sit on my face?" he asks, and my hand spasms in his as the image of me doing just that filters through my mind.

"I think I could keep my eyes open for that," I breathe, as he locks the door and sets the alarm.

Turning me toward him, he mumbles, "Figure you could," against my mouth, while wrapping his arms around me and walking me backward toward the bedroom, where I keep my eyes open for a lot more than just sitting on his face.

"COMING!" I SHOUT, walking with my freshly pink-painted fingers spread wide apart, as I head for the front door when the bell rings. Without looking through the peephole, I swing the door open and feel my body go tight when I see who is standing on my front porch, looking exactly the same as the last time I saw him.

"June," Lane says. I start to push the door closed, but his hand shoots out, preventing me from slamming it in his face. "I just want to talk."

"I have nothing to say to you. Go away." I try again to shut the door, but his hand stays planted against it, stopping me.

"I want to apologize. Please, let me say sorry."

"Done. You've said it, so go." I push harder then growl in frustration when he doesn't move away.

"I know you're pissed at me, but did you get the letter I sent you?"

"I got it, I read it, and I still don't care. We have nothing to talk about. Please step back."

"Are you…" he trails off, zeroing in on my hand. "Is that an engagement ring?"

"Lane, if you don't step back, I swear to God I'm going to scream bloody murder," I hiss, ignoring his question.

"You're getting married?"

"Oh, my God!" I cry in frustration. "Yes, I'm getting married. Will you just leave now?"

His brows draw together and his head shakes. "I was in love with you."

"You wouldn't know what love was if it hit you upside the head. I'm only going to say it one more time. Please step away from my door and leave."

His eyes move back to my hand and his voice drops low. "I fucked up."

He did fuck up—not that I was ever even close to being in love with him. But I did care about him, and who knows what could have happened with time. But then again, even if I was with him and Evan came back into my life, I probably would have wanted to find out where things could go with Evan, because the connection I've always had with him is just that strong.

"Who is he?" he asks quietly, moving his eyes to meet mine.

"That's none of your business."

"Is it your ex? The one you were so hung up on?" he asks on a growl, banging his hand against the door.

"Lane, please go," I beg softly. The way he's acting is starting to scare me.

"It is, isn't it?" he asks, turning red while the pulse in his neck beats wildly.

"Yes," I finally say, hoping he'll leave once I give him what he wants.

"I hope he makes you happy," he snarls, dropping his hand from the door, but he keeps his body where it is and my pulse speeds up.

"Lane, please, just go," I whisper shakily, but he doesn't move his body from the doorway or his angry eyes from mine.

"Step back." Looking over Lane's shoulder, I watch as Evan steps up onto the porch. I didn't hear him pull up, which is crazy, since he rode his bike today, and I always hear him when he's on his bike.

"Whatever." Lane glares at me before moving past Evan down the steps.

Watching his retreating back, I feel Evan get close before he blocks my view. Then, his fingers are on my chin, lifting my eyes to meet his. "Go inside. I'll be in, in a minute."

"Don't do anything that will lead to me visiting you in jail," I whisper-yell, resting my hands against his chest, feeling the anger coming off him in waves.

"Go inside," he repeats, putting his hand to my stomach, pushing me back an inch before pulling the door closed, shutting me inside.

Debating with myself about ignoring his order, I mutter, "Shit," and head back to the living room, so I can call my uncle. That's when I see Ninja through the glass of the backdoor snarling and barking up a storm. "It's okay," I coo, as he runs past me into the house toward the front door, coming back a moment later and taking a seat close to me. I leave a voicemail for my uncle, telling him that Lane is at the house, outside with Evan. When my phone rings a minute later, he tells me that he's on his way and to stay inside then hangs up.

Rolling my eyes at that, I take a seat on the couch. A few minutes later, I jump in place when the door slams and Evan's boots stomp down the hall. "Why did you open the door to him?" he asks, stopping at the mouth of the living room, planting his feet wide apart, and crossing his arms over his chest.

"I didn't know it was him," I explain quietly, licking my lips nervously when his eyes narrow.

"You didn't check the peephole?" His body language and tone make it obvious I fucked up.

"If I had, I wouldn't have opened the door."

"Do not fucking get smart with me right now!" he roars, making me jump again.

"I'm not." I stand, needing and wanting to gain some control of the situation. "I wasn't even thinking."

"He could have forced you inside the house, June. He could have done something to hurt you."

"He didn't." I frown then, like an idiot, continue, "He wouldn't do that."

"Are you sure about that?" he thunders, leaning forward with his hands on his waist.

Swallowing, I close my eyes, because I know he's right. I have no idea what Lane would do. I didn't even know his name was Lane until I was dragged into the police station in the middle of the night. And that guy who was outside on the front porch wasn't the Lane I knew.

"I'm sorry," I whisper after a moment, feeling tears burn my throat as I try to swallow them down.

"Come here." Opening my eyes, my gaze connects with his still pissed-off one.

"You're mad," I state the obvious, while keeping my feet planted where they are.

"I'm fucking furious, beautiful, but I still want you to come here." He points to the ground where he's standing.

"I feel safer over here."

"June," he warns, and my feet move. As soon as I'm close, his arms shoot out, wrapping around me, and his face drops to my neck, where he breathes in deep.

"I'm sorry. I won't answer the door without looking again," I whisper, circling my arms around his back.

"I know you won't," he rumbles against the skin of my neck, holding me tighter.

Running my hands down his back, I ask softly, "Are you okay?"

"I knew who he was when I pulled up to the house and saw him standing in the doorway. I saw your face and could tell you were scared. I wanted to fucking kill him for putting that look on your face."

"He was fine at first, but then he saw my engagement ring and got angry," I explain, and my hands start to shake.

"You have nothing to fear," he vows, pulling away to look at me. "Nothing," he repeats, and I drop my forehead to his chest, feeling his lips at the crown of my head.

"Will you be okay for a few, while I go out and talk to your uncle?"

"Yeah." I nod against his chest and his hands move to my jaw, tilting my head back. "I'm sorry," I repeat once more, while holding his concerned gaze.

"I love you, baby, so fucking much that even the idea of you breathing that motherfucker's air pisses me off." His forehead touches mine and I watch his eyes close briefly. "I'm not mad at you, okay?"

"Okay," I agree, fisting my hands in his tee while his words wash through me.

"Give me a few minutes, yeah?"

"Yeah." His mouth touches mine in a soft kiss, that lets me know we're okay, before he lets me go and disappears down the hall.

"DON'T ANSWER THE door again without Ninja being in the house," Evan instructs, and I tilt my head back to look up at him from my position against his chest in bed.

"I won't." After Evan came back in from talking to my uncle, he didn't mention Lane's visit again. Even after he noticed that the back door had bite marks in the wood around the doorjamb and saliva all over the glass from Ninja's barking, when he was trying to get inside, sensing in his doggie way that his mom was in trouble. When Evan saw the damage, I explained that Ninja had been outside when the doorbell rang. With us not having a doggie door and it being the middle of summer, I had shut the door, leaving Ninja out in the backyard, so I didn't lose the cooled air in the house while he wandered the grass for hours. Something he loves to do. I could tell he was pissed, but he didn't say anything about it until now.

"Your uncle is going to talk to the judge tomorrow about getting a restraining order. Now that he's made contact, we've got a better chance of getting it approved," he says, pulling me out of my thoughts. I sit up, putting my elbow into the bed, so I can look down at him.

"Do you think he'll be back?" I ask, and his fingers run through my hair, sliding it over my bare shoulder.

"I want to say no, but I can't guarantee he won't."

"Great." I sigh, dropping to my back and covering my face.

His hands wrap around mine, pulling them from my face, and his eyes go hard. "It will be okay."

"I believe you." I lift my hands, running my fingers over his jaw, watching as his eyes soften. "As long as I have you, I have nothing to worry about. I know that, down to my soul," I get out, before his head drops to mine and he kisses me, making me forget about everything.

"OH…" MY LEGS tense and my eyes blink open, seeing the early morning light spilling across the ceiling.

"Morning."

Looking down the length of my body, I catch Evan's wicked grin before his face lowers between my legs and his hands cup my ass, bringing me deeper into his mouth. Waking primed and ready from his touch has become one of my favorite ways to start my day. The added fact that he seems to get off on it just as much as I do only makes me love it even more.

"Ev." My teeth dig into my bottom lip and my hands fist in his hair, when one finger then another enters me slowly, and his tongue circles my clit. Raising my hips higher, I silently beg for more.

"What the fuck?" he growls, and my foggy mind takes a moment to register that the doorbell is going off.

"Don't stop. They'll go away," I plead, not above begging.

"Make it fast, baby." His fingers work faster, curling up to hit my G-spot, and his mouth latches on to my clit, pulling hard, sending me spiraling through a short but sweet orgasm while the doorbell continues to chime.

"I'm gonna kill whoever's at the door." He knifes out of bed, tossing the blanket over the lower half of my naked body.

"Okay," I agree, and he grins with a shake of his head, roaming his eyes over me while pulling on his sweats.

"Don't move," he orders, growling, "Fuck," when I raise my arms over my head to stretch.

"The door," I remind him, as he stalks toward me.

"This better be good," he grumbles, turning and leaving the room without another look at the bed, where I'm sprawled out.

"Bitch, get your ass out here!" JJ yells, and I sit up and swing my eyes to the clock on the bedside table. I knew it was early, judging by the light coming in through the blinds, but it's not even 7:00 yet.

"What the hell?" Rolling out of bed, I rush to the bathroom and pull on my robe, tying it around my waist, then stop at my dresser and slip on a pair of panties before leaving the room. When I make it to the kitchen, Evan is standing near the coffeepot, watching JJ, who has made herself at home in the kitchen, where she is currently rummaging through the fridge.

"Is everything okay?" I ask, and her head pops up out of the fridge so she can glare at me.

"I don't know." She tosses some lunchmeat onto the counter, along with a jar of mayo, and then stomps to the breadbox, opening it up and pulling out a loaf of bread. "I haven't seen or heard from you in three weeks, and I had to find out from Brew, of all people, that my girl is engaged. What the fuck?" she asks, putting her hands on her hips.

"I suck," I mutter, feeling horrible for not calling her with my good news. But honestly there has been so much on my mind lately including the fact I found out a few days ago that I'm pregnant. I'm still in shock from seeing the two pink lines on the test I took and have been trying to find a way to tell Evan we're going to have a baby.

"You don't suck, but Jesus…could have called me," she says, opening drawers and closing them until she finds what she's looking for. "I better be invited to the wedding."

"You are," I agree. "Do you want help?" I ask as she massacres the sandwich she's attempting to throw together.

"No." She smushes the two pieces of bread together with turkey meat and mayo in-between them. "When Brew told me your news this morning, I left before I could finish making my lunch." She grabs a paper towel, wrapping her sandwich in it.

"Oh," I mumble, shooting a glance in Evan's direction, who hasn't moved from his position near the coffeepot. I can tell by his expression, that he doesn't know whether to laugh or yell.

"Now, let me see your ring." Holding out my hand toward her, she takes my hand in hers and looks the ring over. "It's beautiful. I'm happy for you," she says quietly, meeting my gaze.

"Thank you, JJ. I'm sorry I didn't call."

"Don't worry about it. You can pay me back with tequila one night." She grins then looks over at Evan. "You did good." He lifts his chin, and she shakes her head then looks at me, smiling. "I gotta go to work, but we'll get together soon."

"I'll call you," I promise, then watch her leave down the hall, carrying the sandwich she made.

"That chick's crazy," Evan mutters, grabbing a mug and pouring himself a cup of coffee.

"She's sweet." I grin, and he looks at the counter, where all of her sandwich supplies are still laid out, and raises a brow.

"I'm thinking she'd kick your ass if you ever called her that to her face."

He was probably right, but instead of confirming that, I just go to the counter and put everything away. Leaning back against it once I'm done, I cross my arms over my chest. "Are you hungry?" I ask, and his eyes rake over me from head to toe, making me shiver.

"My morning meal was rushed. Are you offering to get back into bed and spread your legs for me?"

Looking at the clock on the microwave, I pray I have time, hearing him laugh when I do. "I need to get ready for work," I pout, which makes him laugh harder.

Closing the short distance between us, his hands move to my hips and his face dips to mine. "Go get ready." He kisses me softly, moving his hands down to squeeze my ass. "I'll bring you coffee."

"I don't mind being late," I breathe, pressing closer to him while wrapping my arms around his neck.

Smiling, he kisses me once more then takes my arms from around him and moves a step back. "You can't be late. It's your last day," he reminds me. Today is the last day of summer school, and hopefully, the day I find out if I'm teaching next year.

"I guess I'll just go get ready." I sigh, hearing his laughter behind me as I leave the kitchen and head for the shower, so I can get ready for work.

"HAVE A GOOD rest of the summer, guys." I smile at my students leaving the classroom, gaining, "You too, Ms. Mayson," or "Later," from each of them as they pass by one-by-one. I know they are all as excited as I am to get out of here so they can enjoy a couple weeks of sleeping in and no homework before school starts back up.

Once they're all gone, I grab my bag from my desk and lock up the class. I can't wait to tell Evan that I was offered the full-time teaching position. I knew there was a good chance I would get the job, but with teaching, you never know if you will be passed up for someone with more experience. Lucky for me, my summer of teaching paid off, and I now have a full-time job and my own classroom teaching third graders starting in two short weeks.

Making my way across the lot to my car, my cell phone rings from my bag. I stop and dig it out, smiling huge when I see Evan is calling. "Hey," I answer, then frown when I hear shuffling and muffled voices that I can't make out coming from the other end. "Evan?" I call, gaining no answer in return. My hand that is wrapped around the phone clenches and my vision clouds when someone roars, "You motherfuckers are dead!"

Running for my car, I swing the door open and get in. As soon as the car is started, the phone connects to the Bluetooth and the sound off muffled voices fills the quiet space. "What do I do? What do I do?" I whisper to myself, as I put my car in drive. I don't want to hang up the call, but I need to call the police. I really need to know where to send the police.

"Fuck you, Wes," I make out through the garbled mess of rustling and stifled voices. Praying that my assumption is right and that they are at the bike shop I pull over to the side of the road. Picking up my cell phone I look at the screen, knowing there has to be a way to connect more than one call. Finding the feature I'm looking for, I put the call from Evan on hold and dial 911.

"911, what's your emergency?" a man answers.

"My fiancé called me on accident," I get out through pants, while my hands shake franticly.

"Ma'am, this is 911—"

"I know that!" I cut him off, shrieking into the car. "He called me on accident, but I think he's in trouble. You have to help."

"Okay, calm down and tell me what you heard."

"I couldn't make out much, but I heard my brother-in-law's name and someone saying something about people dying. I think they are at the Broken Eagles' bike repair shop," I say, listening to him type. "His call is still on hold. Can I join your call with his?"

"Do that now, honey," he says, so I press the button to connect the two calls and as soon as I do, two gunshots go off, one right after another.

"Oh, God." I put my car in drive, needing to get to Evan, not hearing anything else the dispatcher says. As soon as I arrive, I see the whole place surrounded by cop cars. Spotting Uncle Nico, I get out, leaving the car on and the door open. I rush to where he's standing, ignoring the officers yelling at me to get back into my car.

"June," Uncle Nico says, as soon as he sees me running toward him.

"What's going on? Is Evan okay?"

"Honey, you need to get back into your car."

"Tell me now!" I scream, and his face softens. Taking my hand, he leads me to one of the squad cars, settles me in the backseat, and then gets down on his haunches in front of me.

"It's not safe right now," he says, gently wiping my face that I hadn't even realized is soaked with tears.

"Tell me what's going on. Please tell me that Evan is okay," I whisper, feeling more tears track down my cheeks.

"We know there are at least two armed suspects inside the building. Right now, that's all the information we have."

"I heard gunshots," I say in a panic, wondering if Evan's been shot, if one of those shots was aimed at him.

"I need you to take some deep breaths and wait here while I talk to my men. Can you do that for me?"

Covering my face, I nod and start to pray.

Chapter 15

Evan

THE BEAST WITHIN me has awoken and is out for vengeance. Seeing blood seeping out of the wound in Harlen's shoulder, I move without thought from my kneeling position and tackle Jordan to the ground, with my shoulder in his stomach. On impact, his gun flies out of his hand and skids across the floor.

I knew something was up when I pulled up to the shop and found the place empty. There is always at least one guy working on a car or bike in the middle of the day, even during lunchtime. When I walked through the compound in search of everyone and entered the common room, the sight that greeted me sent chills down my spine. I didn't have time to think or make a phone call. I barely had time to hit Call on my last call and shove my cell in my back pocket before Jordan and one other man that were holding the guys at gunpoint spotted me.

"Motherfucker," I snarl, getting my hands around Jordan's throat. As I watch his face turn purple and his body jerk, I register the sound of fighting breaking out around me. Jordan's fingers rip at my hands.

"Don't kill him," someone says. But it's too late. Watching his eyes start to slide closed, I feel his pulse beneath my fingers slow and I add more pressure. "Evan." I hear my name through the fog, but my vision has tunneled with one goal in mind. Getting tackled from the side, I roar, fighting back with everything in me, but then a sharp pain hits my skull and everything goes black.

My eyes squeeze tight and my hands move to my head, putting pressure on my skull, which feels like it's been cracked open. "What the fuck?" I hiss in pain.

"Oh, God," I hear June whimper, as her weight settles deeper into my side and her arm wraps over my waist. Holding her to me, I breathe through the pain in my head and freeze when memories of what happened come back to me full-force. "The guys? Harlen?" I try to sit up, but her small body holds me to the bed.

"They're okay," her small voice says, while her fingers run along my neck, and my eyes blink open. "Harlen is okay." She shifts, moving to look down at me, and that's when I realize I'm in a hospital room.

"Why'm I here?" I frown, looking around the small sterile room, trying to recall what happened after Harlen was shot, but I draw a blank.

"You had an episode," she says gently, running her eyes and hands over me.

"Episode?" I repeat, trying to understand what she's saying.

"The guys said you went crazy. They couldn't get you to calm down. You kept going after Jordan, even after he was unconscious and the other man was disarmed."

"Christ." I close my eyes, feeling her head rest against my chest and her arms tighten around my middle.

"I was so scared," she whispers, burrowing closer.

Rolling us to the side, I tuck her into my front and run my hands down her back as I listen to her cry. "It's okay," I murmur gently, feeling her body rock with the force of her tears.

"Wh… When I heard the gunsh… shots, I thought—"

"I'm fine," I cut her off before she can finish. "I'm here. I'm not going anywhere," I vow. Her head tips back and her tear-filled eyes meet mine.

"Don't ever scare me like that again," she demands, and I fight a smile that catches me off guard.

"I won't."

"And you're not allowed to help my uncle anymore. I forbid it," she continues, closing her eyes.

"It will be okay." I kiss her forehead, rest my chin on the top of her head, and then wrap her up in my arms.

"I need to tell the doctor and everyone else that you're awake," she mumbles into my chest, but snuggles into my side.

"In a minute," I mumble back, then close my eyes and wonder what the fuck happened and why I can't remember any of it.

"FUCK, MAN, I'M glad you're okay," Wes mumbles, after taking a seat in the chair next to the hospital bed, where I'm laid up with a sleeping June tucked to my front.

She didn't tell the doctor I was awake. She fell asleep, and I didn't bother waking her; I just pressed the buzzer for the nurses' station and let them know I was up and needed something for my head. Soon after that, the doctor came in to check me over and tell me that they were keeping me overnight for observation. Apparently, in my fight to get to Jordan to end him, Wes was left with no choice but to knock me out, leaving me unconscious with a minor concussion.

"You ever think of going MMA?" I joke, and his jaw clenches.

"You scared us, brother," he growls, looking away from me. "There were three of us on you, and we still couldn't control you." His head shakes before his eyes meet mine once more.

"I don't remember any of it. My last memory is of Jordan pointing the gun at Harlen and pulling the trigger," I admit, running my hand down my face.

"We knew you weren't yourself. I knew I had to stop you from doing something you'd regret. Even if that motherfucker does deserve to pay for what he's done, you don't deserve to live with his death on your conscience," he says quietly, dropping his eyes to June for a second before meeting my gaze again. "If you hadn't shown—"

"Don't say it," I rumble, feeling June's body tense against mine. I know from my talk with Nico earlier that Jordan's plan didn't involve anyone leaving the compound alive. Jordan's father had been taken down early in the morning, and he knew the cops were on the hunt for him and the rest of their crew.

"You know you have my heart, brother."

"Same," I agree, holding his gaze, meaning that shit to the bottom of my soul.

Nodding, he stands, tucking his hands in his pockets. "I better go, and just so you know, the girls are already planning a get-together for when you get home, so rest up while you can." He smiles for the first time since entering the room, and I shake my head, not even a little surprised by the news.

"How's Harlen?" I ask when he reaches the door.

"Guy's a brick house. It'll take a lot more than one bullet to knock him down."

"True." Lifting my chin, I watch the door close behind him then put my fingers under June's chin and lift up. "I know you're awake, beautiful."

"How long have I been asleep?" She yawns, looking around.

"Awhile."

"Has the doctor come in?" She frowns, trying to sit up, but I hold her in place.

"You slept through everyone coming in, including your family," I say, gently running my thumb over her bottom lip then under her eyes. "You look tired."

"I'm okay."

"You should go home and get some re—"

"I'm not leaving you," she says, cutting me off, resting her hand against my cheek. "What did the doctor say?"

"I have to stay overnight for observation," I reply, watching her fill with worry. "It's just a precaution. They want to make sure I'm okay."

"Oh." She deflates, relaxing into me. "*Are* you okay?"

Her soft words give me pause. I know she's not talking about my head, but about my episode.

"I'll talk to someone when I'm released," I reassure her, moving my hand up the back of her shirt so I can touch her skin.

Her eyes search my face for a moment, then her voice softly asks, "Has it ever happened before?"

"Not to me, but I know it's not uncommon," I say, and her face gentles as her hand on my cheek moves so her fingers can slide over my mouth.

"I love you," she whispers after a moment.

"I know you do," I agree, and her head shakes back and forth.

"You don't. You don't understand that it's impossible for me to breathe without you. I can't mak—"

"Baby," I cut her off, not wanting her to go there.

"I'm pregnant," she blurts, and my body freezes. "I'm sorry. I had this whole big plan of how I wanted to tell you tonight, but after today, I really want you to know it's not only you and me anymore. We ha—"

"You're pregnant?" I interrupt, while the words ring in my ears.

"Yes."

"How long have you known?"

"A few days. I was—"

"You're having my baby?" I confirm, cutting her off again and moving my eyes to her stomach briefly.

"Yes." She frowns, studying me. "Are you okay?"

"Fuck, you're pregnant," I rumble, letting the fact that the woman I love is carrying my child wash over me. "Maybe we should have the doctor check you over." I grab the call button only to have it slapped out of my hand.

"I'm not having the doctor check me, we are fine the baby is fine."

She rolls her eyes.

"Fuck your pregnant." I shake my head in disbelief and move my hand to her still flat stomach. "We're going to Vegas."

"Oh, my God. I tell you I'm pregnant, and you lose your mind." She laughs laying down on the bed covering her face.

"I love you, and we're going to Vegas. We're not waiting for you and your mom to plan a wedding. We're getting married now." I loom over her, resting my hand lightly back on her stomach.

"We are not getting married in Vegas. Don't be crazy," she snaps, smacking my arm. "We're getting married in three months. The wedding is almost all planned, and Momzilla will lose her mind if you try to take the wedding from her."

"Momzilla?"

I smile, and she rolls her eyes then slides them back down to meet mine, asking softly, "Are you happy?"

"No, baby. What I am can't be described as happy." I kiss her gently then rub her stomach. "You're really pregnant?"

Her face softens and her hands hold my face. "You're going to be a dad, the best dad in the world." Looking into her beautiful face, I know that as long as I have her, I will work myself to death to prove her words to be true.

"You're seeing the doctor before we leave the hospital." I mutter then cover her mouth with mine before she can reply.

"BYE!" JUNE YELLS, as JJ leaves with Brew to walk across the yard to their house. Wes was not lying about the party June's sisters, mom, and aunts were putting together.

As soon as we got home from the hospital, everyone showed up with food and drinks. Harlen, who was also released today, even made it for a couple hours before Nico's daughter Harmony, who happens to be studying to be a nurse, offered to give him a ride home after seeing his wound was bothering him. The big guy didn't know what to do with the bossy little chick. I had to admit, they fit in that whole "opposites attract" kind of way, but watching Nico watch Harlen with his daughter was comical as hell. I thought the guy was going to lose it. On the plus side the doctor checked June over before I was released and everything looked perfect.

"That was fun." June smiles, shutting the door behind our last guest, and I turn her around and move us down the hall with my hands on her ass. "Are you feeling okay?" she questions, studying me with her hands against my chest.

"Nope," I mutter, dropping my mouth to her neck, licking up to her ear.

"What's wrong?" she breathes, trying to pull her face back.

"I need to be inside of you." I nip her ear and her hands slide around my neck as her body softens into mine. Moving into the bedroom, I lift her then dig one knee into the bed then the other, before dropping her to her back in the middle of the bed.

"You have a huge fucking family," I inform her, ripping her shirt off over her head. "And we have a lot of friends. I thought they would never leave."

"We have a huge family. They're your family now, too." She lifts her hips, panting, so I can drag her jeans shorts and panties down over her ass.

"I've been dying to be inside of you all night. I swear I was ready to kick everyone out hours ago." I unhook her bra and toss it behind me.

"They care about you," she hisses, as I cup her breasts and pinch her nipples.

"I know," I agree, leaning back to help her pull my tee off. "But they could have waited a week or two before showing up," I complain, and she laughs, cupping my cheek.

"Welcome to the family, honey. You will never be alone again." She smiles, and I smile back. As much as I hate to admit it, that shit feels good. "Now stop talking," she whispers, putting pressure on the back of my neck. Giving her what she wants, I kiss her then roam my hand down between her legs, finding her wet and ready for me.

"Ev," she moans, riding my fingers while my mouth covers her breast.

"I'm right here, baby."

"I need you inside of me." Removing my fingers from her, I lick them clean then kick off my jeans and move back between her still spread legs.

"I don't know if I can go soft," I tell her, pushing her hair back away from her face.

"Why would you need to be soft?" she asks, wrapping her hand around my cock, sliding it up and down.

"The baby."

"The baby is fine. Now, please, fuck me." She lifts her hips, and I sink slowly inside her.

"Harder," she begs, and I lean back, searching her eyes, picking up my pace. Her legs lift, wrapping me tight, and her back arches off the bed.

"Fuck," I growl, picking up the pace at seeing that she's close.

"Yesss." Her nails dig into my back as her pussy convulses around me, taking me with her through her orgasm.

"Home," I growl, looking into her beautiful eyes. "You are my home." I slide out then back in, burying my face in her neck and my cock deep.

"You're my home," she whispers into my ear. "I love you."

"I love you too, beautiful." I lean back to look at her, knowing I may have fucked up, but there was no way I would ever lose her again.

Epilogue

Three months later

"YOU MAY NOW kiss the bride."

At those words, I grab June around the waist, dip her backward, and cover her mouth with mine, while our family and friends cheer loudly. When I saw her coming down the aisle toward me, holding on to her dad's arm, I had to clench my fist so I didn't rush forward and drag her away from him toward the altar.

Ripping my mouth reluctantly from hers, I gaze down at her, knowing I'm the luckiest motherfucker on the planet. She's always beautiful, but wearing her off-the-shoulder, form-fitting ivory dress, with her skin glowing from pregnancy, her hair tied up, showing off her face and neck, she's breathtaking.

"I love you," she breathes, running her fingers over my lips, while her eyes fill with tears.

"Always, beautiful, until the day I die." I stand her with me, and a roar explodes around us. Lifting her up into my arms, I listen to her laugh while I carry her back down the aisle, hearing a few chuckles as we pass everyone without stopping.

"Where are we going?" June questions, as I head into the building, where we both got ready this afternoon.

"Your mom kept me from you last night. And today, I stayed away like she asked me to, but now you're my wife, all bets are off," I mutter, heading toward her dressing room. As soon as I reach her door, I growl, "Open it," then kick the door closed and move across the room to the couch, laying her down gently. "How hard would it be for me to take this dress off you?" I question, running my hands up the lace covering her sides and the intricate buttons along her back.

"It took twenty minutes for my mom and sisters to get it all buttoned." She laughs, tugging my face toward hers. "But we can make out." She smiles against my mouth and I thrust my tongue between her parted lips, covering her body with mine.

"If you two don't get out here right now, I swear I will break down this door!" November yells, breaking up our moment, and I look into June's smiling eyes and mutter, "Your mom is a nut."

"That's not my mom. That's Momzilla," she whispers, shoving her face into my neck, laughing when November pounds again. This time harder.

"We better get out there before she realizes the door isn't locked," I grumble, looking toward the door, surprised it hasn't opened already.

"We have a week of just us and a private beach," she says, reminding me softly about our wedding gift from her Uncle Trevor and Aunt Liz, who are letting us use their beach house in Jamaica for a week. A week during which I plan to take complete advantage of our time alone without family and drama. Not that there has been any more drama. Lane has stayed away since he was served with a restraining order, and I've been seeing someone about my episode. The wedding is the only thing that has been keeping me from having all of June, and as of today, that is over. Even though I have to admit, the reception hall and the wedding venue are perfect. All of June's late nights with her mom, sisters, and aunts have paid off. They did an amazing job.

"I don't want to share you with anyone. I didn't like being away from you last night or today," I admit, and her face goes soft.

"Just a few more hours."

"A few more hours," I agree, standing her with me, then move my hands to her hair and smooth it back into place. "You look beautiful."

"And you look very handsome in your tux. I can't believe mom actually talked you into wearing one."

"She didn't leave me a choice." I grin then search her face. "How are you feeling?"

"Fine." She smiles leaning into me. "I got a little sick this morning, but since then, I've been okay."

"I don't like that you were sick without me there to take care of you." I frown, moving my hands to her stomach.

"I wasn't sick, just nauseous, and it's normal, so get that look off your face." She shakes her head smiling.

"It's my job to worry about you," I remind her. Just then, the door swings open and November comes in with her eyes covered.

"You two better be decent!" she shouts toward the wall opposite us.

"Mom, you're safe." June laughs, and November uncovers her face and looks at the wall then swings her head toward us. "What are you doing? The reception is starting any minute."

"We're coming now. I just wanted a few minutes alone with my wife," I tell her, gently tucking June into my side.

"Oh," she says softly, looking between the two of us. "You could have just said that."

"You're in Momzilla mode. You would have stopped us," June informs her, and November's lips twitch.

"True," she agrees with a sigh. "I'll give you a few more minutes, but then I'm dragging you both out of here."

"We'll be out in a second, Mom," June says, and November nods then looks at me, and barks, "Don't mess up her hair. You still have pictures to take," before leaving the room, shutting the door behind her.

"Are you sure I can't take off your dress?" I ask, hearing November shout through the door, "Do it and die, Evan!"

Covering June's laughing mouth with my own, I pray silently that the night ends quickly.

"ARE YOU HAVING fun?" June asks from my side, and I look at her beautiful face then around the large, open room. Seeing all of our friends and family has made me realize how lucky I am. I may have had a shit childhood and fucked-up parents, who still to this day haven't gotten it together enough to think about their son, but I have good men at my back, and a woman at my side who fits me perfectly. And really, what else is there to ask for in life?

June

Four years later

FINALLY CATCHING MY daughter, who I'm pretty sure was put on this earth to make me nuts, I swing her up into my arms and turn to face an older gentleman when he taps me on my shoulder.

"Yes?" I ask, holding Tia's tiny hands down, so she can't bop me in the face as she yells for *candy, candy, candy,* which she is not getting any of. She doesn't need candy. Her on veggies and fruit is bad. Her on candy is my worst nightmare.

"Is that your boy?" the man asks, stepping to the side, and when he does, I feel my lips press tight.

I want to say no, that the little adorable hellion isn't mine, but he is—or he's all his dad's. "He's mine," I murmur, taking my daughter with me toward her brother, Conner, who is apparently using the automatic popcorn butter-dispensing machine to wash his hands in butter.

"Jesus," I hear Evan rumble from behind me, as the weight of his hand settles against my lower back. "I was gone for two minutes," he mutters in astonishment.

"Yep," I agree, trying not to laugh. "That is all yours." I watch him approach Conner, tug his hands out from under the streaming river of butter, and grab some napkins. Our life is insane, complete chaos. There is never a dull moment, but there is also never a moment I don't appreciate what we have.

The End

Until Ashlyn

Prologue

"**H**EY, MOM," I greet, tucking my phone between my ear and shoulder as I shove another dress and matching heels into my suitcase. I can't help but smile while I do because Dillon will likely flip his lid when he sees my choices in attire for the weekend, but there is not one damn thing he can do about it since we won't be in the office. So technically, his stupid rules don't apply.

"Are you all packed?"

"Almost." I sigh, looking at the clock and realize I only have ten minutes to finish before my cab is set to arrive. I wasn't planning on going to Vegas for the dental convention but Dillon insisted that he needed me with him, and like an idiot, I agreed, so now I'm stuck packing last minute.

"Is Dillon picking you up?"

"No. I'm meeting him there. His flight left this afternoon."

"Oh." She lets out a defeated breath and I roll my eyes. My mom is convinced that Dillon and I are meant to be together. *Snort* "Is it just you and him going?"

"I hope so. I swear if the wicked witch shows up, I'll sell her on the strip to the highest bidder, or pay someone to take her out to the desert and drop her off," I grumble, digging under my bed for my BOB, just in case of an emergency.

"Call me if you need an alibi." She laughs and I smile, shaking my head while dropping my BOB into my suitcase.

"I'll call," I mutter, heading to the bathroom so I can gather my shower supplies.

"He's so nice I don't understand why he's with her." she says quietly, and I grit my teeth. Dillon is annoying, bossy, and—fine he can be nice sometimes, plus he's uber hot—but I hate him. Okay, I don't *hate* him but I really, really want to hate him.

"I don't know mom."

"Oh well, so how long are you going to be gone for?"

"Just the weekend. My flight gets back in Monday night around seven."

"Promise you'll call everyday and check in."

"I'll call or text," I agree, grabbing my makeup case from under the bathroom cupboard.

"Please try and have some fun while you're there. Make Dillon take you out to a nice dinner or dancing."

Snorting I mutter, "Sure, Mom. I love you. I'll message when I land."

"Okay, honey,"

"Tell Dad I love him."

"Will do," she agrees softly, before I hang up and shove my cell into my back pocket. Looking at the clock, I let out a quiet curse then get my ass in gear and finish packing, so I don't miss my flight.

DRAGGING MY BAG behind me toward the reception desk, I'm stunned by how many people are here wearing nametags, stating they are here for the dental convention. Dillon mentioned that this weekend was one of the largest gatherings of dentists in the United States, but *sheesh*! This is crazy. Finally making it to the front of the line, I smile at the cutie behind the desk and slide my sunglasses into my hair.

"How can I help you, gorgeous?" he asks once I'm close. I set my purse on the counter and pull out my ID, handing it over to him.

"Hi, I have a reservation." I yawn, covering my mouth while I listen to the sound of slot machines going off in the distance. I love the slots, or penny slots, to be exact, since I'm too chicken to play the real slots.

"I'm sorry," He slides my ID back towards me. "There's not a reservation under your name. Are you sure you're staying with us?"

"I'm positive. It may be under my boss's name, Dillon Keck. He made the reservations," I say, and he starts to type again then smiles.

"Got it. I see here that Mr. Keck has already checked in and requested we give you your own key to the suite upon arrival."

"Uh, what?" I frown, feeling something close to panic fill my stomach. "Are you saying he's staying in that room, too?"

"Yes, it's a suite with two king beds and a view of the strip."

"I don't care about the view or how many beds are in the room, it's one room." I panic, leaning half over the counter, trying to see his computer screen. "Please tell me you have another room?"

"I'm sorry, but we're completely booked. This is one of our busiest weekends of the year."

"Of course it is." I shake my head. "Can you recommend another hotel?" I plea.

He shakes his head no. "Sorry, I doubt there will be any openings most people book this weekend a year in advance."

"Of course, a year in advance that makes complete sense."

"I'm sorry."

"It's okay, totally okay." I squeeze my eyes closed then drop my head to the top of the counter. "It's not a big deal. I can share a room with him, we're both adults, adults share rooms, it will be like a sleep over." I whisper, balling my hands into fists.

"Um, so do you want me to get you your key?"

Opening my eyes I lift my head and, blurt. "I don't like him."

"Um." He looks at me like I'm crazy and I may be.

"And I'm definitely not attracted to him." I keep on and his face softens.

"Call down and check. Sometimes we have people call off their reservations last minute," he holds out the small envelope with the room key tucked inside. "You never know, something might open up."

"Sure, I'll call," I agree, wondering what the hell I did to deserve this kind of karma.

About The Author

NEW YORK TIMES & USA TODAY BESTSELLING AUTHOR Aurora Rose Reynolds started writing so that the over the top alpha men that lived in her head would leave her alone. When she's not writing or reading she spends her days with her very own real life alpha who loves her as much as the men in her books love their women and their Great Dane Blue that always keeps her on her toes.

For more information on books that are in the works or just to say hello, follow me on Facebook:

facebook.com/pages/Aurora-Rose-Reynolds/474845965932269

Goodreads

goodreads.com/author/show/7215619.Aurora_Rose_Reynolds

Twitter

@Auroraroser

E-mail

Aurora she would love to hear from you Auroraroser@gmail.com

Sign up now for Aurora's Alpha-Mailing list where you can keep up to date with what's going on.

http://eepurl.com/by57rz

And don't forget to stop by her website to find out about new releases, or to order signed books.

AuroraRoseReynolds.com

Other books by this Author

The Until Series

Until November – NOW AVAILABLE

Until Trevor – NOW AVAILABLE

Until Lilly – NOW AVAILABLE

Until Nico – NOW AVAILABLE

SECOND CHANCE HOLIDAY – NOW AVAILABLE

Underground Kings Series

Assumption – NOW AVAILABLE

Obligation – NOW AVAILABLE

Distraction – NOW AVAILABLE

UNTIL HER SERIES

UNTIL JULY – NOW AVAILABLE

UNTIL JUNE – NOW AVAILABLE

UNTIL ASHLYN – COMING SOON

UNTIL HIM SERIES

UNTIL JAX – NOW AVAILABLE

UNTIL SAGE – COMING SOON

Shooting Stars series

Fighting to breathe – Now available

Wide open spaces – Coming soon

Alpha Law CA ROSE

Justified – NOW AVAILABLE

Liability – NOW AVAILABLE

Verdict – Coming Soon

Acknowledgment

First, I want to give thanks to God, without him none of this would be possible.

Second, I want to thank my husband. I love you now and always. Thank you for looking after our sweet boy so I could finish this book.

Thank you Mom for everything. Thank you for flying out to help out during the first weeks of JC's life so that I could get this book done.

Kayla, you know I adore you woman. Thank you for all your hard work and for being an editing rock star.

PREMA Editing, thank you for everything from your amazing advice to your hard work. I love working with you. I really love that I learn something new with each edit.

Thank you to my cover designer and friend Sara Eirew. Your design and photography skills are unbelievable. I love that you accept my craziness and that you know what I'm looking for even when I just have a vague idea. This cover is as gorgeous as all the others.

Thank you to TRSOR. You girls are always so hard working, I will forever be thankful for everything you do. Lisa, I love you woman.

To every Blog and reader, thank you for taking the time to read and share my books. There would never be enough ink in the world to acknowledge you all but I will forever be grateful to each of you.

XOXO Aurora